PROFESSOR GOLDEN MYSTERIES

BIG BEAR INTRIGUE

Novel

JEANETTE JENSEN

Professor Golden Mysteries

This book is a work of fiction. Names, characters, places, and incidents are products of the author's imagination, or are used fictionally. Any resemblance to actual persons, events, or locales is entirely coincidental.

Cover painting is an original oil by Jeanette Jensen

Professor Golden Mysteries: Big Bear Intrigue

Copyright © 2018

ISBN-13: 978-1-7328574-0-7

All rights reserved.

Dedicated to Jeanay, my daughter, a university

journalism graduate. Meet her twin Cheantay in

another cozy mystery, Professor Golden Mysteries

Volume 2.

Also dedicated to Natalie, a fellow artist and inspiration

for Professor Golden, and Dr. Goldman character in my up
and

coming Adventure Novel, Holy Land Raiders.

Big Bear Intrigue

Intrologue

FIVE DAYS LATER.

The ground sparkled here and there. She whispered, "Be careful he might have a gun."

Arrival

Professor Golden sat quietly facing the stone fireplace, her eyes reflecting the brilliant blaze, her head capped with a knit beanie. Only her hand, fingers tapping rhythmically, covering the cell phone on top of her elegant lap throw gave evidence of inner anticipation. The doorbell rang, simultaneously Professor let out a jubilant, "Oh," as her feet thudded to the floor from the footstool. She threw the lap throw with her cell phone down into the high backed chair chattering all the way to the door. "Well, it's about time-my goodness what took so long--maybe it was the traffic--maybe it was the..." Flinging open the door her eyes locked on a smiling radiant face. Professor flung her arms around Jeanay almost knocking her over effusing, "Oh, my lovely girl, what took you so long?" She then held her at arm's length staring into her blue-green eyes and light olive complexion. "My look at you, you are so…lovely!" She dropped her hands from Jeanay's arms. "You must be frightfully tired. Oh, it's so good to see you!" Jeanay just stood there, her big bright eyes blinking while holding the hand-pulls to her suitcases in each hand. Waiting for an opportune moment she released her luggage tipping them upright. She then grabbed her aunt, with both arms around her shoulders, and laughed robustly.

"Oh Auntie, look at you just the same as always. Can I come in?"

Professor Golden laughed at herself and answered, "Oh yes, you know me darling don't you, come in, come in, silly me." She locked onto Jeanay's arm as Jeanay grasped the handles of her luggage, and mustered in the door. She awkwardly maneuvered her luggage with the Professor clinging to her muttering the entire time. Chattering on about what the flight must have been like and the ride to her house. The Professor continued to mutter as they deposited the luggage at the bottom of the stairwell. She didn't stop muttering until she seated Jeanay in a cozy chair, near hers.

Jeanay took a deep breath to help relax from her aunt's rambling and the exhausting trip. "Yes Auntie, everything went just fine. The taxi had no trouble finding you. I couldn't get phone tower reception for some reason. That's why I couldn't reach you. I know you're excited!"

"Oh, oh yes, I am. I really must settle down a bit," she amicably responded. "Let me go get you some tea? You really would like that I'm sure. You do like tea, I remember." Professor kept up a discourse as she headed toward the kitchen disappearing into it. "Your mother always insisted her children drink tea--you were nine or ten? Let's see you were in that house on 7th Street." She continued speaking from the colorful Italian-yellow kitchen. It was warmly decorated with homey apple and chicken decorations on decorative plates, wall paintings, baskets, hand towels, and trivets. She bounced happily around the kitchen preparing their drinks. "Such a lovely mother you have, and she must be so proud of you--and she's let you come and stay with me all this way--my goodness what a brave soul she is--just amazing!"

Jeanay smiled with a loving, knowing, familiarity of her aunt's banter as it continued from the kitchen. "Yes Auntie dear," she mumbled softly remembering her aunt's long, meandering chitchat. Professor would talk herself in and around anything it didn't matter if anyone was listening and most weren't. Unfortunately some people would tune her out, after a while, all except for her enraptured students.

Jeanay smelled the wood burning in the large open fireplace. She mused silently to herself. *It's so big you could fit two people in there if they bent over a little bit... Ahh, it feels so good!*

The warmth of the fireplace was much appreciated as this March day was still chill for being so close to summer in California. The radiating heat and crackling orange flames called to Jeanay. She stood up and went to lean against the hearth. She touched the large, fire-warmed stones that her uncle had lovingly built into the wall. Her eyes peered up the rich, dark-hued, walnut wood stairway that rose to an open landing enhanced with an elegantly carved wood handrail. You could stand at the top landing, lean on the rail looking down over the large living room, and see all the way to the kitchen. Her eyes turned to the long picture window which lent itself to a lovely view of the beautiful cobalt, blue lake. Her eyes followed the window view of the lake and continued past the massive dining room table and on into the wide entry of the country kitchen. Jeanay could feel the warm lived-in feeling of the room where she stood. She brought her gaze back to Professor Golden's original artwork paraded along the light beige walls, in gallery style, opposite the lake view windows.

Jeanay thought to herself, *the place seems too big for her. I'm glad she wants me here.*

"Now tell me all about your last days at college," Professor Golden's voice drew closer as she carried in their tea.

"I produced the last news show on campus for the school year. It went really well. I think I'm quite good at it."

"What was your role as a participant in producing?" Professor Golden asked as she handed Jeanay a cup of tea.

"I put the story together, wrote it, filmed the video, edited it, and I personally presented some of it in the video. The video package came together very nicely. They used my piece and some of the others' vlogs which I, also, presented as the main newscaster." Jeanay stood proudly against the fireplace with her teacup and saucer sipping a cinnamon flavor.

"That's wonderful! Congratulations girl! I bet your parents are so proud." Jeanay, smiling, nodded her head. "Tell me how's your mother and my dear brother-in-law?"

Jeanay came over to sit beside her aunt. "They are doing just fine and send you their love."

"Ah, that's so nice. When you talk to them again give them my love. How are your sister and brother?"

"They're fine and working hard. Sis is struggling with which way to take her journalism degree. She's not as independent thinking like I am, so she'll probably go for a job."

Professor Golden nodded in the affirmative. "Funny how you two picked the same area to study, is that a twin thing? Yet you're so different from each other! It's a good thing there are a number of different branches you can choose from."

Jeanay nodded in agreement and then yawned. She set her empty teacup down. "I think I'd like to take my things upstairs. Thank you so much for letting me visit it's a great break from years of studying."

"I wouldn't have it any other way. You just go right on up and get settled in. Did you bring your toothbrush? I have extra if you need one."

"Yes, no, I'm good. I brought it," Jeanay said while she yawned, again.

Professor Golden got up. They hugged each other.

"See you in the morning," they spoke together at the same time and laughed. And then spoke again, simultaneously, "Goodnight."

In The Morning

"Oh, she's just fine." Pause. "Yes mother, I know." Pause. "Really I'll be fine. You didn't want me all by myself so this is best. And yes, she is a little more talkative, probably because he's gone." Pause. "Okay, I love you too, bye-bye."

Jeanay slipped her phone into the side pocket of her flowing, calf-length skirt. Peeking out the silk-curtained window at the lake below, her face awash with anticipation, she longed to take a wade. Placing a book under her arm, her skirt swishing, she proceeded from her bedroom and sashayed down the stairway. *Funny auntie sleeps on the street side. My side has such a lovely view of the lake.* She stepped lightly on the bottom landing and looked around. The house was quiet. *Hum, where could she be?* Jeanay peered out the Tudor windows with their crisscross wood braces. *There she is!* Jeanay spied her aunt outside sitting at a small wood table for two. It was situated against a tall, imposing wall of cedar wood. The wall separated and hid the lake view from people sitting at the table. Jeanay walked out the door by the kitchen, and past the picture windows to the small table, "Hi, Auntie."

Professor Goldman looked up smiling with a mouth full of food. Today's hat, an artist's beret, was tipped at an angle on her head. She gestured with her fork for Jeanay to sit down opposite her. Jeanay spoke as she slipped into the wood-backed chair, and she placed her book on her lap. "I've always wondered why you have this wall here when the view is so spectacular? I mean don't people pay a premium for a lakefront view?"

"Yes, well yes…yes." Professor nodded her head vigorously as she spoke. "I agreed to the property so your uncle could boat and fish to his heart's content. In return, your uncle built it for me. He promised he would build that wall for me so I don't see the wa-wa, water." Stammering she stopped and shivered. "I don't like water. I do like to drink it, wash with it, but that's it! I'll go get your food." She abruptly dismissed herself in an unusually quiet manner.

Jeanay called out after her, "I'll go get my feet wet if you don't mind. Be right back." Jeanay jetted out to the water, flipped off her sandals, she swirled around in it up to her ankles laughing. Professor Golden returned to the table. Jeanay noticed her, and headed back to the dry sand to pat off her wet feet with her skirt. She then joined her aunt at the table where her breakfast sat. The Professor was silent her head down reading a book. Jeanay watched her thoughtfully. "Thank you for the breakfast, it looks great."

Professor Golden looked up she gave her a quick smile then turned her attention back to her book.

"What ya reading?" Jeanay asked, in a playful voice, as she munched on her breakfast.

Holding up her book Professor Golden revealed the title that was in a different language. She then spoke the name in English, "Tanakh The Holy Scriptures."

"Oh, I have one too except it's in English translated directly from that one's Hebrew."

Professor Golden lovingly ran her hand down the old, worn, tattered cover. "I'm afraid I'm a bit messy. It's really worked over, and I've spilled coffee on it too. I love reading it at breakfast with my coffee, both are my comfort food. The Rabbi's would not approve. They keep theirs so pristine out of respect."

"And t-r-a-d-i-t-i-o-n don't forget," Jeanay waggled her finger in the air as she emphasized the word 'tradition.'

They both laughed. "Yes and that too!" Professor Golden added.

"I don't think God would mind. It looks to me like it is love-worn Auntie."

"Um, yes…So you read your Tanakh every day?" The Professor stated it as any Jewish mother would more as a warning that it should be done than a question.

"Oh yes, and I also read my Jewish New Testament." Jeanay held it up.

What was, at first, a smile of approval that started at the corner of Professor's mouth suddenly, contorted into a look of dismay. Professor grabbed her Old Testament to her chest. "That's right, my brother-in-law rejected his faith! It had lapsed from my memory." She looked very sad as she nervously looked away attempting to distract her thoughts.

Jeanay spoke softly to her aunt's distress, "Oh Auntie, really it's not so bad. We love the same God. We just view things a little different."

"A little different! Christians persecuted our ancestors mercilessly through the centuries."

"I know it was horrible. I don't believe they were true Christians. Jesu—" Jeanay abruptly stopped, when she saw a look of horror cross her aunt's face. Jeanay realized her aunt's expression was due to her attempt to use THAT name. She corrected herself carefully, "The New Testament quotes, 'that the Jew is first, and the gentile is grafted in,' you're not replaced. Plus the New Testament is written by all but one Jew." Her hands moved expressively, "Which legitimately entitles it to be called the Jewish New Testament. Besides we're not really Christians…" She inserted a pause and then slowly added, "Per say." Professor lifted an eyebrow, and cocked her head to one side waiting. Jeanay continued, "We're Messianic! Jew and Gentile together, we accept Him--you know," not wanting to upset her aunt with the name "Jesus" again. "And all our Jewish feasts and holidays we also celebrate, but as many having since been fulfilled." Jeanay understood the deep, pain-filled feelings that she also once associated with that "Name." The "Name" tied together the Holocaust, Pogroms, and all the atrocities the Jew's suffered through the centuries from Christians and non-Christians alike.

Professor Golden softened, a little, from the jolt of the topic that had invaded her family. She, after all, loved them dearly. "There have been many called Messiah," she sighed.

Her aunt's slight acknowledgment pressed Jeanay onward. "The Gemara states, 'you can believe anyone is the Messiah.'"

Professor Golden scrunched her face looking pinched. "Yes, that's true, but I've always found that to be a bit odd. How could just anybody be the Messiah? Plus it is confusing that we're expecting two Messiahs; one the suffering Ben Joseph Messiah, the other the King David Messiah."

Jeanay worked to recover from her quote that anyone could be the Messiah. She was not comfortable with that idea as well. "But… The Messiah is acknowledged in the Tanakh that He, the Messiah, must come before the temple is destroyed. And that was dated to be prior to 70 A.D. the year the temple was destroyed."

Professor Golden's expression looked both like she was listening to the scratching of fingernails on a chalkboard, and a doe caught in the headlights of a car.

Jeanay began a new tack, "Do you remember Rabbi Yitzhak Kaduri?"

"Yes, of course, who doesn't? He was the most revered Rabbi in Israel, a healer, and prophet." Professor Golden wondered, nervously, where this was headed.

Jeanay continued hopefully, "When he was young it was prophesied that he would see the Messiah, and he would know who the Messiah is. And, then again to confirm it, a year before he died at 108 he had the same thing prophesied to him.

"Kaduri stated that he had regular visions, of meeting and talking to the Messiah, for a year before he died. And he said, 'I will write His name on a piece of paper that is not to be opened until a year after my death.'

"He added, 'It is encrypted in a code.' It was all written in Israeli.

"He also instructed, 'Take the first letter from each word in this sentence. He will lift the people, and prove that his word and law are valid.'

"When it was opened and deciphered it caused uproar. The code revealed the name, Yehoshua."

Professor Golden drew her breath in quickly, and then she let out a long, slow sigh. Jeanay could not quite tell if it was fatigue from the subject, or acceptance, or shock. Professor continued to hold her book tightly to her chest desperately wishing this conversation were over.

Jeanay spoke quickly, uncomfortably, "Yehoshua, Yeshua, or Messiah. We all know who that refers to--I'll stop. Oops, no, ah, I just want to add please use my English Tanakh to read Isaiah 53. Why do you think Isaiah 53 was taken out of yours by the Rabbis'? What do you think they are afraid of? And check Psalms 22 and the book of Daniel. You don't need the New Testament to prove anything. It's just so clear in the Tanakh who the Messiah is." Uncharacteristically Jeanay wrung her hands, "I'm sorry I've upset you."

Professor Golden placed her Tanakh down on the table without expression, and she stood up looking down at it trying to figure out whether to flee or stay.

Jeanay, also, rose from the table. *I think that's enough. I better give it a rest.* "I'm going to go grab my laptop and look at some newspapers and see what's going on in the world while I eat.

Professor nodded and sat down to finish her food.

Jeanay returned with her laptop to find her aunt seated and immersed in her reading. She studied her laptop while taking bites of food. "Hum, interesting…" Looking up Jeanay smiled, "The foods great! Thank you, Auntie." Professor looked up and smiled. Then they both resumed their silence. Jeanay continued searching online.

"I'm going to go rinse my dishes." Professor Golden got up from the table. Soon the sound of washing came from the sink.

Jeanay called loudly to her aunt from the outdoor table through the open French doors. These doors were situated between the dining rooms table with its picture windows and the kitchen. She could hear the dishes clinking and the water faucet running. "Oh my, listen to this Auntie. It's close to here, Big Bear. There's a missing scientist from the lake's observatory. You could go with me to check it out."

No sound came from the kitchen even the water abruptly stopped.

"It might be an interesting story to investigate, don't you think?"

More silence from the kitchen. Professor Golden stood stock still with both hands grabbing the edge of the sink as her arms and body stiffened.

Jeanay spoke louder, "I really need to find something to investigate. This is close. How would you like to go with me?" She looked toward the kitchen and doorway expectantly waiting…and waiting.

Professor Golden's, tentative, face slowly rounded the kitchen doorway. Her body was uncharacteristically rigid. She hid half-way behind the wall. "Big…Bear…Lake Observatory…a lake…up a curving…switch-back…steep mountain road?" She added a definitive, "I don't think so!"

"Oh, come on, let's have some fun together! Let's go for a couple days, see what's up! You don't have anything else to do, do you?"

Professor steadied herself against the door frame. "I was planning to start another painting…" Then she paused averting her eyes from Jeanay's eyes and quizzical expression. Hesitant she quietly, fearfully queried, "How would we get there?"

Jeanay, smiling, responded to her with a hopeful tone, "Can't we use your car?"

Oh, I wish she didn't melt my heart looking at me like that. Where is that husband when I need him? Professor Golden spoke slowly, "I don't do water. I don't do curves. I don't do heights!" She shook her peppered, long curls back and forth. She expressively moved her hand sideways imitating a sidewinder snake, "Curves." And then her hand moved up and down, "Mountains, uphill--downhill." Professor bobbed her head up and down as if already getting car sick.

Jeanay, in a chipper voice, countered, "That's okay I'll drive. You'll be fine! Enjoy an adventure with your favorite niece."

"An adventure with your favorite aunt that takes her out of her comfort zone?" The Professor wrung her hands. She stepped nervously side to side, in place, pacing, going nowhere.

"Of course you are my favorite aunt!" Jeanay grinned, "Plus you're my only aunt. You have a car don't you?"

"Yes, of course, your uncle's."

"You still have his Mercedes?"

"Yes."

"And it runs?" Jeanay was bowled over by the thought.

"They run forever. He always kept it up—regular tune-ups—brakes, fluids—washed it every week. Waxed it—It was his bab-"

Jeanay interrupted knowing this might take a while if she didn't, "Okay great! So can we leave tomorrow?"

Professor Golden looked rattled. "Tomorrow… Contemplate, contemplate. You can do this. It's just a little drive, up a little," she gulped, "Incline."

"That's right Auntie just a little incline." Jeanay clasped her hands together in prayer placing her fingertips against her lips. She looked up eyes pleading.

The Professor oblivious to Jeanay's pleading antics continued her nervous mantra. "Mountains, trees, fresh air, breezes, trees--lots of trees, roads, green…green everywhere—

"Okay," Jeanay interrupted, "Then that's a go!" She threw both fisted hands and arms up in the air in victory. She bellowed, "Yes! We're going!" Professor Golden paid her no mind. "Auntie, I'm going up to pack after I clean up these dishes. Thanks again, that was delicious."

The Professor was, at least, of the presence of mind to nod that she heard. However, she kept up a soft muttering dialog with herself. Jeanay flipped her laptop closed, and picked up her dishes, silverware, and glass. She walked toward the kitchen where the Professor was leaning back against the door frame staring up into nothingness. She was caught up in her own little world of flight attempting to sooth herself. Jeanay stopped in front of her, and she looked into her eyes, "It's going to be okay Auntie, you'll see. This is going to be fun!"

Professor Golden spoke out loud to herself, "Yes fun, think fun, it's going to be fun, fun, fun!" She grimaced.

Jeanay sighed, "Hum." *What am I to do?*

Professor Golden's muttering continued as Jeanay sauntered into the kitchen. She ran the water cleaning up her dishes. She walked out past her still muttering aunt. "I'm going upstairs to pack, and then I'll look into where we can stay. Don't worry I'll take care of everything. After all, I need to learn to do these things. I'm a newswoman!" Jeanay puffed out her chest with a super hero stance.

Professor Golden was much-too-much into her flurry of thoughts to notice Jeanay's antics which would normally crack her up. The Professor spun words originating from anxiety. Her words slowly started to change and began transitioning gently spinning into words of calm and encouragement. "Okay, we're going to Big Bear... It's going to be fine... It's going to be okay... We'll be fine it's just another day... We'll be back soon."

Mountain Morning

The road up to Big Bear mountain is historically called the Rim of the World. The drive is a cliffhanger as each vehicle winds around on the outer edge of the mountain. The view is spectacular as you look out and down the deep crevice of the mountainside.

The road took them past two seasonal ski resorts as they neared the top of the mountain. Then the road eased into a flat area with a few stores where Jeanay pulled the car into a small parking lot. She stepped out of the pale yellow Mercedes in front of a convenience store. "Ah!" She stretched her legs and arms. "A perfect 70 degrees I bet, perfectly warm, um-um!" Jeanay bent over looking into the car, "You were right Auntie it made it here nice!" Jeanay stood back up and breathed in deeply, "Ah, fresh-clean air! Now I sound like a laundry commercial, no that's an air freshener commercial. Oh no! Now I'm rambling too!"

Jeanay, standing so that her face could not be seen from inside the car, spoke to Professor Golden in a decidedly, jovial voice. "And you made it too! We only had to stop about 10 times." Her aunt was in no frame of mind to pay attention to Jeanay's mildly, annoyed expression attached to the words 'ten times.'

Professor Golden was jarred, she grit her teeth then opened and closed her jaw. She tipped her head to one side gently banging her head above her ear to help unblock her ear drum. "Ears popping, messing-up-my-equilibrium. Homo sapiens weren't meant to go up hills..." Professor stuck her fingers in her ears wiggling them in an attempt to pop them.

Jeanay bent back down and looked at her in shock. "What?"

"Fast, not meant to go up hills fast!" The Professor corrected her slip. She shook her head back and forth her shaggy locks waving around. She tipped her head again, and she continued to wiggle her fingers in her ears opening and closing her jaws.

"We'll bring chewing gum next time," Jeanay tersely announced.

The Professor continued vacillating between a tearful tone and protestation, "Or looking out over cliffs and miles of winding roads—and giant mountain boulders that could fall on you at a moment's notice. And trees, all those trees, anyone of them could topple over." She pointed up and down at the trees, "Up there and down there." She gestured an attempt at trees falling over each other, "Trees tumbling over each other because it's too steep for them and taking us with them to! Rocks, lots and lots of rocks! They could just fall down, on your head no less, any second!"

Wishing to break the ranting Jeanay announced, "Auntie, I'm going inside this convenience store and see if I can drum up any information. It's a really small town here, so there is probably a lot of gossip sharing. Can I get you anything?"

The Professor spoke in a matter-of-fact, staccato voice, "No... I'm fine...or I will be fine! I think... Yes, I'll be fine... Just a matter of getting over it... Yes, that's it... Getting over it... Uh-huh, uh-huh." Professor Golden nodded her head up and down vigorously working to convince herself of this new, hopeful truth.

Jeanay added, "Uh-huh," with a roll of her eyes she made sure her aunt couldn't see. Not that Professor would notice as she was completely involved in her self-talk discourse.

"Me and your uncle driving here, been awhile." Professor took a deep breath and let it out slowly. "It's good, it's going to be okay, it's--all good."

"A drink? Maybe, gum?" Jeanay continued to offer.

"Whatever you think honey."

"You're a survivor!" Jeanay quipped.

"Yep, I'm a survivor, survivor, survivor…" Her mumbling dimmed as Jeanay walked away and entered the store.

An older man stood behind the cash register counter. He was chomping on a mouth full of gum. He squinted at Jeanay as she came in.

He looks crotchety to me. He'll probably be more likely to open up if I buy something first. She moved to the refrigerator's double doors and selected two bottles of mountain fresh water. Jeanay looked at them and checked the label. *Local? Nope, from France. Nothing mountain fresh about this,* she laughed to herself. Jeanay went over to the counter and set the bottles down. She then selected from a counter rack a pack of gum. Looking around Jeanay didn't see anyone else in sight. *Good, we're alone.* Turning her attention to the employee behind the cash register she tried to appear nonchalant as she nervously fiddled with the gum. She asked, "Anything exciting happening up here these days?"

The cashier had picked up a bottle and was swiping it for the price. He looked up quizzically, "Exciting? Not much happens here, pretty quiet."

Jeanay spied a newspaper. "Oh, look at that, a missing scientist? Wow! I wonder what that's about?"

He noisily chewed his gum, in between sentences, and shrugged in disinterest. "Oh, those scientists can hardly understand them, some foreigners. The guy probably wondered too far got himself lost."

Jeanay encouraged herself and asked directly, "You have any idea where they got this information?"

Thinking quietly the cashier bagged up the drinks and gum. He became friendlier, "There's a gymnastics teacher, one of her student's dad reported his co-worker didn't show up for work."

"Ah, I bet that happens," Jeanay nodded.

"Yeah, sure!" He grumped, returning to his usual charm.

"I'll take this too." Jeanay slipped the newspaper under her arm as she paid the bill.

Jeanay carried her bag out to the car and handed the Professor water. She unwrapped the top to the package of gum and took out a piece. "I know this is kinda late, but it still might make you feel better."

"Okay, thank you," Professor Golden responded in a quick, nervous voice. She took the piece, unwrapped it, and slipped the gum into her mouth chewing vigorously.

"The guy inside gave me some info I need to follow up on!" Jeanay looked excited. "He said the scientist is a foreigner, and I need to look for a gymnastic teacher."

Professor Golden had stopped her chatter and now dispensed information in a most professional demeanor. "The foreigner is from Ukraine. They send their scientists here to study the stars. We have clear skies here 360 days out of the year. And it's a perfect spot for an observatory in the center of the lake, no less. This observatory and the one in Arizona have a great center to study from, the later one having unusual sitings."

"What do you mean unusual sitings?" Jeanay queried uncomfortably.

"You haven't taken any of my classes… There are a lot of unusual things happening out in space that are unexplainable. Flashing lights, explosions, moving objects at unusual speeds and patterns."

Jeanay leaned back in her seat and abruptly stopped drinking. "What do you mean?"

"You don't need an observatory to see the spectacle. Infrared military goggles, worn at night, reveal objects moving at unusual speeds and angles, with accompanying explosions around them. Some of the objects are slow enough to be man-made, others are not. Sometimes a moving object is seen to be shot down from one of the other objects."

Jeanay looked quizzically at her aunt. "Nooo," Jeanay retorted shaking her head. "You mean aliens? Spaceships? Noo!! I don't think I can believe that. You've worn military goggles?"

"No." Professor gave Jeanay a look. "Deep space? Don't judge what you haven't studied."

Jeanay frowned and started the car. "We'll see about that!"

"Yes, we will won't we!" Professor Golden shot her a confident grin.

Jeanay looked at her aunt squinting at her. *Well that got her tethered to earth again.* She decided not to take the challenge and instead change the subject. "I looked in the Ad section while I was inside and it has an ad for gymnastics classes. I'm going to call the number, and then hopefully tonight I can catch a class."

"I thought you were finished with gymnastics?" Professor looked blank.

Jeanay's humor and sweet disposition returned. She chuckled, "I am Auntie. I found out the news leak started out at the gym with the gymnastics owner. I'm starting there to track information. After I make the call we can find a motel. That should be pretty easy there is only one main street that goes the entire length of Big Bear separate from 'old town.'"

"Okay, kiddo. I'm about chewed out with this gum. Thanks."

"I'm glad you're feeling better!"

Professor Golden nodded her head in a decisive manner. "I am, now that we're up on a flat surface, yes."

Jeanay started the car and drove slowly so that they could catch the view. An impressive Gothic designed bridge greeted all who entered Big Bear. They passed a section of the blue, crystal-clear lake. Log cabins were perched among the trees and boulders against the mountainside opposite the lake. New more modern homes were planted on the lakeside. These newer homes had their own beaches. These premium-priced, exclusive locations showcased their own private docks filled with rowboats, skiffs, and motor boats. The old and new dichotomy of intertwined housing looked out of place. There did not seem to be any rhyme or reason to the building plan if you could call it that.

The road then curved and took them away from the lakeside. It became a very pleasant, winding road lined with tall pine trees. Sprinkled about were a few oak trees with massive gnarled trunks claiming their space. Decorating the roadside, here and there, were patches of long, bright, green grass. Intermixed with the grass were orange-red-yellow and purple wildflowers poking their heads up through the diminishing snow. There were large patches of wet dirt where the snow had melted. There was a smattering of empty lots with and without "For Sale" signs. Homes, cabins, antique shops, and cafes lined the road. Just before they entered the official old-town "L" shaped strip a large sign overhead read, "Welcome to Big Bear City."

Gymnastics

A small gym was situated a few blocks off the only highway. It turned out to be where classes were offered through the school district, but privately run. Jeanay parked the car in the parking lot of the gym and adjacent park. Jeanay started to step out of the car. Professor Golden popped out with two hats in her hand. "Wait, wait. I brought this hat for you." Professor Golden plopped her wide-brimmed Sun hat on her own head.

Jeanay took the small, white, felt hat from Professor's hand, and pulled it over her hair letting it rest atop her head. "What's this?"

"It's called a Halo hat. It makes you look angelic. A look of innocence when investigating could help? And maybe keep you out of trouble!"

"My, aren't you the smart one!"

"Yes. I'm not at all humble about that!" The Professor threw back her head with emphasis and comedic relief.

Professor Golden and Jeanay walked through the gymnasiums double doors to be greeted by the echoing, loud sounds of moving bodies and voices. It was mostly young girl's voices, happy and excited, that met their ears. An occasional word of command, or encouragement could be heard from several instructors. There was the sound of thuds from equipment that the kids would spin off of, or jump from, as they did their flips. Several parents were seated on raised bleachers watching their children and talking to each other at the same time. Professor Golden hung back and watched Jeanay sit down by a lone parent.

Jeanay turned to the parent and asked, "Hi, how are you?"

"Fine, thank you."

"I was wondering if you could tell me who the contact person is here? I was told on the phone it would be Cathy."

"Oh yes, she's the owner, she's over there." The lady pointed to a tall, fit blond in her forties giving instruction to a row of six girls.

"Thank you, I appreciate that."

Jeanay beckoned for Professor Golden to join her. She, carefully, stepped up the bleacher to join Jeanay and the parent.

"Auntie, I want to wait until the class is over to talk to the lady over there," nodding toward Cathy. "You mind if we just sit and watch? It's fun watching!"

"Sure, I'm up for it. They're such cute little things. I remember you doing this, you were the best!"

"Not really, but thank you."

They sat and watched the tumbling and fumbling and subsequent successes of different maneuvers.

After a while, Cathy clapped her hands for attention. "Okay gymnasts' good job for today. See you Saturday for more. You can go." Cathy moved over to the bleachers and grabbed a towel to wipe her glistening face. Her physique showed what a good work out catching and lifting the kids did for her.

Jeanay got up and walked over to Cathy as the kids filed out with their parents. "Hi, my name is Jeanay. Are you Cathy?"

"Yes, I am what can I do for you?"

"I wanted to ask you a few questions about a newspaper article I read."

"Really? Why?"

"I thought it might help my journalism career by doing a showcase about the scientist reported missing. I think still is missing?" Cathy nodded "yes" in answer to her question. "I would really appreciate your help."

"I really don't know how much I can help you. The person you might want to talk to just left with his daughter. His name is Bohdan. I don't think he would mind talking to you. You can catch him out at the observatory in the morning. Just tell him I sent you."

"Oh that's terrific, thank you."

Professor Golden wandered over to listen to the conversation staying back out of the way.

Cathy raised her hand in thought. "Oh, wait, I better call him and ask if that's okay. They quit tours to the place this year."

"Why would they do that?" Jeanay queered in surprise.

Cathy shrugged, "I don't know, ask him."

Jeanay reached into her bag for something to write her cell phone number on then she handed it to Cathy. "Please call me at this number if there is a problem, otherwise, we'll go out first thing in the morning. Oh, what nationality is the name Bohdan?"

Professor Golden interjected, "Ukrainian."

Jeanay looked at her quizzically.

"I overheard a couple talking in their native tongue on their way out. Word is Ukraine sends its scientists here to study. Remember?"

Cathy nodded her head that the Professor was correct. "Okay, I'll give him a call for you." Cathy turned to leave.

Jeanay added quickly. "Oh, would you mind me interviewing you for my video news package?"

Cathy turned back toward her and frowned. "No, I don't think so. I really don't know anything, besides I've gotten involved enough when I reported this."

Jeanay looked surprised and hurt. "Oh…okay…thank you." Jeanay turned away. As they walked out Jeanay mumbled to Professor Golden, "I gotta get used to being turned down."

Professor Golden cleared her throat and gave Jeanay a look.

Jeanay, now distracted by her aunt from Cathy's turning her down, looked befuddled. "What?" She paused and then guessed, "Oh, okay, you were right about Ukraine!"

"Thank you. I'm going to be right about other things I've said too!" She gave Jeanay a meaningful look.

Jeanay gave a, "Humph." And they walked out.

We Bitty Town

Professor Golden and Jeanay sat in the Mercedes. Jeanay drummed her fingers on top of the steering wheel. "We've made a little progress don't you think?"

Professor sat quietly her eyes batting expressions of doubt flickered across her face. She looked straight ahead hoping Jeanay would not notice. "Tomorrow will tell. The suns going down, why don't we get a bite to eat, then a little drive around, find a place to sleep."

"Yes Auntie, I know." Jeanay let out a sigh and started the engine.

"Doesn't that sound great, a rumble and then a purr. Your uncle just loved that!"

Jeanay drove out the parking lot into pine tree lined streets casting shadows over their car. The homes, here also, were oddly mismatched with old log cabins next to regular track homes next to new log cabins and empty lots. Further up on the hills could be seen bigger expensive homes and more boulders. Each lot was heavily littered with rocks, brush, pine trees, pine cones, and clumps of their needles nestled all over the ground mixed with patches of snow.

An empty, flat plane brought comment, "The Lake must be over there." Professor Golden nodded in that direction and fidgeted in her seat.

"Yes." Jeanay looked back and forth checking out the stores. "I see fast food places. Think I'll turn around and head back the way we came, I think, I hope. I'm a little turned around... Something quaint, maybe with an old town bar where the locals go... You never know what conversations you might overhear that could be a lead for my story."

Jeanay drove around and noticed eateries. "Oh, I just can't make up my mind! This is so important! I just don't know what to do!"

"Pull up to a service station and ask where the locals go." Professor Golden observed.

Jeanay slapped the steering wheel, "I don't believe it. Why didn't I think of that! Thank you."

"You're welcome!" Professor's lips curved upward ever so slightly in satisfaction.

Jeanay pulled into a service station where she saw car repairmen, in greasy overalls, driving customers' cars into the garage to lock them up for the night. She drove up behind a car that had just been moved as the driver was getting out. "Excuse me...excuse me!" Jeanay waved trying to get attention from a tired looking young man. He turned their way begrudgingly until he saw Jeanay smiling at him with her effervescent personality in her halo hat.

The young man smiled and perked up a bit. He came closer and in a deep voice answered, "Yes?"

"Could you help me? I'm looking for a restaurant with a bar, a local's place? Could you direct me?"

"That way," he pointed down the road, "At the end of this street before you get back into old town."

"Excuse me what? I thought old town was the other way. I'm a little turned around."

"Oh, yea." He rubbed his hands on a rag he had been carrying to wipe off steering wheels and car seats after he extricated himself from them. He wiped his brow and tossed his hair back off his forehead. "Okay, so the main drag, drive—ah, old town's street with most of the shops..." Jeanay looked at him listening, but blank.

He paused, looking at Jeanay wondering how to explain, "Did you come up from the front or back of the mountain?"

"There's a front and back?" Jeanay looked puzzled.

He rubbed his arm across his sweaty face unaware that he had wiped off some distracting grease. This gave him time to check his growing annoyance.

"Yes. Okay, did you come from Redlands, or Yucaipa, or Apple Valley?"

Jeanay had no idea what he was talking about. She looked totally confused, and now, concerned with his growing impatience. "Orange County," she blurted out as she gripped harder onto the steering wheel.

"That's front," he gave out a tired sigh of relief and pointed, "Go toward the little town you drove in through. And just before you get to the shops you will see a log building that reads "Blue Skies Big Bear Bar and Grill," lots of locals, sometimes a little rough late at night."

"Thank you that's just what I'm looking for."

"Glad to help," he quipped as he turned sharply on his heels to go.

Professor Golden turned down her window as Jeanay started to pull out which put the young man on the Professor's side of the car. She stuck her reddening face out the window. "And you could be a lot nicer about that young man. You should be ni—"

"Oh, Auntie!" Jeanay embarrassed, interrupted as she set her foot to the gas pedal hard. She exited the station quickly.

"Well, he wasn't a gentleman to you. I won't put up with such rudeness. This society is all about how fast you can do this or that. How quickly you can get rid of somebody, no courtesy anymore. People acting entitled, where're their manners? And don't get me going on being politically correc—"

"I know, I know," interrupting her aunt, again, a little impatiently, "I know. It's okay. He was tired. Besides, a hard working guy in overalls doesn't seem the entitling type… He sure had beautiful red hair and blue eyes. I guess the Halo hat didn't help. I tried to look as angelic as I could."

Professor Golden calmed down. "Oh, yes, you're right, he was tired. I must be tired too, hungry. It's been a long day."

"We're going to take care of that," Jeanay assured.

"He noticed you, should've used the Garbo hat," Professor noted. Her niece looked mystified. "Before your time, honey," Professor Golden added, "Before my time too."

"Ah." Jeanay grunted. "So you think he noticed me," Jeanay smiled.

"Uh-hum," Professor grunted and then went on to explain, "She was a sexy movie star. The brim goes up on one side and on the other side goes down over the eye. Sexxxyyy!" She snickered then laughed.

"Here we are!" Jeanay neatly parked the car in the parking lot.

Upon entering the rustic building Jeanay talked with the harried waitress-hostess who then escorted them to a table that bridged the restaurant to the bar.

"This might be interesting don't you think?" Jeanay looked around.

"A little too loud for me!" Professor Golden cringed. She looked around at the wood tables, wood chairs, wood panels, and wood bar. The walls held little of interest on them. The light was dim, but shining at a pleasing level from antique fixtures. The only interesting thing was the unusually costumed waitresses garbed in clothing from the western time period. The costumes included raucous, exposing bar dresses, prairie dresses, and elegant ladies dresses. *Amusing, this might keep me distracted from the dreary interior's noisy hubbub. Oh be nice, be nice, find things you like, why don't you? You're not bored at least. Look who you're with, not lonely, right? Right!*

"Sorry about the noise I asked specifically to be near the bar," Jeanay spoke with her eyes on the menu. A few minutes later she glanced up, and noticed her aunt's attention was not on the menu, but still distracted by her surroundings. She placed her hand on Professor Golden's hand, and lightly rubbed it to redirect her to her menu and called, "Auntie…Auntie! Have you found anything you like?"

A little startled Professor Golden looked at Jeanay, "Hum?... No." Professor Golden lowered her head to look at the menu. Still glazed over from her surroundings she looked up into Jeanay's expectant eyes. "Did you find anything you like?"

"I'm narrowing it down to a couple items." Jeanay looked back down into the menu.

"Okay, give me a moment." Professor buried her head in the menu to study it this time.

Jeanay hummed to herself feeling quite content they would have food soon, and because she was in the perfect spot to catch any gossip that might wend her way. The waitress came to take their order and upon completion reached for their menus.

Professor Golden clung to her menu, "Oh no, no, we'll keep the menus." She shook her head "no" to Jeanay who was about to hand off hers to the waitress. Jeanay looked quizzically at her aunt. Professor leaned forward and whispered, "Easier to hide behind, be discreet, while we eavesdrop. Really quite rude, embarrassing you know, eavesdropping that is!" Jeanay smiled back at her amused, she cared less about courtesy than about getting her story. She nodded "okay" to Professor who sat back quite satisfied with helping her niece. The Professor placed Jeanay's menu on top of hers, protected.

The waitress returned with glasses of water and tried again to take the menus with her. A little tug-of-war ensued between her and the Professor. "Did you ever hear the client is always right?" That provoked the irritable waitress further. The Professor heightened her tone, "What if I want to get dessert later?"

Jeanay spoke up to the waitress, "It's okay." She added her palm to the top of the menus that both women were holding. The waitress resigned herself with a sigh, and a shrug, and left them alone. Both ladies started laughing at their antics and the waitress' stubborn reaction.

Professor Golden rolled her eyes, "I wonder what bee got up her bonnet?"

Jeanay started laughing loudly, "Literally!" The waitress' costume ensemble included a bonnet head adornment.

"You're too much Auntie!"

"I know!" The Professor had joined in the laughter.

"Maybe it was a Professor bee."

"Why you don't think she liked me? Professor Golden jested as she shook her head, "I don't think she did."

"Are you sure you don't want a little wine. It has been a long day and we still have to get a room."

"Oh no, it will just get me going. Talking, talking, you wouldn't want that now would you?"

Jeanay laughing shook her head, "You got that right!"

The Professor gave her a playful, perturbed look which lent to an amicable silence.

The food looked and tasted delicious. They were both busy filling their mouths when Professor Golden stopped suddenly, then she pulled her hat forward to cover her eyes. She whispered, "Jeanay…Jeanay!…Jeanay," finally getting her attention.

Jeanay, poised with a raised, food-laden fork hovering in front of her mouth, stopped.
"What?" Jeanay whispered back peering under Professor's hat barely able to see her eyes.

Tossing her head to one side in a little jerk indicating the customers seated to one-side of them, "Listen, they're talking about the incident."

Shocked Jeanay pulled herself up short and wide-eyed. Her fork, ready to enter her mouth, was gently lowered back down on her plate. She lifted her water glass taking a slow drink as she listened to the conversation wafting over from the next table.

"I really don't understand what you're saying," the lady spoke. "Why haven't they found out anything else? It gives me the creeps that someone could just up and disappear, foreign or not, and nobody knows anything?"

The man across the table answered, "You know he was a little strange not like the other scientists that have come here."

The woman answered back, "Was he that way before he came here, or after he made some local friends?" The man didn't answer so the woman continued, but this time indicating the bar area and nodding directly at a person sitting in the bar, "You know who!"

Her companion put his elbow on the table, and he used his hand to shield his face from the person indicated in the bar, "Alright! Possibly, could be bad company, none of our business."

Professor Golden and Jeanay quickly turned their heads to look into the bar. Each was analyzing and looking each person up and down trying to figure out who was being indicated.

"Auntie, I've got to find him!"

Professor whispered back, "I know, I'm working on it. That one is into a conversation with her. Don't think it's him."

"Who, who?"

"The couple at the bar."

Jeanay nodded in agreement and added, "I don't think it's the guy reading the book at that table."

"What about the guy in the Grizzly bear outfit?" Jeanay was looking to the right of the bar.

Professor Golden was looking to the left of the bar, "Perhaps," but then she noticed Jeanay was not looking in the same direction. She turned to look at Jeanay's point of interest and exclaimed, "Oh!" Then she turned back to look at her Grizzly bear dressed man which then turned Jeanay's eyes toward him.

"Oh, great! Now, what do we do?" Jeanay's gaze locked on her aunt.

"You watch yours, and I'll watch mine. We report to each other then see what we come up with."

They both ate silently and watched.

Jeanay held her drink up to her mouth as if to sip, but, instead, used it to talk behind as a cover. "What's yours doing?"

Professor Golden held a menu up in front of her face, "Drinking."

"So's mine."

"Told you these menus' could come in handy. You better use one. You can't keep drinking or you'll get water logged. Besides, it looks weird."

"I know… Don't you think it would look weird with us both eating and looking in the menu at the same time?" Jeanay argued in a whisper.

"No, people look for desserts," Professor argued back in a whisper. She switched theme, "Something's bound to give one of them away, but then what? Why are we whispering?" She handed Jeanay a menu.

"I don't know…" Jeanay took the menu and covered her mouth with it.

"You don't know what?"

Why we're whispering or what I'll do. I'll have to figure it out as we go along. Jeanay returned to her normal voice. "I AM after all a Newswoman."

"Yes honey, but you're not in intrigue, just news!" Professor's normal voice warned her. "I'm getting so nervous!" Professor's foot started tapping the floor.

Jeanay leaned over her menu to her Auntie. "I know, isn't it exciting?"

Professor looked at her, and she spoke an emphatic, "No!"

Then one of the grizzly outfitters got up to pull out his wallet. He pulled back his furry coat revealing a large knife, in a sheath, hanging from his belt. Both women sucked in their breaths in fright. Jeanay emboldened herself and quickly started to get up. Between clenched teeth, she breathed, "I've got to go stop him." Then she shrunk back into her seat, "Or maybe not. I could follow him?"

Professor Golden grabbed her arm. "No, you don't!" Then she leaned out of her seat across the aisle to the couple who had been talking earlier. "Hi, sorry I don't have time to be friendly, tell me who is that man over there standing up in that grizzly outfit?" Jeanay looked at her aunt in surprise. The couple, stunned, looked at Professor Golden in surprise as well. This time she asked forcefully and urgently, "Is he the person you were talking about?" This provoked them to make a quick response. They looked at the intended person then shook their heads "no."

"Oh." Both Professor and Jeanay let out a sigh of relief.

Professor Golden impressed with her own emboldened action turned back to the couple. She asked, pointing to the other grizzly figure, "Then who is he?"

"Oh him, you don't want to know him!" The woman shook her head as she answered. The couple looked at each other awkwardly.

Jeanay nodded her head up and down in the affirmative vigorously, but it was her aunt who continued talking.

"Oh yes, we do. You see my niece is doing a news story on…" Professor Golden, nervous, one foot taping rhythmically, "On unusual people attracted…to um…this wilderness place, beautiful place! And he is dressed so perfectly. Like, like…um…like the waitresses…and he would be a perfect candidate. Ah. Ah. You know, don't you…perfect… It really is a lovely place you have here. We, we—"

The pair looked at each other wondering when this would end. "Gunther Travis," they both blurted out his name. Realizing the conversation was going to continue emitting from this sprite, awkward, mature lady. And not wanting to be impertinent, but wanting very much to stop her.

Relieved, and unnerved from her own outburst, Professor Golden quickly got up and shook vigorously the closest person's hand. "Thank you, thank you!" Then she sat back down. The couple looked relieved that their intrusion was over.

Jeanay looked at her aunt and mouthed the word, "Thank you." She pulled out her cell phone and wrote the name down. Professor Golden dipped her napkin into her water muttering, "I don't believe I did that." *What this child has gotten me into. My, my, what would her mother think?* She patted her brow with the wet napkin attempting to calm herself. *At least I kept her from that strange man, for now.*

After Professor Golden had recovered she asked, "So what's next news-lady?"

"Let's wait for him to leave. Oh look! Look he's leaving I can't believe it!"

"You're not going to follow him," Professor Golden was emphatic. Professor's feet came down hard on the floor as if digging in her heels. She put a restraining hand on Jeanay as Jeanay was getting up from the table.

Jeanay replied anxious, "Why not? I can't think of anything else to do."

Professor's voice was pitched higher than normal in worried alarm. "Well, I forbid it that is far too dangerous."

Jeanay paused for a moment uptight and perplexed, "Okay then, I sure hope someone in here knows where to find him. I'll ask when he leaves."

Professor Golden let out a sigh of relief as relieved Jeanay sat back down. They waited patiently slowly finishing their meal as he paid his bill and walked out the door.

Jeanay got up and went over to speak to the bartender. The bartender shook his head. She opened her purse and pulled out a bill pushing it toward him. He looked at her with the bill in hand and shook his head in an emphatic "no." Deflated Jeanay walked back to their table.

"That didn't look promising, what happened?"

Jeanay sat down hard and let out a peeved sigh, "Shoulda' worn that Gar—

"Garbo hat," They both finished the sentence together and laughed.

"He almost seemed insulted that I offered him money!" She shook her head in confusion. "Maybe that's just a Hollywood myth? I guess they're tight-lipped around here, private, small town protective sort of thing?"

"Okay, we'll see about that!" Professor Golden snapped and got up. She walked over to the bar and started chatting and prodding the barkeep. She took off her Sun hat and waved it around nonsensically. When that didn't work for her she started deliberately chattering about everything and nothing. The bartender looked exceedingly annoyed.

Shortly thereafter the Professor came back beaming. "He lives around the corner, ha, ha."

Jeanay looked incredulous at her aunt. "How did you find that out?"

"I told him that if he didn't tell me where he lived I would just keep talking!"

Jeanay gazed at her aunt with amazement and a new found respect. She started laughing. Then the professor joined her laughing. "Okay, you can laugh at me THIS time."

Observatory Observed

Jeanay yawned, stretched her arms out and yelled, "Observatory d-a-y!"

Professor Golden was jolted out of her dream filled sleep. She gave a startled yell, "Auugh!"

"Oh, sorry, sorry Auntie."

Professor Golden moaned, "Oh, don't do that! It's too early!"

"You know those scientists are going to be up at the crack of dawn. We gotta get there right away. I sure hope Cathy got a hold of him and we're clear to go. I better check my phone." She picked up her cell phone and checked it while talking. "Which hat is it today? I need a lucky charm. No call, we're good to go."

Professor Golden stretched, groaned, rubbed her blurry eyes and sat up on the edge of the bed. She sat there working to clear the fog out of her head and slowly got up. She went over to one of her suitcases pulling out some cloth, and she twirled it around her fingers. "How about a Turban, might remind him of his homeland?"

Jeanay got up and grabbed it with delight. "Perfect!" Looking at it she exclaimed, "My lucky, lucky charm, or at least you better be." She spun around in a circle.

Professor Golden let out a belly laugh enjoying the exuberant antics of her new pal, forgetting she was headed for water.

Jeanay pulled the car up on the crunchy gravel next to the lake. "I'm sorry we don't have time for breakfast first."

"I couldn't eat this early if I tried." Professor Golden patted her over the shoulder bag, "I always bring reserves, if needed." She turned, and for the first time noticed the water. "Yipes!" Startled she lurched in her seat 'petrified' was written all over her face. She froze spluttering, "I, I, I-I-I-I-I, wa-wa-wa-wa-water… no bridge? Don't like bridges anyway! 'Cept from a picturesque distance."

"It's okay Auntie," Jeanay patted her aunt's leg. "Really, it's okay. I can go over there alone."

Professor Golden nodded her head in short little jerky up and down movements, "Oh—oh—good, good." Then she frowningly shook her head back and forth "no." "No, no, you might not be safe. Oh what am I going to do? Your mother would never forgive me!"

Jeanay jerked back a little in surprise and indignation. "Of course not, that's ridiculous! I have to do my job! Besides, these scientists aren't dangerous. He has a child in gymnastics."

"You don't know about the other one!"

Now distracted by her aunts imagined plight and fears. Jeanay shook her head trying to clear out her aunt's phobias and keep focused on her own task ahead. She looked over at the observatory. "My biggest problem is how do I get to them? I see a rowboat, but then there's all my equipment for the news package. Maybe if I just give a toot someone will come out." Jeanay gave a honk on the horn. Rather quickly in response, the door opened. "Oh look! Someone's coming out!" Bohdan waved and Jeanay waved back. Then he stepped into a motorboat and started the engine. "He's got a motorboat! He's coming to get us. I've got to get my stuff out quick, so we won't keep him waiting."

"You're going! I'll wait here!" Professor Golden's head was down studying her hands as she rubbed them nervously.

"Oh, right." Jeanay paused thinking hard.

Professor Golden, out of the corner of her eye, saw Jeanay's pinched expression. "W-H-A-T?" She said with suspicion.

"I really wish you would come with me, you know science stuff better than I do. You might pick up on something."

"No!" Professor Golden blurted out determined and stared straight ahead. She wouldn't look at the lake or Jeanay, only the dashboard.

The motorboat roared toward them. Bohdan landed it efficiently at the wood landing, killed the motor, hopped out, and quickly wrapped the rope securely to the mooring. His neatly tailored white shirt had its long sleeves rolled up to keep them dry. He smiled broadly at Jeanay and Professor Golden, who returned it with a pained nod, whereas Jeanay flourished a generous smile. In his light Ukrainian accent he spoke English quite well, he welcomed, "Hello, come ladies and have a look at what we do."

"My aunt declines your offer. Would you mind if I brought my equipment and did a video interview with you."

"I didn't know I was getting myself into a video. That might not work! I hate to disappoint you, but a video of this place could go out on the Internet, and my government would have to authorize that first."

"Oh yes, I didn't think of that!" Jeanay put her hand to her forehead to cover her disappointment as she fought to think fast. "That's okay I'll bring my trusty laptop to take notes."

"All right with me," Bohdan planted one foot back in the boat and one on the landing, to steady it for her, offering her his hand after she retrieved her laptop.

Jeanay lifted her laptop out then shut the trunk to the car with her remaining equipment secured. She went over and took his hand as she seated herself. "Oh, this is so beautiful!" She looked around at the crystal-clear water and pine trees lining the lake along the adjoining hills. The still silence was suddenly jarred with a shrill shriek and a snort that emanated from the car.

"Wait, wait," Professor Golden waved a scarf in the air as she almost tripped over herself getting out of the car. She slapped the lock button and slammed the door. Her thick hiking sneakers ground quickly across the gravel path in short steps. She yelled, "Wait, wait, for me!" Then under her breath, "This might be the death of me, but I won't let it kill me. Oh, what I do for love."

Professor stopped at the edge of the boat huffing. She demanded, "Okay help me in!" She looked straight up to avoid looking at the water. She held one hand to her throat and the other held out for someone to take. In the extended hand, she held a scarf.

Bohdan looked at Jeanay in question.

Jeanay, wide-eyed from the scuffle, frowned slightly and out of one side of her mouth pursed softly, "She's afraid of water."

Bohdan looked surprised, "Oh!"

Jeanay reached out her hand for her aunt. "I got ya, I got ya! Just lift your leg over the side, and I'll guide you to the seat."

Professor Golden took her hand and eased her leg over the side as Jeanay placed her other hand on Professor's calf guiding her leg down slowly. Then the Professor dropped Jeanay's hand, and she spread her arms out wide waving them to balance as she continued to stare at the sky. Jeanay dodged her aunt's flailing arms, so as not to get hit.

Professor placed one foot on the seat. Jeanay pulled on the Professor's waist to get her foot off and over the seat so she could sit down. This rocked the boat slightly. "Oh!" "Oh!" Professor responded in little hysterical huffs.

Bohdan couldn't help but smile at the funny antics. He was choking back outright laughter. Jeanay was too busy trying to maneuver her aunt to find anything amusing about it. Finally Professor Golden felt steady enough to reach down and feel around with both hands to seat herself. She immediately tied the scarf around her eyes that she had been holding in her hand.

Jeanay looked at her in dismay. "Auntie you can't do that! Please! You look so um, um…"

"Ridiculous—I know. But at least I'm here."

"So you are," Jeanay sighed and sat down beside her aunt.

Bohdan looked to Jeanay for a sign to proceed. She gave him a nod and he started the engine. Professor Golden grimaced and held on tight to her seat. The boat gave a smooth ride. It neatly sidled up to the side of the observatory and its generous deck. Bohdan hopped out and secured the boat's rope. He politely ignored the ensuing drama.

Jeanay instructed, "Okay Auntie, reach over feel the deck and step out. I'll hold you by the arm." Before she could reach Professor Golden she was climbing out on all fours. Jeanay jumped out exclaiming, "Oh my, oh my!" She reached for her aunt's arm aiding her as she slowly stood up with the scarf still covering her eyes.

Professor Golden then commanded, "Take me inside!"

Jeanay guided her to the door as Bohdan quickly sprang to open it. They entered the surround hall that accessed the entire circular building. Desks were built into the curved wall rendering a pleasing design to the eye. Professor Golden pulled her scarf down to hang around her neck and with a sigh leaned back against the closed door.

"Doctor Bohdan may I introduce my aunt her Eminence Professor Golden." Jeanay was hoping this introduction would impress him and not leave such an awkward impression of the prior events. Professor blinked her eyes at Jeanay's introduction of her and she smiled. She shook Bohdan's hand and then added, "We do what we have to do." Bohdan generously gave a nod of his head in the affirmative still quite amused.

"So what is it that this observatory studies, exactly?" Jeanay got right to the point with Doctor Bohdan.

Bohdan went into his practiced speech. "Scientists refer to this place as (BBSO), the Big Bear Solar Observatory. It is operated by a group from the New Jersey Institute of Technology called the Center for Solar-Terrestrial Research (CSTR). Yes, lots of acronyms. In short, we study the sun with instrumentation and data resources from its surface and extending to Earth's atmosphere."

Another voice startled them coming from a white lab-coat clad figure. The thick accent asked, "You here for crazy Oleg?"

Bohdan cleared his throat. "Let me introduce you to my associate, astronomer Dr. Bondar." Then he turned to the ladies, "Professor Golden—"

Jeanay quickly interrupted, "Her Eminence."

Bohdan taking cue corrected himself, "This is her Eminence Professor Golden and her niece newswoman—"

"Excuse me that's newsperson," Jeanay corrected.

He continued, without breaking stride, "Newsperson Jeanay Golden."

Dr. Bondar shook their hands. The introduction had distracted him from his question, and he returned to his desk.

"We can take a seat over here." Bohdan lead the way to chairs lined up at the desks where they took their seats.

Jeanay spoke first, "Thank you doctor for seeing us."

"You may call me Bohdan. I don't know what more to tell you than our associate disappeared. The same thing I told the police which you read in the newspaper, I'm assuming."

Jeanay crossed her legs and opened her laptop, "Just a minute please." Seconds passed and her laptop was uploaded.

"Your associate, Oleg Kushnir, did you know him for very long?"

"No, he was relatively new here. Our country rotates many of its scientists to give equal education. And other scientists bring new ideas to our study of the solar system. I am one of the few tenured here."

"Okay. You've had some time to reflect since the police report. Have you had any new thoughts, or questions come to your mind about your associate?"

Bohdan thought for a few seconds. Then using his hands expressively as if they could help him speak the words he was searching for. "Oleg was a little more to himself than most. But he is a nice person. Very intelligent, a little more, how do you say... nervous, excitable. I surprised he did not leave us a note, or indicate he would be gone."

"Could he have fallen in the lake?" Jeanay asked matter of fact.

"The police have swept the lake and sent out search groups. They found nothing."

Jeanay continued, "How about wild animals in the forest?"

Professor Golden gave a noticeable shiver of fright. She spoke in a disapproving tone. "I live on a lake, and we don't allow wild animals."

Jeanay kept a straight face though she wanted to kick her aunt.

Bohdan's polite, mannered persona broke. Looking at Professor Golden with a most incredulous, drawn-out, tone of voice he asked? "YOU live on a lake?"

Professor's face became drawn and flustered.

Jeanay leaned into him and spoke quietly, "It's a long story." She nodded her head up and down looking at him in earnest not wanting to go there.

Professor Golden wiped her face with her scarf and shuffled her clothing around distractedly.

Bohdan checked himself and resumed his quiet demeanor. "When search parties went out they found no evidence of any human or animal, how do you say...foul play."

Jeanay pushed in, "What do you think happened to him?"

Bohdan, in silence, appeared conflicted. Holding very still, sitting slightly forward his arms resting on his legs, his clasped hands together.

Professor Golden looked at him oddly waiting and wondering why there wasn't more forthcoming. They heard a snort come from across the room. Heads turned toward Dr. Bondar. "Really Bohdan, you so nice, too nice!" He petulantly continued, "Oleg he nuts. He come here and stayed late at night looking at stars. This, a solar observatory, and he look at stars! The more he look the wackier he gets!"

Professor Golden asked quickly in surprise, "Meshuga?" Only Jeanay knew that meant crazy in Israeli. The men were too involved with each other to pay her any attention.

Bohdan got up quickly trying to stop the conversation. "You should not be saying these things!"

Bondar spoke loudly, "Oh, why not!" Waving his hand in the air Dr. Bondar mused flippantly, "Maybe he goes to Arizona?"

Jeanay and Professor looked back and forth at the two men wondering what that statement might mean.

Bohdan, one hand on hip and the other in an open gesture, scolded, "You do not know anything."

Professor Golden and Jeanay nervously wondered if the two men might exchange blows.

Dr. Bondar, insulted, stepped forward with a red face and then, checking himself, he suddenly decided to change course and went back to his seat.

Both ladies breathed a quiet sigh of relief.

"Please, doctor, explain what that was all about?" Jeanay asked in earnest.

Bohdan sat back down with a sigh, "Uh!" he paused, "Oleg was fine when he got here. He got bored, so he'd listen to radio programs while he was doing his observing. One of the programs he came across, well actually a new acquaintance in town told him about, and gave him access to, started changing him. It's a pay program. Now, what was the name of it?"

"How does that work, I'm not that familiar with radio? Jeanay inquired.

"You pay and set up an access code, like a password, and then you can listen to it online."

"Oh, simple, sort of like program and movie service companies, Netflix, Hula. I get it," Jeanay nodded.

"Yes, like that."

"What is the name of the station?"

"It goes by the host's name, I think it was Noory."

"What was the radio program about?"

"It was about aliens and other phenomena."

Jeanay and Professor Golden turned to each other eye-to-eye. Professor gave a knowing nod.

"I know that sounds ridiculous, but he got, how you say?" Looking down at his hand making a hook out of one of his fingers, "Hooked. He would come out here late at night to watch the sky and celestial bodies."

"What was this referral to Arizona?"

"All astronomers around the world know each observatory and what it studies. Oleg heard from the Noory show something we had not been told. That the Vatican Observatory is looking for aliens to bring the Messiah and World Order."

Jeanay could not hold back her shock and her mouth dropped open. She turned staring at her aunt who tipped her head to one-side and gave a look that said 'I told you so.'

Still shocked Jeanay turned back to her interviewee and asked, "Do you believe this too?"

"Probably not." Bohdan shrugged.

A big thud and a thick file folder hit the desk, dropped indelicately beside them, from Dr. Bondar. Jeanay flinched. "Check this out, he left behind."

Jeanay picked it up and flipped it open. There were drawings of space, stars, and other objects with trajectory equations. She shook her head, "Not my thing." She turned to Professor Golden, "I think this is yours though, Auntie!"

Professor took it from her hand and started reading as she flipped a few pages through it. She then turned to Bohdan, "Did the police look at this?"

"Yes, but they didn't take it. They thumbed through it looking for clues like suicide intentions."

The Professor full of interest asked, "Can we keep this?"

Bohdan replied, "It's not official, just his notes on his hobby, so we don't need it, take it, don't know how it can help, but a word of caution. Be careful how you use this and publicize it. Our government has been calling and is very upset. We don't need anything to ruin our studies or relationship with your government."

Jeanay nodded in agreement. "Of course... And would you know this friend of his?"

Dr. Bondar quickly interjected, "Big furry guy!" Then he facetiously added, "Maybe they got abducted! Ha!!"

Deciding to interrupt Professor Golden stepped in, "You do know there are recorded, unusual, phenomena with both science and military."

Dr. Bondar stopped and studied Professor Golden for a second. Then he rolled his eyes and went back to his desk.

Bohdan sighed, "You'll have to understand this has been quite trying, and he's not at his best. I will get you back to your car." Then he turned to Professor Golden with a smile. "And I will be very cautious and careful to get you back with as little disruption as possible."

Professor Golden tucked the file under her arm and smiled, "Thank you!"

Scary Man

Professor Golden and Jeanay sat quietly in the Mercedes, after being dropped off the boat, thinking about the possible scenarios of a disappearing scientist. Jeanay spoke first, "Oh shoot, I forgot to ask them why they don't offer tours anymore."

Jeanay removed her head scarf. "I can't even wrap my mind around the Vatican searching for aliens! If that's really true and he was spreading their secret mission could they have silenced him? NO, no, no," shaking her head vigorously. "Too ridiculous, but so is the whole alien thing! Aliens, abductions…" Jeanay squirmed in her seat. "Ah…let's just work with human possibilities. Who would want a scientist gone?"

Professor Golden decided to speak, "Maybe he just walked away from it all? It sounds like he became unhinged, mentally challenged, couldn't handle it along with his responsibilities. He gets embarrassed that he's having issues potentially creating problems for his country and their program participation."

"Yes, but the embarrassment might keep him anchored to stick it out. Couldn't he just opt out of the program? What do you know of the Ukrainian government? Maybe they took him out, if you know what I mean," Jeanay alluded.

"Covertly? You mean his government removed him?" Professor laughed, "I doubt that. They are proud and they have their reputation to keep intact with our government and the joint programs. He did have some kind of clearance to go through though, but they could simply replace him." She pondered, "If they did anything the scientists sound clueless."

"True, they didn't look suspicious, or like they were trying to cover anything up. Still, I can see their country being pretty upset about this." Jeanay lowered her voice demonstratively dramatic, "Maybe he upset his fellow astronomers, and they got rid of him—or his country got rid of him. Conspiracy! That would be a great story!" Her normal voice returned, "Ah…Oh, I don't know. Let's go get something to eat I'm starting to get hungry, how about you Auntie?"

"Sounds good to me!" Professor agreed with a nod.

The drive was short, just a mile, to a country breakfast cafe with big picture windows affording a great view of pine tree lined streets and hills.

Taking a bench seat Professor Golden sighed, "I need my coffee before I can think about another thing. I can't believe what I do for you. Jump in a boat…huh…be in a little, tiny building, surrounded by water, sitting on top of a lake. Oh no, I didn't even think of all that before, I'm getting dizzy." Professor Golden looked a little peaked and steadied herself with both feet as if she were going to swoon. She started taking little breaths. Then one foot started tapping rhythmically. "I mean all I thought of at the time was getting across the water for you, didn't want you to be alone. Oh, for heaven's sake I don't know what I was thinking." In heavy gasps she added, "Infact, I want to stop thinking right now.

"Auntie, Auntie!" Jeanay started fanning her with a menu. "You're here, you're just fine!"

A young waitress hurriedly came over, "Everything okay?"

Jeanay reassured her, "Yes, yes she'll be just fine. A cup of java could help fix things up quick," she spoke in a hopeful, encouraging tone, she added, "One for me too!"

"Okay, you got it!" The waitress rushed away and then came back in a flash with two full cups. "Here is cream and the sweeteners are right there on the table next to where we keep the menus, salt, pepper, and jelly tubs." She set the cream down slowly and quietly as if it might help calm her shaken customer. She looked on wide-eyed chewing a fingernail hovering over them.

Professor Golden grabbed the cup of coffee with both hands and took long black sips.

"Everything better now?" The waitress asked nervously.

Professor nodded her head in the affirmative and stopped gulping for a second to respond, "Comfort food, good! Thank you."

"Okay Auntie, let me put in your sweetener and cream?"

Professor Golden looked up at the waitress her toe-tapping slowed down, "Butter, may I have butter?"

The waitress looked at her as if she were very peculiar, and answered, "Sure?" Then she looked to Jeanay with an expression of "what for?"

Jeanay volunteered, "Sometimes she just likes it black with grass-fed butter and her stevia sweetener. It's called Bullet."

"We don't have grass-fed butter or stevia, just plain butter." The waitress bit at her nail.

"That's okay whatever you've got is fine," Jeanay affirmed.

Professor's toe-tapping stopped as she was sufficiently distracted and nodded, "That's fine!"

"Be right back." The waitress whirled around happy to be able to get away and do something else. She returned with butter on a small plate.

Jeanay pulled out a stevia bottle from Professor Golden's purse for her. Ordering their breakfast went off without a further hitch. The Professor relaxed. While she drank and enjoyed eating she studied the file she had brought along. Jeanay was pleased to sit quietly and look at the scenery, watch the other customers, and rest her brain.

Professor Golden was deeply engrossed in studying the file when Jeanay interrupted her. "Oh my goodness, my news-package has no videos yet! What am I going to do?!"

Startled Professor Golden's foot slapped the floor. Looking up flustered she exclaimed, "Oh!"

"I don't think that was about my problem." Jeanay waved her hand apologetically, "Sorry, thinking out loud, engrossed huh? You got something?"

Professor tapped one hand on the table thoughtfully. "Yes!"

Jeanay perked up. "Yes?"

"Oleg has kept quite a record here of diagrams." She turned a page around to show Jeanay. You can see he is indicating stars here and then these other objects, obelisk-shaped, with lines showing their movement AND the mathematical velocity of their movement. They are moving at amazing speeds!"

"Right, jets, rockets?" Jeanay's eyes widened, shaking her head, "Oh no, Auntie."

"W-e-l-l, he also describes what he sees."

"If this is true, and I'm not saying it is." Jeanay gulped, "Doesn't it seem odd he would leave this behind for people to find if he left of his own free will?" Professor Golden nodded her head up and down very much like a Bob Head. A Bob Head is one of those dolls whose head is on a coiled wire and bobs, gyrates when moved.

Professor's foot started to tap again. "I guess w-we need to make a grizzly visit." She started into her incessant chatter mode as she opened up her shoulder bag and plopped out some bills onto the table. Her head started to bob, again, as the words tumbled out oblivious to others around her. "I can't believe what you're getting me into. I must be crazy, yes, that's it crazy, meshuga! This is what I get for being an aunt and a god-mother."

Jeanay came around and looped her arm through her aunt's arm. She walked her out while Professor continued to talk to herself. Their waitress gave them a look and slowly backed up. Jeanay nodded to the money on the table.

Professor Golden ramped up, "So we're going to drive over to a Grizzlies house, and just ask him if he knows a weird guy who is freaked by aliens. Your uncle he warned me. Thi-this was a-a strange family—Oh don't get me wrong I love you all. Love, love, love you all." Jeanay squeezed them both through the front door, as quickly as she could, and walked them briskly, arm in arm, to the car. "Oh, he's just a man, like any other man, he's probably fine—even though he wears bear clothes." Professor's head bobbed even more, "And lives in a cabin. Tall at least six foot, probably traps Grizzly Bears. No, wait! There are no Grizzly Bears here…Brown Bears just brown ones, they're smaller and they're black not brown, but still called brown. But, but who cares we're in the mountains. The mountains are nice everyone should live in the mountains."

"We're at the car, Auntie." Opening the passenger door and hoping this would curtail her aunt's verbal unwind or wind-up depending on who was viewing her.

Professor Golden spoke in a spastic, high-pitched voice, "Okay, okay, uh-huh, uh-huh, we're at the car. I'll get in the car, uh-huh, get in the car Natalie. Everything's going to be fine Natalie, just fine."

Jeanay shut the Professor's door, hurried around to her own door, got in the car and put on the radio. "What kind of music would you like? I know soft classical. Classical music will be calming!"

"Oh don't mind me." Professor chattered in a low, barely intelligible voice.

"I'm trying, I'm really trying!" Jeanay patient at first was now having difficulty holding back her annoyance. Under her breath, she mumbled, "Wish I'd brought earplugs. Don't think she can even hear me, *thank God*." Jeanay noticed her aunt was winding down, and then she finally sat silent. Jeanay breathed a deep sigh of relief, "Ah."

The ride was quiet except for an observation, here and there, of a point of interest to Professor Golden. Jeanay's amicable response was supplied. Shortly, thereafter, Jeanay pulled the car up in front of their restaurant's location from the night before. "Okay Auntie, I don't know where to go from here, you have the location."

Professor Golden was apparently calmer now. "Yes, there are little log cabin duplexes amidst the buildings along here. He is in the one closest to the restaurant." Her nerves kicked in again, "Do you know what you're go-going to ask him?"

Jeanay got out and straightened her clothing. She bent over and looked through the car window at her Aunt. "I've got a few ideas. I just don't know how I'm going to get his permission to video him. I haven't exactly had good luck with that. I think I'll start out without the camera."

"That's probably best," Professor agreed, "It's broad daylight. I think I'll stay here. You're probably safe. Give a holler if you need me to call the police."

"What? You think I might need the police?"

Professor Golden twisted her hands in her lap, "You never know…I've had needs for police…with different situations."

"Go on, but unlock the trunk. Never mind I'll do it." Professor Golden opened the glove-box compartment and pushed a button on the inside. A familiar pop sounded. The trunk released and opened without it going up all the way.

"Should I wear a hat?" Jeanay asked jittery.

"Only if you got a Grizzly Bear hat and I sure didn't bring one!" Professor grouched.

"Oh, you're so funny!" Jeanay tapped her foot to relieve her nerves.

"Ha, ha I'm funny." Professor was in no mood to joke.

Jeanay grabbed her cell phone and started to reach for her laptop, but decided not to. "Let's just go for the notepad," she breathed. Putting on bravado, and holding her head up high Jeanay marched up to the door and knocked. She heard the floor creak inside the house, but no one answered. She knocked again, and she waited fidgeting as she looked at the peephole high up above the center of the door.

Slowly the door opened a crack and a bearded face revealed one eye peering through the slit. A deep voice asked, "Yes?"

In her friendliest voice Jeanay proceeded, "Hi, I'm a college graduate..." Moving her head back and forth in an attempt to see his face, which she hoped would prompt him to open up the door. "Sir, could I get you to open the door a little, please? You're scaring me." He opened the door wider, so his whole face could be seen. "Thank you. I'm trying to get more information for my first story, which I hope will get me a job, and I heard you are a friend of Oleg." As soon as he heard "Oleg" he tried to close the door, but Jeanay had anticipated that and had put her foot in the door. The door banged her foot, and she bent over yelling in pain, "Oh, ow, ow, ow!"

He flung the door open. "Oh, I'm so sorry, are you hurt?"

"A little bit," her crumpled face softened him. "I hope you can give me just a little information? Anything?"

He sighed, "Yes, Oleg and I are friends. I don't know what happened to him. He's a bright guy. I'm sure he'll be okay."

In a hopeful voice Jeanay asked, "I was told he had some trouble at work?" Then a quick-fire succession of questions and answers ensued between them. She used her cell phone as a support for her notepad, which she scribbled on furiously.

"I don't know anything about that."

"He was interested in UFOs?"

"Don't know anything about it. But there are UFOs out there!"

"Can you tell me about them?"

"Nooope!"

Jeanay gave up in disgust, "Okay...thank you."

"Yep, watch yourself out there."

"What do you mean by that?" Jeanay looked startled.

Gunther shrugged, "UFOs."

"Oh, oh, right, thank you." Jeanay shrugged.

"Welcome!" He shut the door.

Jeanay sighed and walked back toward the car. To her surprise at the corner of the building was Professor Golden holding up, in a menacing fashion, an umbrella in one hand, and Jeanay's video camera in her other hand. Jeanay excited asked, "What's this?"

"You needed video, you got video!" Professor stated in triumph.

"And…the umbrella?"

"You don't think I'm going to let my niece go to a stranger's door and not be protected. I'd be banging this thing on his head if he gave you any trouble. Bam, bam, bam!" She slapped the umbrella against the building in demonstration of fierce intent.

Jeanay brightened and laughed loudly hugging her, "You amaze me. You're wonderful! ...Though I'm supposed to ask for their permission first."

"And that's worked? I think you need to rethink that! Leave that notion behind back in college. People don't seem to be friendly to it."

"Yea, I know what you mean. The stories I did for university were pretty friendly stuff, not like this. Here, Auntie, let me put the equipment away while I try to figure out what to do next."

Fetch & Stay

"Auntie, I'm tired of driving around in circles. Let's park and walk I can think better that way."

"Okay. My legs need a good stretch. And there're other notes I haven't told you about in Oleg's file that might provide more room for thought."

Jeanay spoke as they got out of the car, "Really? That's good! I don't think I learned anything that will help from Mr. Travis. He seemed nice, then he seemed weird like those folks made him out to be, probably scared me for nothing."

"People think you're weird if you believe in UFOs," Professor Golden said in a non-committal voice. "That Grizzly Bear coat and hat he has doesn't help."

"Unless, he wants people to leave him alone," Jeanay thought out loud.

"Hum, yea! Paranoia can lead one to...react in different ways."

Jeanay looked purposefully at her aunt, "I know."

Professor Golden looked up at Jeanay a little startled, "What do you mean? That sounded a little personal?"

Jeanay stopped and stared at her, "You and WATER!"

Professor Golden turned and walked on with a pensive look trying to ignore Jeanay. She took a few more steps and then stopped, "Oh wait!" She turned around, "We need hats for this."

Jeanay replied, "We do? What kind this time?"

"Fedoras," Professor Golden spoke emphatically, "A Panama Fedora for me."

"Fedoras? I thought that was a man's hat?"

"They have them for both. I'll give you the female one." Jeanay turned around with her aunt, and they returned to the car.

Professor Golden reached over to the back seat into her bag and rummaged through it. "Here it is. Your uncle loved this hat the best, wore it so often." She pulled it out and lovingly stroked it as if caressing his cheek. The top of the crown was indented as large as a fist. The hat tapered inward at the crown, and fluted out toward the wide head band and brim.

"Oh, that's sharp Auntie. I think it might make you look like a real, live, sophisticated detective."

"You think?" Professor Golden smiled then put it on and tipped it to one side provocatively.

"Yes, I do! And where's mine?" Jeanay clapped her hands in sudden glee, "I just love hats."

"Here it is. Slightly tapered and elegant wouldn't you say?"

"Yes, say…" Jeanay put it on and tipped it to the side as well, "How's that?"

"Perfect!" The Professor beamed.

Jeanay looked around her as they started walking. "Look at these cute shops, very distracting. What's that over there?" Jeanay pointed at a place across the street from them. Professor Golden turned and looked with a blank stare. Jeanay read the sign over the door, "Fetch & Stay Chow. That's a strange name, don't ya think?" Professor just stared at the place puzzling over it. "Let's go check it out!" They crossed the street.

Professor Golden looked in the window. "There are dogs in there."

Jeanay shaded her eyes to look into the window, "A pet shop? No, not with all those tables! Hum, food on the tables and dogs eating under the tables. Sooo…dogs, and people eating, a dog restaurant? I've never seen or heard of this kind of place. How unusual! Let's go in."

A waitress noticed them come in the door and came over to them. She asked politely, "Where's your dog?"

"We don't have one," Jeanay answered her expecting to be seated.

"I guess you didn't read the sign, on the outside, by the door." The waitress held up her fingers and made quotation mark motions as she spoke. "You're not 'IN' without a dog. Borrow or rent a dog if you don't have one." She stood like a guard in front of the ladies.

Professor Golden was put off. "Oh," she scoffed.

The waitress pointed out the door. "You can be served at one of the tables out on the patio without a dog."

Both women stared at the waitress in disbelief.

The waitress sighed, "The owner is a dog lover, and she got tired of not being able to take her dog into restaurants. So she decided to open one that had a reverse policy. She's a non-conformist you might say. It gives me a job."

Professor Golden came out of her stupor of disbelief. "Oh, yes…well…I see. Come on Jeanay let's sit outside."

Jeanay, frazzled, looked at her aunt, "Okay, if you say so, but there're no dogs out there." Jeanay's voice went into an excited animal lover's voice. "Some of them are so cute in here!" Several of the dogs looked up and waged their tales at her in response. "Oh see, see their so cute!" She reached out just itching to pet one.

Jeanay's voice trailed off as Professor Golden grabbed her arm walking her the other way back toward the door, while Jeanay looked over her shoulder at the attentive dogs. "Not now Jeanay."

"I'll bring you the menu," the waitress almost sighed with relief.

Jeanay let out a disappointed sigh and turned her head around. They seated themselves at a table, and much to Jeanay's delight, a couple came and sat down near them with a dog. Jeanay turned to them, "Ooh! Your dog's so cute. May I pet her?"

The lady answered, "Sure, she's friendly."

Jeanay leaped from her chair and knelt down petting the little dog. As she made cute little noises over the dog it responded by wagging its tail violently. "Ooooh, your just so cute aren't you."

Professor Golden looked on amused and spoke to the couple. "You aren't going to sit inside, the preferred seating?"

The gentleman answered, "No, my wife likes her Bow-Wow out here."

"Excuse me?" Professor looked at them with a peculiar expression waiting for an explanation.

Jeanay appeared to be ignoring them all playing with the dog, without looking up she asked, "What is it?"

"Coffee," the wife laughed thinking she was answering both Professor Golden and Jeanay.

"What, your dog, Bow-wow, is coffee?" Jeanay looked at them puzzled.

The wife sputtered, "What? Coffee?—Oh, her names not coffee, or Bow-wow, or do you mean what kind of dog is she? She's a long-haired mutt is all we know."

Jeanay looked even more confused. Professor caught the meaning and explained, "Jeanay they call the coffee Bow-Wow here."

"What? Oh?" Jeanay laughed and continued to engage herself with the mutt.

The husband turned to speak to the Professor. "You must not be a local, first time here? Food's good, you'll find the menu unusual, to say the least."

"Oh?" Professor Golden answered loudly not sure what to make of it.

The waitress walked out the front door and handed Professor Golden the menus. She also brought their place settings. "May I get you anything?"

Professor Golden jumped on that, "I'll have a Bow-Wow."

"Me too," Jeanay quipped.

The waitress gave a surprised look and then with a sly smile asked snickering, "With or without fleas?"

Professor hadn't opened the menu. She was startled by the unusual question, "Oh." Then she quickly opened the menu and looked for that.

The wife came to her rescue as the waitress was having too much fun to be helpful. It was one of her few perks with a vigorous, demanding job. "That's sugar."

Jeanay belched out a loud laugh, "Fleas please," then shook her head in a kick over it.

Professor responded, "Without fleas!"

"Any cow juice?" The waitress asked ever so slightly snide with a crooked little smile.

Professor Golden looked up at the waitress and nodded her head up and down. "Oh, I get this one. Yes, cream."

Jeanay laughed delighted with the dog, waitress, and her aunt. She got up and dusted her hands off. "Enough fun I guess. I better get back to serious business."

The couple looked at her. *Serious business?*

"Thank you for letting me have fun with your dog," she smiled. They returned her smile.

Jeanay went back over to her table and sat down picking up the menu. The Professor started giggling. Jeanay looked at the menu, and then up at her aunt responding to her giggle with, "I see."

"So what do you want Jeanay a 'No-No' or a 'Sit and Stay'?"

Jeanay looked the menu over and let out a belly laugh. "No, I think I'll have a 'Dry Bone and Fetch'.

"Oh, that's a good one also darling." Professor Golden was so taken with the menu that she launched forth laughing so much she had a hard time speaking.

Here's how the menu read.

Fetch - Omelet
Sit - Eggs Benedict
Stay - Biscuits and Gravy
Rollover - Eggs over Easy
Scratch - Scrambled Eggs

Dry Bone - Toast
Gravy - Butter
Lie Down - Bacon
No No - Double Bacon and Cheese Burger
Bow-Wow - Coffee
Fleas - Sugar
Moo - Cream

The waitress came out with menus and settings for the couple across from them plus a treat for the dog. Then she took the Professor and Jeanay's order without further ado and went back inside.

Professor Golden started the order of business. "Okay, shall we look at the facts surrounding the conversation you had with Gunther and, also, about the additional notes I read?"

Jeanay nodded her head, "Sure." Then her eyebrows arched upward in question, "Are there connections?"

Professor Golden nodded, "Yes, well possibly, certainly interesting conjectures. Gunther's comments about UFOs and Oleg's drawings of objects that look both familiar and unfamiliar to our solar system has prompted him to make a theory that includes mention of quantum physics, quarks, and Planck's Theory."

Jeanay lifted an eyebrow in skepticism, "Oh, so only an opinion, and at that, only an idea without sufficient evidence or proof. You need to explain Planck's Theory I have heard of the other things."

"Okay, first let me explain Planck's Law, an electromagnetic radiation from heated bodies is not emitted as a continuous flow, but is made up of units of energy. Keep in mind a body is an object. Now, Planck's theory states all electromagnetic radiation is quantized and occurs in "bundles" of energy which we call photons. Light is quantum particles.

Professor Golden continued, "Albert Einstein, and scientists since, advanced Planck's Theory and made possible the development of quantum mechanics, which is a mathematical application of the quantum theory that maintains that energy is both matter and a wave."

Jeanay responded, "Okay, so it's tied into quantum physics which is the branch of physics concerned with quantum theory. It's hard to believe energy can be both a wave and matter!"

"And is not continuous, but is in bundles. Oleg also indicates the theory of quarks to be very disturbing?" Professor frowned, "That's odd."

"In what sense is that odd? They were discovered, right?"

"Yes, but by the quarks very nature they cannot be accurately tracked, their movement is erratic and even disappears. That's what he has a problem with. Let me qualify that they are yet to be accurately tracked, but that time will come, and I emphasis the word yet. Why would he find that disturbing? It just is! Oh well, each to his own."

"How can you be so sure they will someday be accurately tracked? Quarks are incredibly small being the smallest part of a neuron and proton."

Professor Golden shrugged as if it were a matter of fact. "I just am. Then he talks about…" Professor looked at Jeanay it was apparent from her expression that she was not accepting her last answer. "I'll qualify that. When scientists discovered atoms they decided that was the smallest particle possible. It wasn't!" She watched Jeanay's face change to a look of acknowledgement and then proceeded, "Then he notates discoveries about photons as having disturbing new facts."

Jeanay spread her hands out with raised eyebrows, "Really? So?"

Professor Golden continued, "The new factual discovery is that photons are aware they are being watched and they will change course accordingly."

"What—no!" Jeanay pushed back from the table. "Creepy! They are sentient?"

"Yes, certainly interesting. We could talk all night about the possible implications." The Professor was revved up, her motor purred with this type of discussion.

Jeanay waved her hand, "No, no, no! But please go on with what he says."

"Okay. Then he makes note that a credible scientist, Dr. Lear, has removed alien implants from people." Professor delivered this quickly thinking Jeanay's reaction would be farcical, derisive, or frightened.

Jeanay, wide-eyed, sucked in her breath and held it. Professor waited, and then she spoke concerned, "Breath Jeanay, breath!" Jeanay let out her breath and started breathing. "I have more, can we go on?" Jeanay nodded apprehensively. "He goes on to note that when a Christian woman, living isolated in the countryside, saw two Greys she shouted out, "Leave in Jesus name!" and they fled.

"Greys? What is a Grey?" Jeanay stared at her Aunt, and accused, "You know about them don't you!" A chill went up her spine. *I'm not sure I want to know the answer. I wish I hadn't asked the question.*

"Yes, I know about them. They are very tall, thin, odd looking, with human-like features."

"What do you mean human-like. No never mind, don't answer that. I don't want weird images in my head... You've seen them?" Jeanay asked, petrified.

"No. I've seen drawings based on their description."

"And you believe they really exist?"

"Have you forgotten that I was a science teacher, and part of my curriculum was phenomena?"

"Yes, but I didn't think of phenomena in these terms." Jeanay's arms swirled above her head and she flicked her fingers in mock, simulation bursts. "I thought of it as bursting things going on out there, in space, stars forming, and planets. Not this, I don't like this!" She shook her head in defiant disapproval.

"Neither did our scientist! You have something in common."

"Oh, yes, right…You don't think he was abducted? Oh, what am I saying! This is ridiculous!" Jeanay started rubbing her temples.

"Honey, he could have just needed to get away and think, or look more in-depth into these things. Lots of people study this. They look into the sky, they don't disappear, they're not abducted."

"Oh, yes, right. Wait!" Jeanay looked up suddenly at her aunt, "You DO believe it!"

"Jeanay, I know of people who stopped studying this as they were convinced there was a sinister side to it. I, personally, never investigated it. I've never met anyone who wrote about it. And I have never experienced any of it myself. I just study the material and teach speculation about the possibilities. That ladies response and outcome to her encounter should reassure you."

"Yes, but if that's true then there is a sinister side to this," Jeanay declared. "Maybe instead of beings from other planets it's dark angels, or that thing in the bible about Nephilim, Genesis 6, that messed up the earth, so that God called for a flood to clean up the contamination," Jeanay speculated.

"I don't know," Professor Golden shrugged and continued, "Another subject for another day. Now I do believe in the bizarre discoveries about photons and quarks. That's been proved, to a degree, which needs more in depth investigation. Not to disprove it, but to understand it. Now back to your journalism. You have new information that you can use to go back to the people you have spoken to and ask more specific questions. Get closer to the truth. Work the pieces of the puzzle. You can do this!"

Jeanay took a deep breath, "Okay, your right. Thank you, Auntie, for giving me more leads."

Professor Golden put her hand on top of Jeanay's hand. "You're welcome, my young reporter. And you, of all people, should be relieved that using Jesus' name dispels strange things!" They both smiled. Professor patted her hand to redirect her attention to the food being served, "And now the food is here." They both looked up eager to try their doggy food.

The Hunt Is On

Jeanay pulled up in front of the observatory. "I don't know how to get in since they aren't expecting me. I could swim, take that rowboat I guess," pointing to the boat tied-up at the beach's edge.

"Why don't you just call them?" Professor Golden held her cell phone in front of Jeanay's face. "Their number's on the Internet."

Jeanay looked sheepish, "Great investigative reporter I am!" Professor Golden kept a straight face.

"Thank you." Jeanay dialed the number on her phone, not long thereafter the door opened to the observatory.

"I'll stay here!! You can handle this without me," Professor Golden said, in no uncertain terms, not allowing herself to look at the water.

"You got it." Jeanay got out and waved to Bohdan who got in the skiff and swiftly steered toward her. When he arrived she chatted with him for a moment, and then she joined him in the boat. *Good, he's going along with me talking to them together. I'll see what kind of reaction I get.* The engine was too loud for any conversation pleasantries. Jeanay stepped out on the landing as soon as the boat rolled up to the footing.

Bohdan stepped out and tied the boat to the landing post. "Come on in I'll get Bondar." Jeanay followed him inside and took a seat where other chairs were that could accommodate all three of them. Bondar followed Bohdan over to Jeanay with a grumpy expression on his face. They both stood there and stared at her. Jeanay squirmed in the chair. *Should I get up or ask them to sit.* Jeanay's confidence was slipping. She cleared her throat. "Thank you for seeing me. Gentleman, doctors, please, please sit down with me. I need to have you clarify a few things that were in Oleg's file."

Bondar complained, "Oh bother, we try to be nice giving you his file, now we get our work interrupted?"

Bohdan turned to Bondar, "She's trying to help find him. You only gave her that file to get her off your back." Bondar rolled his eyes and shrugged. They ignored Jeanay and continued to banter.

The men being distracted with each other gave Jeanay time to take the opportunity to slip her cell phone out of her bag and turn it on unnoticed. The video started to record them. *I sure hope they don't notice.* Jeanay nervously interrupted, "Excuse me," clearing her throat, "Excuse me, please." The men stopped to listen. "How is it that, I'm referring to Oleg's notes, he has a problem with the part of science that deals with quarks and photons?"

Bondar snorted and waved his hand up in the air, "Because he's nuts. All scientists know about smaller particles in protons and neutrons. And photons have been studied far longer. This not to bother us, but him he gets some spiritual thing out of it. Then he go off and create problem for our government with United States." Dr. Bondar threw his hands up in the air in exasperation, "Why he have to go and do such thing?"

"What is your government's standing in this?" Jeanay queried.

Bohdan took his turn, "We have a long-standing relationship with the U.S. Our government is waiting for local police to find him."

Jeanay grew bolder as her interview subjugated her nerves, "When they do find him, hopefully, what will your government do?"

Dr. Bondar crossed his arms and spoke with contempt. "They take him back to Ukraine and put him in mental hospital…where he belong."

Jeanay waved her arm toward the ceiling. "So you don't see anything unusual out there, space, that bothers you?"

Dr. Bondar answered, "No, scientists know it is much unexplained out there, nothing come from it. Someday we will have perfect understanding of undocumented phenomena and it will be fine." He turned away, "I'm finished now," and went back to sit under the telescope.

Jeanay watched Bohdan's face for an indication of which direction she should take. Instead, uncomfortably, he offered that direction. "I have seen what books talk about, and military reports say, and they are denied as fraudulent. I wonder, on personal level, but do not let it get in way of my work. Oleg took this in how you say...in stride, until he made friends with Mr. Travis, who studies and tracks what he calls UFOs. Then it bothered Oleg for the first time that these moving things people photograph are out there. And that on our earth, in a smaller molecular environment, there are particles that disappear and move around in relative non-traceable patterns." Bohdan shrugged, "Are these types of behavior related?" Bohdan shrugged again, "And photons, which we thought were stable wave-patterns, to then find they, are also particle matter. And this particle matter also has the intelligence to differentiate and make decisions. Even now photons are being studied and found to respond to stimuli. For Oleg, this was too much information to process, and he made it have too much meaning. He went unstable."

"Did you try to get him help?"

"No, we would have had to contact our government and get permission. I did not want to jeopardize his job. In hind sight, that might have been the better choice," he conceded.

"You were embarrassed it sounds like to me."

"That too, I not proud to say," his accent slipped into grammar faux pas under stress. "So there you have all we know and all that Oleg let us know."

"Okay Bohdan, thank you. I appreciate your time."

Bohdan brightened, "Ah, you are velcome. If you find out anything you will tell us?"

"Yes, I'd be happy to," Jeanay assured him.

Bohdan got up and offered his hand to shake. Jeanay started to rise to her feet, as she did she discreetly slipped the phone behind her to rest on the seat, and shook his hand. "Thank you for running me back and forth. You have been very kind." Bohdan nodded acceptance of her compliment with a smile. He turned to leave. Jeanay took that opportunity to turn around and retrieve her phone and to discreetly turn off the video. She then texted her aunt they were on the way out and back to her.

Jeanay waved to her aunt as the boat approached her. She squinted her eyes to see more clearly. *What is she doing? Oh my, what is she doing behind the car?* Peeking barely above the trunk of the car was the video camera on its tripod with Professor Golden standing behind it. As they neared the embankment the Professor stepped in front of the camera hiding it. The boat docked, Jeanay stepped out and turned to nod to Bohdan as the boat headed back to the observatory. He gave a farewell wave.

Jeanay turned and grinned at her aunt, "What are you up to? Let me see."

"I got a great view of you heading back. Now, why don't you stay right there with the observatory in the background, and give us an update while I tape you? How did it go?"

"What a great idea! I'll show you." Jeanay pulled out her cell phone and brought up the video.

"Good girl, that was smart and tricky!"

"Why, thank you, Auntie. I'll splice it into the video you're taking, later."

Jeanay whipped off her Fedora and straightened her outfit.

"Is my hair okay?" She flung her golden locks from side to side.

"Your hair is fine." Professor Golden's hand was poised on top of the cell phone, size camera as she looked through its lens."

"Okay, I'm ready, turn it on."

Professor Golden pressed the "on" button and nodded to Jeanay.

"This is the famed Big Bear Observatory." Jeanay turned slightly and slowly waved her arm toward the building like a model directing the audience's attention to the prize. "I am standing on the North Shore. The investigation of a missing scientist has led me here today. I have interviewed the associates of the missing scientist, Oleg Kushnir. We will now go to that interview to help give us information into Dr. Kushnir's life leading up to his disappearance." She paused, and then directed, "Cut."

Where Do We Go From Here?

Professor Golden and Jeanay packed the video camera into the trunk. "You look a little tired Jeanay. I'm feeling adventurous after that nifty idea to record you. I'll drive…where to?"

"Well, you saw the video. The only clue left, that I can see, hinges on Gunther Travis which I'm not too thrilled about."

Professor Golden nodded her head in the affirmative, "True, as long as you're putting aside abduction or drowning in the lake."

Jeanay rolled her eyes and stated categorically, "I'm not going to even mention the other thing, whereas we can conclude that the police search ruled out drowning."

Professor drove the Mercedes out of the observatories parking lot. Jeanay stared at her aunt to see if she was serious about her statement, or just wanted to be agitating. Her aunt seemed oblivious as she steered the car. Jeanay mulled over her comments shaking her head, "Just head to Travis."

"Um, huh, that's where I'm headed." Undaunted her aunt had a merry look. "I'd forgotten how nice his car drives." There was a short ten-minute drive. "Oh, look at this we're here already. I'll get the camera out and follow you to the door, remaining discreetly out of the way of course."

"My Auntie you're getting bold."

"Why not! Beats sitting at home," Professor blurted out uncharacteristically.

"That's a nice change of tune," Jeanay commented joyfully and then asked sweetly, "You miss teaching?"

"I did until now!" Professor Golden beamed at Jeanay as she opened the car door.

Jeanay pursed her lips in a satisfied expression finding this information gratifying.

Professor Golden got out of the car and scurried to the trunk. She grabbed the handheld video camera from the trunk and slid up next to the wall not far from the door of Gunther's lodging. Jeanay marched up to the door and knocked. Professor clicked the "on" button and poised herself as if she were ready to get struck by someone. If anyone had noticed they would have found her to be quite comical. For all the effort no one answered the door.

Jeanay returned to her aunt, "I'll be back."

"You'll be back from what?" The Professor sensed what she was up to. "Oh, no you don't, I'm coming!" Professor Golden switched off the video.

"Okay, see if you can work your magic with the bartender again." Jeanay winked and strutted into the restaurant bar next door with her aunt. They proceeded to the bar.

The bartender turned around to greet them. As he turned he was caught in surprise. "Oh no, not you two, are you ganging up on me?"

Jeanay laughed, "No, no! We just want to know where to find Gunther he doesn't seem to be at home?"

Professor Golden gave him a sweet, little smile.

The bartender grinned, in derision, and continued drying out a serving glass. He put it down forcefully startling both ladies. "Not a problem. He's gone!"

Jeanay, alarmed, sucked in her breath loudly. "What do you mean by that?!"

Professor Golden made a fist and slammed it down on the bar, "Yea!" It was a hilarious attempt at being tough.

Jeanay couldn't help herself she tried to force back a smile at her aunt's antics. Then the bartender made a gruff, "Haw." Professor Golden reacted with a glare, and then she started laughing at herself ignoring his scornful tone.

The bartender leaned back on his haunches and crossed his arms.

Jeanay called his bluff, "Oh, the silent treatment eh. You just might be in cahoots with him... obstructing the law." Jeanay tapped her finger on the bar and leaned forward in an accusing loud, long whisper, "M-a-y-be mur-d-e-r," and then quickly added in a firm voice, "Professor, go call the police!"

The bartender looked shocked, "Professor? You?" Incredulous he looked Professor Golden up and down. He shook his head in disbelief, "Police?" He reconsidered his stance, "He left for his cabin."

Professor Golden shifted her weight and stamped each foot, side to side. She looked puzzled and exclaimed, "We were just at his cabin," then looking to Jeanay, "We were just at his cabin, weren't we?"

Jeanay looked at her aunt with a shrug, "Beats me." Then looking at the bartender she demanded in a frustrated voice, "Will you please tell me where he is!"

The bartender leaned forward and spoke tersely, "Up the mountain, he has a cabin."

Jeanay sat there waiting for more, when it didn't happen, at the end of her rope, she jumped off the bar stool and stood straddling the floor in defiance. Her arms shot out at each side of her straight down toward the floor, her hands balled into fists. She shouted, "Up which mountain? Tell me now!" Uncomfortable with her own demonstrative behavior she quickly changed her fists to open handed begging, "Where?!" She asked in consternation.

The young man, not sure what to make of her double-action, duplicitous stand, drew back and conceded, "Follow Sugar Loaf Ridge!"

"What?" Jeanay yelled back. "What does that mean?"

The bartender shot back loudly, in defense, intending to get rid of them as quickly as possible. "I don't know I've never been there! That's just what he told me."

Jeanay, who became suddenly quiet as if a switch were turned off, replied, "Oh, all right."

Professor Golden, wide-eyed, had been jerking her head back and forth between the two, her feet rocking, her fists clenched against her chest moving them back and forth like a boxer, but in miniature movements. Out of her element in an unreality to her known life she looked unhinged.

Jeanay slipped her hand into her aunt's balled fist, "We're finished here," she declared. They walked out hand in hand with Professor's head bobbing in unrelenting nerves.

Christmas in May

Once outside the bar Professor started bouncing, "Whoa, hff, hff," making huffing noises in little, triumphant puffs. I didn't know if I was going to have to start swinging or try to drag you out before he started swinging. I'm so pumped, don't know what I'd of done, first I was terrified then something came over me almost superhuman. Never felt that before, exhilarating!" She flexed her little shoulders like a boxer.

"Sounds empowered! Auntie, wow look at you," Jeanay smiled feeling her adrenaline flush settle down. And thankful for her aunt's head bobbing nerves to have settled.

"Yea! I don't know what I was, how about you?" Professor asked elated.

Jeanay was much more serene as she spoke, "I don't know what I was either. Didn't know what I was doing. I guess you could say something came over me too." Jeanay thought out loud as she and Professor Golden walked to the car parked outside near the restaurant. "And now, I've got to find out how we can get to Sugar Loaf Ridge."

"The motel has a local, one-page, fold-out map of the area. I noticed it in our welcome package on the table in our room," Professor Golden offered as she calmed down and returned to her cerebral thinking.

"Now how did I miss that?" Jeanay looked mystified.

"Jeanay I'd like to leave the car here and walk through town. There are so many darling gift shops we haven't made time on our little trip to enjoy not that it hasn't been interesting so far."

Jeanay chuckled, "Right… Sure, I think it would be nice to take a break and look in the souvenir shops. That would also give me the opportunity to ask around about how to get to Sugar Loaf."

They walked not far from the car before a coffee shop, a movie theater with only two movie screens, a game arcade full of noisy kids with their parents, a postal store, a candy shop, an ice cream store, two art galleries, several restaurants, and souvenir shops filled their vision.

Jeanay pointed at a store, "Oh look, a Christmas store, I love it, let's start there," she bounced toward the store.

Professor Golden trotted behind Jeanay to keep up with her, she replied, "That's odd, a year-round Christmas store? Always something new they think of these days. Remarkable they could make enough money year-round with that! Oh well, that's a tourist town for you."

They went through the front door, stopping short, to take in the winter wonderland of decorated, lit trees with ornaments galore. Sparkling lights met their eyes. Soft Christmas music met their ears. The outer walls were fitted with display cabinets and filled with assorted ornaments of glittering angels, round ornaments, little toy soldiers, and a myriad of every ornament toy imaginable. A friendly voice greeted them from the cash register, "Welcome."

Jeanay walked over to a shimmering, gold and white angel and fingered it delicately. "Mother and I love angels. She's got them around the house. I think she'd like this one."

"Yes, your mom would love that. I'm going to walk around." Professor Golden stepped away. They both looked around not walking far from each other to share "Oohs" and "Awes" over different items. Then the Professor stopped abruptly noticing a woman near her. "Hello, hello?"

The lady turned around, "Oh hello."

Professor placed her finger against her temple lightly tapping it in concentration. "Aren't you the lady from the aerobics wait, no-no, the auditorium, the gymnastics, yes, the, gymnastics classes?" Professor Golden finished fishing from her memory and caught Jeanay's attention as well.

"Yes," Cathy answered, while politely taking in Professor's maze-like, tracking.

"Cathy," Jeanay called out cheerily and walked over to join them.

Cathy responded with a small smile. "Hello, how has your manhunt been going?"

"We've found out a few things, but not enough." Jeanay looked at her hopefully.

"Oh, well the police haven't either. Don't feel so bad. How do you like our little town?"

"We haven't had much time until now to check it out. That is other than the Bow-Wow place. Dogs are my thing." Jeanay admitted.

Professor Golden laughed, "All animals are your thing!"

"True," Jeanay smiled and nodded.

Cathy laughed, "You mean the Fetch and Stay Chow Restaurant. Cat's are more my thing!"

Professor Golden got an inspiration, "Maybe they'll bring in a cat place. I heard they are popular in Japan, and Los Angeles opened their first one."

Cathy looked at her in surprise, "Seriously? You're kidding!"

"No," Professor Golden shook her head. "They have them behind glass with their own set-up of toys, beds, and catwalks. They play and the customers laugh at their antics. They have to wash their hands to go inside to pet the cats. The places are called..." Professor looked up to the sky pulling on her memory, "Cat Cafes. Yes, that's it!" She looked proud of herself.

Jeanay laughed, "Yes, that's right! I saw something about that on T.V."

Cathy looked impressed, "I think I'll have to go visit Japan."

"L.A.'s closer," Professor Golden offered pointedly.

Cathy looked a bit embarrassed giving a slightly, sheepish grin. "Yes it is, but it would give me an excuse to visit Japan," she cleared her throat.

"Japan's more fun," Jeanay remarked wanting to keep them united. Jeanay decided to change the subject not wanting to lose Cathy to meandering around the store just yet. Knowing her aunt was sometimes not people sensitive like this situation indicated. "Just making a joke or just giving the facts," the Professor would say not understanding how anyone could mistake it. As Cathy started to step away to relieve the awkwardness she felt, Jeanay intervened, "We are trying to find Sugar Loaf Ridge. Could you tell me how to get there?"

Cathy described, "Sugar Loaf is a nice short drive from here toward the backside of the mountain."

"Backside, I've heard that before, a little confusing for a first time here," Jeanay confessed.

"Well, that's true. Actually, we have two backsides, one to Las Vegas through Apple Valley, the other Yucaipa which goes on down into Redlands."

"Oh great," Jeanay looked even more confused.

"It's simple really. We have only one main road that runs from the front bringing people from Riverside-Orange County, to the back taking them to Redlands-Palm Springs, and another way to get to Las Vegas. Which way did you come?"

"It was the front way, from Riverside," Jeanay replied turning to her aunt, "Right Auntie, although I did see a Redlands sign?"

"You're right dear."

Cathy continued, "Okay, so continue on from the way you came up, pass the airport, and take the signs that say Yucaipa. A few miles out of town you will see a sign for the Sugar Loaf turn-off. That part's simple. Now, the ridge is another matter. You have to hike to it and there aren't, really, any good paths or signs. It is lovely up there. Makes you feel closer to God."

"Oh," Jeanay exclaimed, "No wonder!"

Cathy looked puzzled, "No wonder what?"

Professor Golden looked at Jeanay wondering as well. Then she guessed, "A place to hide?"

Jeanay gave a slight nod of agreement, "That to," and added, "A closer feeling to God!"

Jeanay and Professor Golden looked at each other, eye to eye, with understanding.

"What?" Cathy asked loudly looking back and forth at them.

"Can I help you?" The cashier had noticed them and interrupted.

Being thoroughly distracted by the cashier Cathy handed her an ornament, "Yes, I'd like to go ahead and buy this."

"Certainly," the cashier walked to her cash register with Cathy following behind her.

"Come on let's go, Auntie!"

"You bet. Wait. Don't you want to buy that angel for your mother?"

"It can wait."

They both waved and yelled to Cathy, "Bye," then they walked, arm in arm, out the door.

Cathy turned around to see where they were. *Gone,* "Hum," *place to hide, closer to God, I wonder what that was all about?*

Sugar Loaf Ridge

"Now you watch for the Yucaipa and Sugar Loaf signs too Auntie."

Professor Golden nodded, "Uh-huh," as she stared out her side of the window.

Jeanay had taken the wheel. She furtively looked for signboards. "All roads seem to point back to Gunther Travis," she murmured.

"Pure speculation, but we haven't found evidence leading to anything else. I looked on your laptop for articles about violence here in Big Bear. There have been noted fights, a few deaths, shootings, etc. Not very many, but they have all been related to people who knew each other, arguments, disputes, that kind of thing. Alcohol or drugs were usually involved."

"Wow Auntie, you thought of that? I'm impressed! You're turning into an investigative reporter."

Professor Golden smiled her quirky little smile. "Thank you!"

"So, Auntie, do you think they had a dispute?"

"Maybe, Oleg did seem to be a little unstable that rubs people you know."

"But Gunther was the troublemaker with the UFO stuff," Jeanay tossed back.

"All the more reason for a good fight," Professor Golden tapped her fingers rhythmically on the door handle where she rested her arm. Suddenly, she pointed repeatedly, "There! There Jeanay, there's the cut-off!"

"Ah, okay, got it! Jeanay turned the car sharply. "Not far now!" Jeanay's voice was full of anticipation and excitement.

They parked the car in the dirt at the roads end. Professor Golden opened the glove compartment, pushed the trunk latch button, rummaged around in her bag in the back seat, and got out of the car. Jeanay was the first to reach the open trunk. "Here's your boots," Jeanay held them up high, by the laces, dangling them in front of the Professor. She had her hiking boots on already. She slung the video camera and tripod bag over her shoulder.

Professor Golden took her boots from Jeanay and set them down, "Thank you and here are our hats. Mine is called a Trapper." She pulled on a faux fur hat that was white fleece lined and had flaps that came down over her ears. She handed the other hat to Jeanay. "And this is yours, it's called Desertwalker. It will make you look like Sherlock Holmes with the brim in the front and back."

Jeanay held the hat out at arm's length between her thumb and fingers to study it. "Oh my goodness," then with a chuckle she slipped it on her head. "I guess we're properly dressed now." Then in an attempt to imitate the voice of Sherlock Holmes, "The adventure awaits. Come Watson."

"Good thing we have a break in the weather. It's always cooler up here or our hats would be too hot. And young lady you need to remember that's my hat! I'm only sharing it with you."

"Ha, we'll see about that!" Jeanay slammed the car trunk closed in mock defiance. "The game is on!" She marched forward and then made an abrupt stop looking up at the mountain.

"Forget something?" Professor Golden held up a compass in one hand for Jeanay to see. "Gotta make sure we can find our way back."

"Where'd you get that?

"Now who's Sherlock Holmes?" Professor imitated Sherlock's voice, "My dear."

They both laughed.

"I bet we can't use our cell phones out here," Professor commented.

Jeanay looked a little worried, "Oh!" She stood very still, and then bowed her head.

"Are you trying to figure out which way to go Jeanay?"

"No, I'm praying…"

"Good idea." Professor decided to look up into the heavens the usual way she, and the Jews pray always looking for a sign from God.

Jeanay lifted her head and looked around, "Now I'm trying to decide, but everything looks the same."

"Let's just walk and look for a cabin, have some faith," encouraged Professor Golden. "Let me change my shoes." She went to the car seat to sit while she put on the hiking boots.

The pine trees were skyscrapers their topmost branches gently swayed as a soft sound whooshed through them. There was no breeze near the ground you could only hear it in the treetops. The air was clean, crisp, pine-scented, comfortable and clear. The birds were busy flying around chirping, some exchanged scolding with a squirrel over territory. A woodpecker could be heard in the distance rhythmically knocking his way into a tree. Bugs scrambled and bee's hummed around them. Wildflowers sprinkled the hillside, here and there, dashing the ground with patches of color in yellow-gold, lavender, blue, and red. The flowers had emerged defying the receding, sparkling snow where patches of brown earth exposed them.

The ladies worked their way up a mile when the clip-clop of horse hooves resounded in their ears. They looked up in surprise to see a lady riding atop a palomino mare with a white mane and tail. The horse's powerful muscles rippled as it placed each nimble hoof strategically, purposefully square in the dirt avoiding rocks and dead branches. The woman sat in the silver-embellished, ornately carved, brown leather saddle. Her horse had a matching silver-link forehead band on the bridle. The rider positioned herself, leaning back slightly, to help her horse maintain better balance. The mare shot out a spray of vapor from her wide nostrils in surprise at their presence. The spray had the sound of a rumbling, swoosh blast alerting her rider that they were not alone. The rider, who had been looking down studying the path raised her head and gently pulled back on the reins to stop. Spotting the couple she patted her horse on the neck, a sign of approval, for its protective signal.

The lady wore matching brown boots and a cowgirl hat. Her hat was decorated with silver medallions linked entirely around the hat band matching the ones on the saddle. Her hair was tucked up neatly underneath her hat with a few white ringlets hanging down. Her clothing started with a neatly pressed, form-fitting, white, tailored shirt worn over jeans. A blue-green-white checkered, three-quarter length, fleece jacket was tied behind the saddle in place of a western style bed roll. Normally the white collar of her shirt was lifted high above the white fleece jacket collar, the ensemble accentuating her cheekbones, but not on this warm day. She smiled at the Professor and Jeanay who were standing stock still watching the impressive pair.

When the horse had alerted her rider, Jeanay laughed, "Horse snot…How beautiful!"

Professor Golden looked at her out of the corner of her blue eyes with her head still pointed toward the horse, and then she moved her eyes quickly back to the mare. *Does she mean the snot or the horse?*

Jeanay stepped forward, "Hi, my name is Jeanay and this is my aunt Professor Golden. Can I pet her?"

The rider smiled and nodded, "Hello, my name is Jube. What are you two doing out here? There aren't any marked tourist trails here."

Professor Golden stood her ground and answered, "We're trailblazing our own, like you."

"Ah yes, so you are."

The woman's horse stomped her hoof as Jeanay raked the fur on its neck with her fingers. "In a hurry to get home are you?" Jeanay spoke to the horse.

Jube laughed, "She likes her oats. She knows she's headed for her treat."

"She's gorgeous." Jeanay skyrocketed into her pet-mode, but with added reverence being in the presence of such a magnificent creature.

Professor Golden cleared her throat and spoke to Jeanay in a prodding manner. "Perhaps a little information might help?"

Jube picked up on the question and asked, "Oh, are you lost?"

"No." Jeanay responded thoughtfully, "But we are looking for a Gunther Travis. Do you know him?"

"The name doesn't sound familiar," Jube shook her head. She looked puzzled, "Didn't he give you directions?"

Professor Golden quickly interjected, "We wanted to surprise him."

Jeanay lifted her eyebrows. *Ooh, quick save!*

The woman looked away as her horse got antsier and started a little dance to get her riders attention. "There are a few cabins over the ridge," she pointed in the direction they were headed. "On foot, it may take you a good hour. You don't look prepared to stay overnight so I would hustle if I were you. You can follow the trail we made coming down. These are my only set of tracks since I went up a different way."

Jeanay pulled her attention away from the horse long enough to say, "Thank you, I really appreciate that!"

"You're welcome," Jube smiled.

Jeanay could hardly contain her excitement over the encounter as she gazed into the horse's soft, large, brown eyes with long, black lashes. The horse met her gaze penetrating Jeanay's blue-green eyes. The mare was the one to break their locked gaze. She nickered in anticipation of home and pawed her hoof on the ground. The palomino raised and lowered her head up and down impatiently. Jube released the reins that had kept her horse in check. The mare took her cue and trotted forward.

Professor Golden and Jeanay turned their heads following the fleeting horse and rider as they continued on, until out of sight, around the bend down the mountain. The mesmerizing clip-clop of hoofs moved away from them becoming fainter and then undetectable.

Ridgeline Surprises

Jeanay reached the top of the ridgeline first. She bent over with a hand on each knee puffing. After she caught her breath she yelled down below her, "Almost there Auntie, you're doing great!"

Shortly a huffing Professor Golden caught up with her. She found a large rock and sat down hard on it. Professor used her scarf to pat the perspiration on her forehead while she breathed deeply to catch her breath. In labored, short breaths she asked, "Do… you see… a cabin… down… there?"

Jeanay was standing up straight now looking down on the other side of the ridge they had walked up. With her hand shading her eyes she reported, "No, but I see chimney smoke!"

"Then chimney smoke here I come!" Professor Golden retorted as she struggled to her feet. "Ugh, I think I'm going to be sore tomorrow."

"Ohh-kay!" Jeanay answered reenergized. Rubbing her calves she added, "Me too."

A little while later the ladies neared the cabin. "I think I hear someone chopping wood," Professor Golden noted the rhythmic sound.

Jeanay nodded in the affirmative, "And I see a flannel shirt and jeans wielding an ax.

Who is it?" Professor squinted to see more clearly.

Jeanay spoke slowly, "It…is…a little hard…to figure out with that knit cap. He's standing up and turning a little. Oh wait, I have binoculars in my backpack," Jeanay pulled them out and adjusted the lenses. In nervous anticipation she announced, "It's our man, Gunther…" Jeanay bit her lip, "What should I do. What should I do?" Then encouraging herself, "Okay, I can do this. You can do this Jeanay!" She shook her whole body in an attempt to shake off her nerves. Decidedly she blurted, "I'm going to snoop around the back and video through the windows."

"If you're going to do that then I'm going to go distract Gunther."

Jeanay grabbed Professor Golden's arm. "No, he might recognize you!"

Professor Golden stood her ground and stubbornly insisted, "No, he won't. You were the only one who talked to him. I was back behind the car with the camera."

"Oh, that's right! Okay, Auntie. I think he's a nice person. No… wait! If he's hiding something he might not be nice. You stay here!"

Professor Golden countered her niece. "Jeanay he's only going to think I'm a hiker passing by. It won't hurt me to talk to him." Then more gently, "That way you can take it slower checking out the cabin."

"Uhh!" *I don't know whether to go with that suggestion or not.* "Oh, okay!" Having decided, and mildly petulant, Jeanay pulled out the video camera. She took stealth-like steps toward the cabin avoiding little branches, sticks, and leaves.

Professor Golden waited until she saw Jeanay round the cabin. Then Professor walked toward Gunther speaking out loudly, "Hi, how are you?" Startled Gunther turned toward her quickly with the ax menacingly poised in the air. Professor jumped back stumbling, "Oh, oh!"

"Oh, sorry ma'am, I didn't expect anyone to be out here." He lowered the ax slowly and placed it against his leg with the head on the ground by his foot, his hand on top, and leaned on it, "You alone?"

"Yes." Then thinking that might not have been a safe answer, her heart pounding, "No, my party is around here somewhere. Why do you ask?"

"We don't get many people out in this neck of the woods. It's more popular near the ski lifts and lake."

"I see. It sure is quiet and beautiful out here!" Professor exclaimed loudly trying to steady her nerves.

He nodded, "Most of the time." Gunther stared silently at the Professor not sure what to say next. He felt her presence a little odd, out of place, but not alarming. Her next question settled his mind about this interruption.

"I was wondering if I could use your restroom?" *Great, now what have I done? It's just so awkward with him staring at me like that.*

Gunther paused considering the request. "I'll have to go in and clean a few things up, if you'd wait here for me please." Gunther crunched through the snow and overgrowth in his heavy boots. He disappeared into the cabin.

Meanwhile, Jeanay who had been inspecting the back windows peeked around the side of the building. Seeing her aunt alone she beckoned to her. Professor cautiously stepped her way over to Jeanay hoping no sound of her footsteps would give her location away.

Jeanay didn't even think to ask of his whereabouts as she whispered in excited tones, "There's someone in there. I couldn't see the face, but, I think, from the back of the head it was a man."

Professor Golden whispered back, "I'm going to use his restroom then I can take a look around."

"You're what?" Jeanay squeaked dropping her whisper for a second.

"Shh, its okay, he said I could after he cleaned up a few things."

In a defiant whisper Jeanay shot back, "Ahh, no! We should just go and tell the police about this."

"Have we switched rolls?" Professor Golden asked in surprise. Jeanay shrugged not sure what to make of this. Professor's bold attitude continued, "And just what do we tell them? There are two people up in a cabin. And we want you to check them out? Really Jeanay, look at us, they'll think we're cuckoo. I know I can be a little wound-up, but not cuckoo!" Professor Golden's tenuous confidence started to slip, "Maybe your right." She looked around uncertain of her bearings, in a tentative voice, she whispered, "What else can we do?" She paused to think knowing the clock was ticking. "I'm stuck, we're stuck! Then firmly she finished with a flourish of conviction, "I've got to go he'll be out in a minute!"

Jeanay stared speechless at her aunt not knowing what to say, do, or think, but fearing imminent danger. Professor Golden shook herself, and she stepped away from Jeanay toward the front door. Wide-eyed Jeanay whispered, "Be careful he might have a gun!"

Jeanay pulled back quickly behind the corner of the cabin as Gunther stepped out. He looked for Professor where she had stood by his woodpile. While he was scanning for her Professor Golden eased herself clear of the house. With her eyes on him she pinched her arm in pain to distract her nerves. Her facial expressions comically displayed her discomfort. Gunther had his hand up shielding his eyes from the sun looking for her. He then turned and spied her, "Oh, there you are. You may go in now. It's back to the left." He indicated by pointing as he held the door open for her.

Professor Golden covered the red mark on her arm. "Thank you," she gave him a charming smile and walked in the door. The small, open combination kitchen-living room had a nice rock fireplace with a comfortable little blaze going. The room was put together bachelor style, sparsely furnished with a rocking chair, a leather sofa-bed, and a fur throw. The kitchen held a counter that ran the length of the wall with a farm sink, a few rustic wood cabinets, and a wood burning stove with an old coffee pot sitting on it percolating. A worn, scratched table and chairs bridged the living room kitchen area. The walls held a few mountain artifacts including a wood-carved moose, a wood-carved mountain scene, and a wood-carved coat-of-mail. The interior had a pleasant smoky scent.

The Professor turned around to see if Gunther was still there, he was. She walked back where Gunther had indicated and opened the door. She noted he was still watching her. She also noticed a closed door across from the one she was opening. Professor went in and locked the bathroom door leaning heavily against it. Her nerves started to kick in. One leg started to bounce spastically. She placed her hand on top of her leg and pushed it down to stop the movement. "Shh," she shushed her leg. The calming effect surprised her, so she quietly kept shushing herself until her nerves settled enough to let her gently open the door. Her head bobbed slightly, and her eyelids batted in apprehension, "I should've listened to Jeanay," she whispered. *What am I doing here?*

Professor Golden quietly unlocked the door and peered out to see if anyone was watching her as her head continued to bob and her eyelashes to flutter. No one was around, Professor Golden eased out the door and tip-toed to the other door. The creaky, wood floor was a challenge to walk on undetected, but it distracted her from her mounting nerves as she traversed it. As she stood before the closed door her teeth started to chatter, she gritted her teeth. The Professor took a deep breath and put her hand forward to latch on to the doorknob, but her hand was shaking so bad that she drew it back. *You can do this Natalie, you can do this! It's good, it's all good!* She placed her hand back on the old, rusted doorknob her fierce grip silencing her shaking hand and slowly, quietly opened it.

There sat a man in a rocker reading a book. The man looked up startled, "Oh," he dropped his book with a loud bang looking back and forth as if looking for help.

"Oh," Professor Golden gasped startled from the loud noise and flung herself back against the door banging it closed. She began to stutter, "O-o-o-oh, e-e-e-excuse m-me, I m-m-must have gotten the w-w-wrong door, this isn't the restroom!" She said in a convincing, embarrassed voice. No actress, sincere in the moment she was out of her element, she wanted to disappear.

Wide-eyed Professor Golden looked around the small room still backed up against the door trying to gain her composure. The young man's rocker sat on an oval throw rug handmade from green rags. A single bed was covered with multi-colored squares of bright cloth stitched into a quilt. An oil lamp sat dark on a small table by the bed with its oil and wick waiting to be lit. On the table sat most notably a Bible. A few other books and magazines littered the floor.

The Professor, nervous and shy, stepped forward bravely and held out her shaking hand. Her voice quivered, "Hello, I'm Professor Golden and who are you?"

The man deliberated about offering his hand and remained seated his eyes bulging in shock and despair. There was an awkward silence. Professor Golden stepped forward further, admirably, to his chair still holding out her hand. Then, resigned, he took her hand to shake it. "Hello," he spoke as he glanced at her and then looked down.

Professor Golden looked over the young man's shoulder and saw Jeanay, at the window, pointing at him excitedly and nodding her head up and down vigorously. *I think Jeanay has found her man. Now I wish I had paid closer attention to the newspaper picture of him, but I'm glad she did.* Then Jeanay mouthed "get out," as she swung her arms wildly pointing to the forest. Professor nodded and then looked down. *Ah, yes, science books on the floor.* Professor turned her direction from the books back to him. "I really must use the restroom now, nice to meet you," she announced awkwardly. He gave her an uncomfortable nod. Professor caught Jeanay's eye and gave her a head nod toward the bathroom.

Professor quickly returned to the restroom. She went over to the old-fashioned, wood window and pushed it up. *Too small to climb out, rats!*

Jeanay had caught the head nod and was waiting at the window. She looked into her aunt's face from outside and bounced excited, "It's him! IT'S HIM! I'm sure it is! I saw his profile when you surprised him, and I've seen his picture in the newspaper. Good work Auntie!"

"I think I might have heard a slight Ukraine accent in that one word "Hello" even though he wouldn't give me his name. That alone was suspicious, not to mention the science books on the floor. I wonder why he's here?"

"Did he look like he was being kept here, locked in?" Jeanay worried.

"No, he looked comfortable and very concerned about me barging into his room."

"Yea Auntie, that was impressive!"

"Thank you, darling."

There was a knock at the bathroom door. Professor Golden jumped and slammed the window shut. She winced at her haste reaction. The voice of Gunther asked grumpily from the other side of the door, "Everything okay in there?" Professor Golden opened the door in response, she stepped forward slowly. Gunther didn't give an inch, "I thought I heard voices and the window slam?"

Professor Golden started giggling nervously, "Yes, you did I talk to myself quite frequently." She put her hand up to her nose and pinched it closed as she spoke in a nasal tone. "Yes, a bit stinky in here right now had to open the window. Sorry, sorry." She dropped her hand from her nose. She squeezed sideways with only an inch to spare in passing by the tall, large, imposing figure. He looked after her puzzled and suspicious as she moved toward the front door. "Yes, yes, some people find my self-talk annoying. Even I find it annoying sometimes. Yes, yes, talk, talk, talk," she shrugged and gave funny little chuckles then nervously backed out the door. Her voice had an unusually high pitch to it, "Thank you. Thank you." Professor cleared her throat then gave a small wave and with quick little steps exited from view. Once outside she sighed in relief, stuck her arms down stiff by her side with her hands open toward the ground and shivered, at the same time, letting out an "Ugh," as she walked briskly up toward the ridge.

Gunther with a concerned, perplexed expression moved to the door where he could watch her. He followed her outside and watched her disappear over the crest of the ridge. He went back inside. The younger man was standing in the bedroom doorway, "What you think that was about?"

Gunther scratched his head thoughtfully, "I don't know, seems odd."

"She ask my name. Is that American protocol? She introduce herself," The young man offered innocently.

"What? She was in your room? What was her name? Gunther asked alarmed.

"Professor Golden."

"A professor! Maybe your people are involved. You need more time. I don't like the sound of this." Gunther went over and grabbed his rifle.

The younger man was alarmed, "What you going to do with that?!"

"Oh, I don't know! Scare her?"

"What good will that do? Maybe it's time for this to end."

Jeanay was already on the other side of the ridge nervously pacing, back and forth, waiting for her aunt. When Professor Golden saw her she waved and hurriedly joined her. Jeanay fidgeting asked, "What do we do now?"

"Jeanay, NOW, we have sufficient evidence to get a hold of the police."

A loud male voice bellowed, "No you don't!"

The ladies didn't move, frozen their eyes widening in fear. Then they simultaneously swung around to face their antagonist.

The younger man came over the hill after the bellicose one yelling, "No…Gunther…stop!" An unmistakable Ukrainian accent met their ears.

Gunther turned around to look at Oleg and yelled, "You need more time!"

Professor and Jeanay, stricken, looked at each other and then knowingly nodded in agreement. Screaming they threw themselves on top of Gunther. The force dislodged the rifle and it flew to the ground out of reach of the girls. Oleg picked it up and placed the handle on the ground with his hand around the barrel ending the threat. The girls and Gunther, wide-eyed, face to face, within breaths of all three stared at each other in bewilderment. In embarrassed, awkward silence the three slowly got up and brushed off their clothing. If it hadn't been so frightening it would have been hilarious.

Cabin Fever

Professor Golden stood with her hands on her hips. "You could have seriously hurt us with that gun!

Gunther meekly answered back, "It wasn't cocked it couldn't fire. It was just meant to scare you off."

Professor wasn't finished she got in his face, "Scare me off, or give me a heart attack."

Jeanay intervened much to Gunther's relief, "Please, Auntie it's over. We're okay. Let's just move on with this interview, please? They, after all, agreed to this. I'm sure to make up for all we went through."

Professor Golden nodded her head with crossed arms.

Oleg and Gunther did the same in awkard silence.

"Okay, start it rolling." Jeanay sat opposite Oleg, in the Ridgeline cabin, and nodded to Professor Golden indicating to turn on the video camera. "Oleg, you are a scientist at the Big Bear Observatory?"

"Yes, I am."

"Did you know you were listed as a Missing Person?"

"I have been called missing by the news, and as you see I am not missing, now."

"What led to you leaving your research?"

"I have been working little too hard. I need break." Oleg spoke in his not so perfect English.

We have a quote from a reliable source who overheard someone say to you, "You need more time." Can you tell us what that meant? Did this have anything to do with your research?"

Professor Golden snickered to herself *'reliable source.' Poetic license, no that's journalism license. And she's worried about asking people for permission to video them.*

Oleg spoke slowly and carefully to keep his English as accurate as possible, "Yes, no," an abrupt flip. "You might call it, how you say, a, a mid-life crisis. I want to apologize to anyone who was concerned about me. I will return and-and put this right with local authorities and my government that has been so gracious to send me here."

"You said, 'Yes and no,' would you explain the 'yes' part."

"No." Oleg squirmed and changed position crossing his arms.

Jeanay felt the standoff and pushed, "I have a log book that shows diagrams of space, calculations, and objects that you drew. What do you have to say about that?"

Oleg looked startled, unhinged. He shook his head and sat silent.

Jeanay frustrated charged, "We have science people who have looked at this, and they say it indicates you were studying UFOs. Have you seen UFOs?" Asking out of interest for herself not just for the video.

No answer.

"Are you looking for a UFO silent collusion with the Vatican?"

Wide-eyed he looked at her in disbelief, "No!"

"Mr. Kushnir you look scared."

"No." He squirmed in his seat. "I must speak to my country."

Professor Golden batted her eyelashes and turned away to cover her mouth from laughing out loud. *I don't believe this girl! Gutsy!*

Jeanay was starting to feel sorry for him even though she was frustrated. So she switched tactics. "Where have you been hiding-out, I mean staying?" The inference was a little underhanded. Jeanay was surprised with herself.

Oleg looked desperate to leave as he confessed, "I have been staying in friend's cabin here in Big Bear."

Jeanay then turned to the camera, "You heard it here first, both the discovery and the return of Oleg Kushnir. This is Jeanay Golden reporting from Big Bear."

Professor Golden stopped the camera.

Gunther looked pleased about the interview being it was his favorite topic that came to the forefront while Oleg looked wretchedly distressed. The two men left quickly.

Jeanay packed up her equipment and asked her aunt, "Well how did you like that Auntie?"

"Do you mean the part about quote, 'reliable source,' or 'hiding-out,' and the 'Vatican,' really?" Professor Golden looked incredulous.

Jeanay looked at her and batted her eyes, "A little over the top?"

"Oh, I don't know it just seems a little much, but I'm not a newsperson."

Jeanay conceded, "Yea, maybe so. I've got to learn my way and listen to my conscience."

"That's the first time I've been that close to a man since your uncle."

Jeanay looked at her aunt surprised with the quick change of subject, intrigued she thought quickly trying to catch up to speed with her aunt's thoughts. She laughed, "You mean when we both knocked over Gunther Travis?"

Professor Golden nodded sheepishly.

They both burst out laughing.

Professor continued, "I'm glad it's something we can laugh at, could've turned out disastrous. You were so brave."

Jeanay returned, "So were you."

"I was a nervous wreck brave."

"We were both a nervous wreck brave!" Then Jeanay asked, "Notwithstanding your partial critique, overall how did you like the shoot?"

"I'm sure glad it didn't end up that way," Professor rolled her eyes.

Not understanding Jeanay sat back and gave her a peculiar look. Her Auntie nudged her with her shoulder, "Just kidding I know what you meant. Nice ending."

"Ahh," Jeanay laughed understanding now, "Shoot, shooting, rifle. Why Auntie, I do believe your sense of humor is improving, very clever."

"What? Improving?" Professor Golden sat upright stiff, not sure what to think, she contemplated the remark with side to side movements of her head. She looked like a little bird perched on a branch trying to decide which way to go.

Jeanay nudged her back, "Now don't go get your feelings hurt, that's a compliment."

"Well," she exclaimed, "I don't know!"

"Really Auntie? Jeanay started laughing, "You take yourself so serious it's hilarious."

"I do?" Professor was not sure whether to be offended or not.

"Yes you do. And you're adorable too," Jeanay knew how to get on her good side when she had, perhaps, stepped over the line.

Professor Golden started laughing, "Okay, okay, I'm just so funny."

"Oh Auntie, don't get me started," Jeanay had laughing tears start at the corner of her eyes, "You have no idea!"

"Humph, well I…" The Professor didn't know what to think, but Jeanay's giggle bug and laughing were so contagious that it won her over.

Jeanay wiped her wet eyes, "I just have to stop laughing, I just have to," she breathed. She held a hand on her stomach's sore, laughing muscles. "I still have a lot of editing to do. This isn't the end of the story."

"Yep, not by a long shot. At least we can agree on that."

Jeanay stopped abruptly and looked at her aunt.

"Gotcha," her aunt answered in gleeful satisfaction.

Where Did He Go?

The observatory stood in the background with the lake between them. Jeanay stood straight looking into the camera while Professor Golden took up her videographer position.

"I am coming to you with a follow-up to my investigation of the, lost and found, Big Bear Observatory scientist. I am happy to report to you that the Scientist, Oleg Kushnir, has returned to Ukraine. He has decided to leave the scientific field of research to enter the ministry. He states that he believes the only way to accurately know and safely deal with our universe and its phenomena is spiritually. I quote from Oleg, 'Science has too many unanswered, unknowable mysteries. Science is the ultimate expression of God with mysteries we will never fully know, or understand in this life.'"

Jeanay spoke with enthusiasm and joy, "So there you have it a happy ending to the Big Bear Observatory mystery. This is Jeanay Golden coming to you from the Big Bear Observatory situated in the lovely Big Bear City district." She smiled at the camera then stood still and held her pose for a few seconds. "Okay, cut Auntie."

Professor Golden waved with a smile on her face and clicked the camera button off.

"I'm going to put you in the credits, Auntie. I couldn't have done it without you! Too bad he wouldn't talk about the mysterious sightings that made him crazy for a while."

"The ufology? I don't think he wanted to be that well known or talked about," Professor Golden winked.

"I think I'll discuss the notebook on video as part of my presentation then I'll splice it in. We can video that when we get back to the motel. The little patio would be a comfortable spot for that." Jeanay stretched and yawned.

"Sounds good. Great job Jeanay!"

"Why thank you!" Jeanay bowed. "Okay assistant let's pack it up."

"Sure thing, boss," Professor Golden grinned and saluted Jeanay.

Horse Stable Mystery Epidemic

Lady on the Horse

Professor Golden and Jeanay decided to celebrate the successful conclusion of their investigation and resolution to the Big Bear Observatory mystery. They sat eating, on the patio, at Fetch & Stay.

"Look at all the dogs. Isn't this wonderful?"

Professor Golden gave Jeanay a little smile in answer.

"Oh come on Auntie you love dogs."

"A few too many at one time for me. I prefer more humans over the dog factor."

"Dog factor, hum, dog factor, they need to add a hot dog to this menu!" Jeanay mused playfully.

"Very funny Jeanay," Professor laughed, "What would it be comprised of?"

"Let me see how about chili on it for the hot, and dog for the wiener? Ha, ha, that would be great!

"A little obvious, but not bad Jeanay, um…clever to have a hot dog on the menu, but isn't that a standard chili dog? Still, you ought to tell the owner."

"I think I will!"

"Or spice it up first with lice or worms for onions," Professor said with a straight face.

"Oh yuck! That's so macabre, really Auntie!" Jeanay squinched her face. After thinking about it she started laughing, "But it is kinda funny in a yucky way." Jeanay's cell phone started chiming. She dug through her bag, "Ah, there it is," grabbing it out of her purse.

Professor Golden turned away to feel the pleasant breeze on her face. The skies were brilliant blue and clear. *Where's the pine tree scent? Guess I've gotten used to the scent, too bad, sure smelled good. My little niece has her first news-package out of school. I'm so proud, so will her mom and dad be.* She sighed. *I hope I make it down the hill in one piece.*

A little pooch started making begging noises at the table next to them. The owner had the long-haired lap dog on her knees. In response to the whining, she slipped a piece of meat on to her fingers, and under the table, for the dog to lick. Professor Golden responded to the sight with a shiver of disapproval. *"Yuck, doggy germs while eating? Unbelievable!"* Professor rolled her eyes and looked away in distaste.

Jeanay placed her phone down on the table. "Well—wow! That was interesting. I'm glad we decided to stay over for a few days to have some fun."

"Why is that?"

"Do you remember the horse and rider we talked to on the trail?"

"Yes, I don't think that would be easy to forget."

Jeanay laughed, "Right! That was her on the phone."

"How'd she get your number?"

"She tracked me down through a news station that carried my story, Ch-ching, money's coming in, ya-hoo!"

"Excuse me, I thought it was OUR story," jested the Professor.

Jeanay gave her a straight face then a loud guffaw, "Of course," and slapped the table. "Okay, now seriously. She has a mystery disease at her ranch. She owns the Lakes End Stables."

"Oh dear, that's too bad! Where is it?"

Jeanay gave Professor a meaningful look, "At the lakes end." Her Auntie blinked back, and they both started laughing.

"Jeanay this is up your alley. I bet you're ecstatic."

"Oh, come on Auntie you love horses too, and dogs."

"Only when they're my own, don't trust other people, or their dogs and horses."

"Why?" Jeanay asked disbelieving her.

"I find most people messed up. And when it comes to animals, well, people don't know how to train properly unless they've also been trained properly. I don't trust people! So I couldn't possibly trust their animals!"

"Really, wow! I never knew that. I guess I'm a little more trusting than you."

"I'd call it naive. I've had more life experience."

Shaking her head in disagreement, "I'd call it trusting," insisted Jeanay bending forward nodding her head for emphasis.

Professor gave her a loud, good-natured, "Ha." Then she asked, "So what's with the stable my little investigative reporter?"

"Some of the horses and a dog are getting sick, oddly, all with different symptoms, no apparent link. Oh, shoot! I forgot to ask her if I figure out the problem will I have her permission to publish it."

"Ridiculous, she couldn't expect a reporter to keep secrets!" Professor Golden's incredulous tone increased, "She knows you're a reporter. That's what you do, report!"

"True, on the one hand if we clear up the mystery and she fixes the problem my publishing won't be an issue, but if it doesn't work out that way, well..."

The Professor pulled an imaginary cap onto her head.

"What's that you're doing?" Jeanay frowned and lifted her head to note the peculiar motion.

"I just put on my inquisitive cap," she answered playfully, "Give me more specifics?"

"Oh, oh," Jeanay jumped in excitement in her chair, "You could be really great help here. Do lab tests on the animals, etc."

Professor Golden's hands waved expressively to slow Jeanay down. "Whoa, whoa, whoa here, first I didn't bring any equipment, and you're jumping the gun. All I want at the moment is information."

"Oh, yea, sure. We can figure those things out later."

"Y-E-S," Professor Golden beckoned with her hand to get Jeanay to spill more information.

"Okay. Here's what happened, or should I say what's happening, on-going—"

"Stop Jeanay, now you're going on like me. Oh dear, I'm rubbing off on you, not good, not good!" Professor shook her head.

"Sorry..." Jeanay looked sheepish realizing the similarity then she cleared her throat. "The horses are getting sick. Now here's the strange part. Most of their symptoms are different. She's had several vets come, and they can't figure it out. She can't afford any specialized veterinarian clinic expenses to figure it out either."

"Oooooh! There's your angle for her permission."

Jeanay looked at her aunt with a blank expression.

"Free to her, at our expense, we run more tests. You don't include that in your bill." Professor was speaking with her head nodding and hands moving. "Then you will have free carte blanch to do whatever you want to with her story."

"Oh, that's a good one! I LIKE that, yep, I think that will work! You're such a genius, Auntie."

Professor Golden smiled with appreciation it had been a long time since she'd heard those words.

Jeanay pondered quietly, "I wonder how we should start? We're not vets."

Professor Golden took off her imaginary hat and picked up another imaginary hat. She spoke while putting it on her head with one hand in the front and the other in the back. She whispered huskily in a secretive, commanding voice, "But we have powers of deduction Watson, my Sherlock Holmes hat, the famous Desertwalker." Professor chuckled enjoying herself. Then she returned to her natural voice, "We'll make a list of the horses and their symptoms. Of course, we'll talk to the stable owner and the vets. Then, have some faith that the answers will come."

Jeanay had been laughing at her aunt's antics and with the last statement nodded her head in agreement her eyes shining in speculative hope. She added a decisive, "Humph," with a snappy nod of her head in agreement. "Auntie, I don't remember you being so funny."

Professor Golden beamed into the face of her niece, "It must be the company I keep."

Lakes End Stables

The yellow Mercedes pulled up in front of the gas station's garage. An attendant walked over to the driver's side of the car. The redheaded, overall-clad, young man leaned over. Wanting to get a closer look at the pretty occupant he planted his elbows on the open window ledge and patted the car, "I remember this yellow Mercedes." He peered into Jeanay's eyes and asked, "How can I help you this time?"

Jeanay looked at his name tag, this time, and sweetly asked, "Can you tell me how to get to Lakes End Stables? The internet reception is sketchy around here." Jeanay busily took notes as he described how to get to the stables. Beguiling, Jeanay looked up into his face and smiled, "Thank you Ardan." She flashed her flecked blue-green eyes into his bright blue ones.

"Oh, you are welcome, any time." Ardan gave a happy tap on the open window ledge twice and stood up to go. He nodded good-bye with a satisfied smile.

Jeanay smiled in return. She set down the directions and put the car in drive waving as she drove away with Professor Golden. "Okay, the stable seems comparatively simple to find. I like small towns with easy to find places when cell reception isn't perfect."

"And cute guy's?" Professor Golden had been exceedingly amused watching them.

"Yep."

"Arden, first name basis now! That was quick. Nice Irish name." Professor Golden was having fun giving Jeanay a hard time.

"Irish? Quick. Quick? Oh!" Jeanay responded in mock exasperation.

A few miles later Jeanay remarked, "I think the stable will be around the bend."

The car dipped as they left the pavement to lightly descend onto the dirt and gravel road. A half mile later an attractive, sprawling ranch home met their gaze. It was set back from the road, with large corrals, on either side of the drive stretching forward to the graveled lane.

Professor Golden was the first to loudly proclaim, "Oh my goodness! They have mules, donkeys. And llamas?"

They looked up at the overhead sign that spanned the dirt road between the wood corrals. Jeanay read it, "Lakes End Stables, private," with, private, printed under the name. "Yes, this is most definitely it." Her voice went into a high-pitched, rolling, animal lover tone. "Ooh-look at all the pretty horses too!"

After passing the corrals the driveway traversed into an oval circle which reached around each side of the house to the back stables. The ranch style home's front yard consisted of an old vintage wheel barrel and rusted wagon that had large wooden wheels. Colorful plants were strategically placed around and within the antiques. Adjacent to the side of the house was a large woodshed, these structures were separated from each other by the gravel driveway. The shed was later to be discovered as the original properties only structure, now turned general store. Inside, the store offered horse nutrients, shampoo, grain, saddle soap, brushes, worming medicine, harnesses, bits, bridles, ropes, leg wraps, etc. The products lined the shelves and hung on the walls on nails. An old, working cash register, with a pop-out drawer, sat on the lone counter by the door in front of the only window.

The stables were behind the shed and house. The road design which looped around and behind the house lead to a large, spacious barn with stalls and continued on to rows, and rows of partially covered piped stalls. A horse lover's paradise met their gaze. Several oval corrals were behind the house for exercising the horses along with a circular horse walker. The walker is a device that a number of horses can be tied to, so they can be walked around in a circle without the aid of a person leading them. This was used to warm up horses before a ride and cool them down after a ride, or dry them after a bath. There were various hoses and faucets for filling the water troughs and cleaning the horses and the grounds. Right behind the house was a large chicken coup raised off the ground. It contained different breeds of chickens, large breeds, and small bantams. They pecked the floor's straw and plastic feeders as they made their contented clucking sounds.

Jeanay drove around the entire structure commenting, "Wow, pretty impressive! Wow…wow, wow!"

"Yes, it does have a really nice feel," Professor Golden agreed. Then she pointed, "I think that's where people park, possibly. Nothing is designated, park where you can?"

"Okay, looks good to me." Jeanay pulled into the inconspicuous area indicated. "I don't think we need to worry about getting a ticket in this place."

"We should be so lucky. Hope a horse doesn't kick the car!"

"Aren't you the optimistic one today," Jeanay smirked then she made a quick text, "Just letting her know we are here."

A minute later, out of the house's back door, strode a woman in a black hat, black boots, matching black clad western jeans, and a white dress shirt.

"That's her!" Jeanay got out of the car. With an affirmative nod Professor Golden joined her.

Jeanay, in equal stride, walked to Jube offering a handshake. The stable owner, in kind, offered her black, leather gloved hand. Then turning to her aunt Jeanay officially introduced them, "This is my aunt, Professor Golden. Auntie, this is Jube the stable owner." They smiled at each other.

Professor offered her hand to shake, "Yes I remember. I recognize you from the trail, nice to meet you, again." She asked, "Is that Ruby?"

"No," Jube shook her head, "It's Jube."

"Oh, I'm sorry I heard wrong."

Jube laughed, "Quite alright, most people give it a second take. As a kid I loved to eat Jujube candy. Somehow my family and friends started calling me Jube and it stuck."

Professor Golden chuckled softly and smiled with a friendly, amused smirk, "Certainly interesting."

Jeanay smiled, "Ah...nice, I like it."

Jeanay's attention was then drawn away to people leading their horses past them to a large arena. A stable tenant was hooking up a horse to the walker. Horses nickered and snorted inquisitively watching them from their stalls as they munched on hay. A small corral, further away from them beyond the rows of stalls, had a rider and horse trotting around in it. Workers were busy mucking out stalls with their pitchforks tossing the waste into wheelbarrows. Others were spraying the area with water to clean and keep the dust down. Another station had a cement area and drain with spray nozzles to wash the horses off.

"Let me give you ladies a tour," offered Jube.

Professor Golden replied, "Great, let me grab a notepad first."

They waited for her to retrieve her notepad and pen from the car. Jeanay was excitedly distracted watching all the activity around her. "It's been so long since I've ridden," she sighed.

"We can take care of that," Jube assured her. She swept off her hat and shook her thick mane down her shoulders, like a star in a classic movie, her elegant features framed by her long silver hair.

"That would be incredible, you have no idea!"

"Oh yes I do," Jube chuckled. "This place is a lifelong dream. And, with your help a lasting one! I hope."

"We'll do our best!" Professor Golden joined them overhearing Jube's last sentence about her property. "And we need to make sure that we can video and report what we find." She looked meaningfully at Jeanay signaling her to get on board.

Jeanay quickly added, "As long as it helps." *I don't want to risk my chances to ride at this point. I wish you had waited on that, dear Auntie!*

Professor Golden's eyebrows arched in question. *As long as it helps, what's that about?*

Jeanay gave her an innocent look and a shake of the head "no" to try and get across that it was bad timing.

"What?" Professor squinted, shook her head, frowned and lifted her eyebrows at her, not understanding.

Jube noticed and gave a sideways look and then bending over flipped her hair up under her hat again. She used this gesture to cover the awkward signals and to give her pause to register her feelings. *Hope that wasn't significant to my cause.*

Jeanay let out a cloaked sigh of discomfort.

"Follow me." Jube took off in the lead.

Guests

"These are our guests," Jube's arm swung out to indicate the horses in her barn and stalls as she spoke.

"How nice calling your horses guests," Jeanay smiled.

Jube came to a stop in front of a flashy, white mare. Its compact body and dish-spoon nose indicated it was of the Arabian horse breed. Jeanay reached out to stroke her soft muzzle. A throaty cough came from the mare. Jeanay, poised to pet her, pulled her hand back startled as she looked at Jube.

"It's okay, she's friendly. She coughs all the time," Jube recited sadly. "She's my other sweetheart, along with my palomino mare you saw on the trail."

Jeanay stroked the mare's nose. The horse, inquisitive, nuzzled her hair its hot breath tickled her neck. Professor Golden stood close smiling.

"There does not appear to be any reason for her cough. One of our other guests, also, has a cough and a small lump on his neck. The biopsy showed it to be benign. It's not going to be removed at this point as it possesses no mortal threat."

Professor Golden took notes. "Have their throats been swabbed and put under a microscope?"

"Yes, there is no microbe detected, but they both have a red irritation. We're administering a lubricating mist, mostly just for their comfort, nothing therapeutic," Jube reported.

"Hum," Professor Golden frowned with a quirk-some, contemplating lift to one corner of her mouth. "How about their white blood cells are they elevated?"

"I'm not sure. You'd have to ask our vet."

"What would elevated white blood cells mean?" Jeanay asked.

"Inflammation, immune system fighting a pathogen," Professor explained. "We will have to check the feed."

"Ah," Jeanay nodded.

Jube moved on as Jeanay and Professor followed her, she stopped a few stalls later. "Over here we have a Tennessee Walker who has a red rash on one side of his belly. Again, tests returned negative for any disease or insect infestation. We treat it with a soothing allergy cream."

Professor Golden looked up from scribbling in her notepad. "What a black beauty, such smooth gait's in the breed. Is he gelded?"

"Yes, we don't allow studs here. They are a little too rambunctious, unpredictable. We do allow a stallion to come in for stud service. We have a small enclosed area that includes a special stall to isolate him and the breeding mare," Jube explained in proud tones about her ranch.

"You have a really nice, professional set-up here," Jeanay looked impressed. Professor Golden nodded in agreement.

"Thank you," Jube answered proudly.

"Now we'll need to head over to the stalls at the back. We have a Piebald Pinto whose four hoofs turned softer. This breed's white hoofs are already soft she sure didn't need this turn of events. Her owner can't ride her because the added weight could cause hoof-splitting damage."

Jeanay cringed, "That sounds painful!"

"Perfectly awful!" Professor agreed.

"Yes," Jube acknowledged, "She is swollen starting above the hoof. The blacksmith said it was best not to try and shoe her. So he packed padding in and around the hoof, as you will see, and wound tape around the padding for support."

They reached her stall. "She walks really funny," Professor Golden observed.

"Kinda delicate, what a shame," Jeanay spoke shaking her head.

"Pity," Professor added. She couldn't think of anything else to say, so they just stood there looking at her feet and petting her.

Jube turned their attention to another horse. "Now this Roan over here, although his coat is burgundy his nostrils are not supposed to be this pink,"

"Is every horse affected?" Professor Golden wondered.

"No, not everyone," Jube exclaimed, "Not the new ones come to think of it!"

"How about the chickens, do they have any signs?"

"No, they don't! But one of our dogs has an itchy belly. The vet said it could be an allergy to fleas and to give Benadryl. We got rid of the fleas, but not the itch."

"Interesting…" Professor Golden looked off, and tapped her chin several times with her pen, thinking.

Jube looked most distressed. "I'm so glad the newer guests don't show signs. I've been puzzling over that and desperately hoping they won't develop any. If the word gets around I may lose business. It would put a short end to my dream."

Professor Golden looked at her with intensity, "Short end! What do you mean?"

"I've only been here a short time. This is a dream I saved for. The stable was doing poorly, it had few guests, not a great reputation and in great need of repair. I have made repairs and added special features. The stable has really been filling up with both local permanent clients and seasonal ones. The seasonal clients are the icing on top of the cake putting money back into my savings," Jube explained with gratitude in her voice.

"So the horses already here, before your takeover, had these symptoms?" Professor returned to the earlier theme.

"Oh." Jeanay caught the significance.

Jube did not catch the drift of her meaning, perplexed she answered, "Yes," with a question in her voice looking at Jeanay and then Professor Golden.

"These illnesses may have started to put the stable out of business before you came. Did you check around about the former owner's reputation before you purchased, or did you look the horses and place over?" Professor Golden proffered straight as an arrow.

Jube looked a little embarrassed. "No not in person. I jumped at this chance. I looked at photos of the ranch online from another state, and I studied their spread sheets. They gave me such a good deal! I mean look around you. Isn't this the most beautiful place on earth? And to own a stable sitting at the top of the world, it's heaven! ...I figured they just weren't good at business."

Jeanay sympathized, "That's okay we'll check things out further and do our best to figure out how to help you." She turned to the Professor, "Right Auntie?"

Professor Golden bore a terse expression. "We'll do our best."

Jube nodded not sure what to think.

"Oh, Jube, one more thing, the dog with the rash was it here before you came?" Professor inquired.

"No, Sadie's my dog. Jube gasped, "Oh, no!"

The Professor's mind was percolating, she thought for a moment, "What does she sleep on?"

"She has a dog bed, but loves to sleep on the dirt."

"I see. And what does the Tennessee Walker sleep on?"

"Mostly dusty hay."

"Does the horse and dog sleep on one side over the other?

Jube looked off into the distance thinking, "Sadie sleeps on one side more than the other. Horses sleep standing, but they do roll and lay on their sides sometimes. I'll have to check into the horse."

"Okay, thank you Jube we can take it from here," Professor Golden answered in a stoic voice." Professor wiped her neck with her scarf and turned to her niece, "Jeanay let's go sit down on the bleachers.

They parted ways with Jube and sat down silently gazing at the horses and riders circling in the arena before them.

Professor Golden spoke, "Jube's dog joining the infected changes the complexion of this puzzle. I'm just not sure how. If no new cases had risen since the new owner we could have been looking at contaminated feed."

"A dog wouldn't be eating hay or grain." Jeanay mused.

"Right! It could lay on the hay, hum. That could fit, but still it seems farfetched. Something is contaminated and as far as we can see only infecting animals. Professor rubbed her temples in thought.

Clucking sounds caught the Professor's attention. She turned to watch the chickens scratching around in their elevated pen where the floor was covered in straw. "I just love those clucking, chicken conversations, so calming," Professor Golden stared at them, "Hum…"

Jeanay looked at her and followed the direction of her gaze. "What?"

The Professor pointed at the cage with the pen in her hand. "Those chickens do not seem to be affected by these various symptoms."

"True, that is what Jube said." Jeanay was trying to make a connection, "Could be not all species would be affected?"

"Yes, could be, but do you see how the area is highly elevated above the dirt with wire as the flooring covered with thick layers of straw. They are not touching the dirt. I think we should take some dirt samples from around here and have them analyzed."

"But how could dirt be a problem for animals?" Jeanay puzzled.

"Beats me for now," Professor Golden shook her head. Maybe our friends at the observatory have equipment I could borrow?"

"Sure, only... I'm not so sure they think we are their friends. Still, it wouldn't hurt to ask." Jeanay reached for her phone.

"This place should have little plastic or paper cups around we can use for the samples. Would you go and ask Jube where to find some?"

"Okay, be back in a jiffy."

"Jeanay," Professor called after her before she had gone far, "Wait."

Jeanay yelled, "Yes?"

"Ask her if any people are getting symptoms."

"Ah, okay," Jeanay nodded her head. *Good thinking!* She activated a call on her cell phone to the observatory as she continued to the ranch house.

Jeanay surprised Professor Golden ten minutes later carrying white Styrofoam cups with Jube tagging along. Jube was pulling off her riding gloves as she neared the Professor. "Jeanay mentioned, you asked if anyone had rashes etcetera? I do!" She held out her hands for inspection.

Professor Golden took hold of her wrists and turned her hands over to look at both sides without touching them. "When did you notice these red spots?" She looked up into Jube's eyes.

"I'd say about three weeks after I came here. I wear the gloves outdoors all the time now. I thought they would go away after wearing gloves, but they are only fainter."

"Fainter? Hum. Do they itch?" Professor Golden inquired.

"Not much, just a little. I don't notice it if I'm keeping busy. I also apply an allergy cream from the drug store."

"Prescription?" Professor asked. Jube shook her head. Professor Golden gently released her wrists, "Okay, thank you."

Jube started easing her gloves back on. "So you think it's related?"

"Possibly," Professor replied.

"I wouldn't have put that together," Jube interlaced her fingers together and squeezed them tightly, "Now I'm even more nervous. Should I check with my workers? None of them have complained of anything, but they always wear gloves while they work."

"No, that's okay. We'll discretely check with them," Professor volunteered witnessing her discomfort.

"Okay, thank you," She pointed several times nervously toward the house. "I think I'll go in and rest for a while. This is a bit much."

"Sure, we'll be leaving soon to test the samples. Right, Auntie?"

Professor Golden nodded solemnly.

Jube headed back to her home. Jeanay silently waited for her to go back inside her house. "Why are you so glum? I think you're scaring her."

"I'm concerned that this is really serious Jeanay. I'm sorry. I'm not good at covering up my thoughts, or emotions even though I try to. Let's talk to a few workers. Oh, there's one." In a loud, high pitched voice, Professor Golden called out impulsively, "Yi-who." She waved at a girl hosing down an area.

The girl turned to see if she was being spoken to and shut off the hose valve. When they approached she responded, "Can I help you?"

Professor Golden, totally unprepared, walked briskly toward her with Jeanay not far behind. "Yes, do you have a rash?"

Jeanay turned red and sputtered, "My colleague, Professor Golden, and I have been hired to do a study of the property and people who work here for—for," trying to think quickly, "Insurance purposes."

Professor Golden, insensitive, caught on to her blundering and retracted a bit. "Oh yes, yes, so sorry, I got ahead of myself. We are checking on the workers to make sure they are in good health for our insurance agency."

Jeanay winced and frowned at her aunt. *I tried to save this.*

The worker looked a little surprised. She brushed back her black hair across her brown skin with a gloved hand. "No, I don't have a rash." She gave a little cough.

"How long have you had that cough? Are you feeling okay?" Professor, undaunted, oblivious asked.

Jeanay gave the Professor a livid stare down. *Now the poor girl is going to think she could lose her job. Oh my word!*

"Yes, I feel fine. I sometimes cough from the horses kicking up dust."

Professor Golden nodded to her blinking her eyes rapidly, "Oh yes, of course. Thank you."

"Let's walk," Professor Golden urged Jeanay.

"Yes, let's please do!" Jeanay puffed at her aunt, "Discreet, you did say we'd be discreet! Was that what you call discreet?"

"Okay, we didn't prepare properly." Professor observed, "Nothing you, or for that matter I said made any sense."

"You think?" Jeanay looked at her incredulous.

"I said YOU too."

"Well, humph, I was trying to cover for you," Jeanay retorted.

"Okay, thank you," responded the accused trying to disarm the conversation, "We were both trying."

Jeanay conceded silently as she unwound from the embarrassment. "I think I heard a rough cough from that man over there. We must be careful not to make them afraid their answers would affect their job. It is possible some are not here legally."

"Why do you say that?" A distracted Professor asked as she was trying to formulate a different approach.

"She looked scared when you asked about her cough after the insurance company was mentioned and a bit skittish when you added the word agency to insurance. The word agency might have sounded threatening."

"Oh, yes you might be right. I didn't think of that. You took all that in? How?"

"I just did," Jeanay rolled her eyes. Her aunt's thick skin toward others feelings was perturbing though, she knew her aunt would never intentionally do harm. *I sure wish she could read others better, I wonder why she can't? Maybe she's just in her head most of the time.*

Their conversation blinded them to how close they had come upon another worker. As they approached the middle-aged, gray haired man Jeanay heard small short coughs. He noticed them heading toward him with both their eyes fixed upon him. He stopped shoveling manure, stood up straight, and leaned on his shovel. "Can I help you?"

This time both ladies stopped short, looked at each other, realizing they still weren't quite sure how to approach getting the information they needed without scaring people.

Jeanay had a thought and spoke hesitantly, "We are here from environmental services. We are checking to see if there are any medically, yes," thinking as she spoke with unconscious nodding, "Related, medically related body, bodily," making a circling motion pointing toward her own body, "Things to report." She laughed nervously and jauntily added, "Safety first you know."

Both the Professor and the man stared at her in silence. Professor thought, *Now, I don't look so stupid.*

Jeanay shot out her arms invitingly, "Anything? Oh, and this doesn't affect your job." She made hand motions like an umpire signals 'safe' in a baseball game then shaking her head emphatically "no," she repeated, "Can't affect your job."

He gave no response. Leaning on his shovel he studied them suspiciously.

Jeanay then looked at her watch and said in a sing song voice, "We're on a deadline here!"

He stared.

Impatient Jeanay added, "And it's a felony not to answer."

Professor Golden dropped her jaw in surprise at this felonious statement, whereupon Jeanay looked at her imploringly.

The worker looked shocked and petrified. "Jes, I have a little cough."

Jeanay jumped on it, "Oh, oh, for how long?"

He answered, "Jes, a little after I start working here, is dusty." He threw an arm out indicating the surroundings.

Professor Golden had a thought, "Did you work here before the new owner?"

The worker looked up and off toward the horizon, worried, as he thought and wondered how his answer might affect him. "Jes!"

"Do you have a rash?" The Professor quickly included.

He shook his head.

Jeanay looked at the Professor, "Is that it?" Professor gave her an okay nod. "Okay then, that'll do it, thank you." Jeanay smiled, and lightly touched his chest, "And you should get that cough checked." They walked away quickly.

"I hope he stops worrying about his job." Jeanay observed.

"You're unbelievable Jeanay!" Professor Golden was incredulous.

"Thank you. Surprised myself," she smiled.

"I don't mean it that way!"

"What?" Jeanay asked in sudden defense.

"Environmental agency? Bodily? Felony? You scared the bejeebers out of him! And you thought I was frightening!" Professor Golden was bouncing her head her curls were jiggling.

"Oh, well he wasn't being cooperative! In my defense…but I guess you're right, sorry." Serious at first, "Guess we both could use a little help. We blew it." Then Jeanay started laughing.

"Oh, you stop it now," the Professor was serious, "Stop it!" She was unaccustomed to finding herself funny in a tactless situation.

Jeanay's laugh became infectious. The Professor started to loosen up failing to remain serious she gave herself over to laughing. They were red in the face by the time they reached the benches where they had left the Styrofoam cups.

"Okay, okay, let's settle down to the job at hand. And we didn't blow it we got valuable information." Professor Golden handed half the cups to Jeanay. "After we take samples from here let's walk down to the lake and take samples from the shoreline."

They completed taking samples from the surrounding area both inside and outside the stalls and arena. When they reached the shoreline Jeanay remarked, "Oh, look how there's sparkles in the dirt here and there!"

"No noticeable shine to the stable's dirt, and they're not that far apart from each other, interesting!" Professor Golden observed.

"Fool's gold Auntie?"

"Um, I don't know, huh! Let's just get back and let me mail this to a lab."

Jeanay nodded.

Un-stable

The next day Jeanay was dropped off behind the stable's ranch house where the row of stalls started. A large, black Great Dane bound toward her with his long tongue hanging out. He wagged his thick tail fiercely. Jeanay went into her doggy voice, "Oh boy, what a pretty boy you are." She patted and stroked him in an excited frenetic manner matching the wild tail wagging. "I didn't see you yesterday, ooh, ooh, you beautiful thing you." She looked up and around talking, to herself, while stroking the dog whose head reached her waist. "Now where should we go? What should we do?" She talked again to the dog, "Oh, that's interesting. That looks like a vet's vehicle. We need to check that out!"

"Jeanay, Jeanay." Jeanay turned around to see who was calling her.

Jeanay waved, "Hi Jube."

Jube caught up with her. "Ah, I see you have met Wags."

Jeanay started laughing and facetiously asked, "Where'd you get that name?"

"Haven't you noticed that tail wag? When it hits you, it hurts!"

"Ah, yes…I have," they both laughed, "It could give a real good bruise."

"He's one of my ranch dogs, the greeter. I'm surprised you didn't get an introduction yesterday." Jube patted his head, "Where's your aunt?"

"She has to prepare the dirt samples to send in the mail and do some soil testing herself. One of the scientists at the observatory that we got acquainted with is letting her borrow his daughter's microscope."

"Oh. Great! She must have been a bright little thing in school. I never was much for chemistry. Well, I've got to see how far the vet has gotten with the rounds."

Jeanay asked, "I was headed that way can I join you?"

"Sure," Jube nodded.

They walked into the barn and went down the wide central corridor between the enclosed stalls with Wags walking between them. Up ahead was seen the backside of the vet and the front raised head of an upset horse trying to get rid of a tube that the vet was holding in its mouth. Jube offered, "He's worming the horse. The paste isn't bad tasting, but they still don't like it." The white paste was exuding from the corners of the horse's mouth. "We have to keep all of them wormed regularly. Some of the owners prefer to pay him to do it."

Jeanay nodded, "I used to do it for Auntie she had horses for us to ride.

They came to stand next to the vet. He glanced their way and smiled a big, bright, flashing smile. His chiseled, young face caught Jeanay's attention. A little lurch occurred in her chest and the flashing smile unhinged her. In a jittery voice, she let out a nervous, "Oh, Oh." She started to giggle in a high-pitched odd laugh, "Haa, hee, haa, hee." Jeanay started stroking the dog standing beside her while still looking at the vet. He turned his head back to the horse and then back to Jeanay giving her another smile. Jeanay's cheeks turned hot red. She pet the dog furiously as her eyes darted away from his gaze to trace the roof line. Wags looked up at her cocking his head sideways watching her.

Jube looked at her and then caught on. *Oh, my!* Hoping to break the tension Jeanay was emitting she cleared her throat and spoke, "Let me introduce you two. Dr. Masters this is Jeanay, Jeanay Dr. Masters."

Dr. Masters turned to her briefly as the horse tossed its head to get the syringe out of its mouth, "Hello." He had to turn back quickly to his uncooperative patient.

Jeanay answered, "Hi," in a strained voice and started giggling.

Well that sure didn't help. Jube crossed her arms in contemplation.

Jeanay's hand momentarily rested on the dog and then took up stroking him rapidly again. The dog seemed to calm her and her stroking slowed down.

Jube noticed the effect Wags was having on Jeanay and found it amusing. Not wanting to let Jeanay know she turned away to smile. Then she turned to Dr. Masters, "I'll go get the list of owners that want the worming and we also have a pregnancy check."

At the word "pregnancy check" Jeanay started giggling, again, and turned red, again. She felt an urgent need to leave and in that attempt she started stumbling over herself to depart. She stuttered, "I-I-I-I-gotta go." She waved blindly and fairly flew out. Wags looked back and forth not sure whether to follow her or stay. Dr. Masters turned his eyes on Jeanay to watch her leave.

"You sure do impress Dr. Masters." Jube watched her depart and noticed his gaze.

Dr. Masters laughed good-natured, "I guess so." He lowered the empty humongous carpule from the horse's mouth and wiped his hands on a rag. "I hope she comes back."

"Really?" Jube flashed a grin at him, "Now don't break a heart Derek."

"Naw, but it sure is nice to be, so very, appreciated. I'm flattered," his cheeks flushed.

Jube gave a loud, good-natured, "Ha! You should be." Dr. Masters returned the comment with a good-natured boyish grin.

Meanwhile, Professor Golden drove up and saw Jeanay petting a large dog. She parked the car nearby and walked over to Jeanay. "Brought you a cowgirl hat," she twirled it around her gloved hand's forefinger. "This one's for you to keep," she said with a broad grin.

"Oh, Auntie how thoughtful, it's so beautiful. And by the looks of you we almost match, thank you so much!" Jeanay's face was radiant over the loving gift.

"Sure, you're welcome. They had these great hats in the shed's store." She brushed dust off the hat with her gloved hand, "But it sure is dusty in there." Professor handed the hat to Jeanay. "You can see the dust swirling in the air when you open the door. It catches in the light streaming through the door and that little window." A horse on its lead rope walked by them stirring up the dirt. Professor covered her mouth with her fist to cough, "Speaking of dust." She waved her hand in the air trying to part the dust in an ineffective attempt to move it away from her nostrils. "Oh, the joy of equestrian life, just don't breathe too deep Jeanay," the warning came through in her tone.

Jeanay frowned, "Any particular reason?"

"Possibly, but I want to be sure. It's just a precaution until the lab work is completed. That's why I want you to wear these gloves." She pulled out a set of gloves from her waistband. "We should probably be wearing masks as a precaution also, but I think it might…"

"Look weird?" Jeanay filled in.

"I was going to say scare people or look suspicious, but that too since we have been going around questioning people and taking samples. It's been a long time since I've done any lab work. This is good practice for me. I sent the prepared slide samples off to a lab so we can get the results faster than waiting for them to do the preparation. They will send the results via email to me. And then the reports will come to the ranch by way of snail mail. I decided not to do any testing myself."

Professor abruptly changed course, "What have you been up to? Do any riding yet?"

Jeanay took the gloves from her aunt's hand. "No, I just met the vet," Jeanay's face flushed. She pulled the gloves on each hand with her head down.

Professor Golden looked at Jeanay's flushed face then cocked her head to the side to study her expression. *I wonder what that's about?* Professor felt something wet touch her arm. She jerked her arm away instinctively, "Oh!" Professor wiped her arm off then she looked down and jumped, "Oh, you're big! So who are you? Mr. Wet nose."

Jeanay put her hand on either side of the dog's neck and ruffled it affectionately. "Meet Wags Auntie isn't he gorgeous!"

Professor Golden smiled wryly, "As long as he minds his manners he's gorgeous."

"Of course Auntie," Jeanay pointed a finger in front of Wags face and waggled it back-and-forth. "Now you mind your manners for Auntie, Wags." Her cute tone, as if speaking to a child, prompted Wags to wag his tail rapidly with his big, pink tongue hanging out.

Wags tail was right by Professor Golden's leg. His rapid, happy wag struck her leg with painful blows. She grabbed her leg, "Oh-ow-ow-OW! Oh, my goodness," Professor jumped back hopping on one leg while she rubbed the other throbbing leg.

Jeanay gasped, "Oh dear! I'm sorry Auntie." Jeanay pursed her lips scolding him, "Wags you failed already! Bad dog!" She shook a fisted finger at him. He looked up into her eyes, tipped his head to one side, and put a paw over one of his eyes. Jeanay rolled her eyes and burst out laughing, "Oh stop, you're killing me! Who taught you that?"

Professor Golden rubbed her leg silently. She stifled a pained, amused smile at the dog's apparent acknowledgment of his indiscretion. *More likely he's learned how to be cute than disciplined.* Recovering slightly she asked, "Shouldn't we talk with the Vet, Jeanay?"

"Oh sure, YOU can," Jeanay gulped and turned away embarrassed. She pointed in Dr. Master's direction, "He's over there."

Professor looked up while still rubbing her leg, "Where?"

Jeanay started walking to the elongated row of enclosed barn stalls where she had come from. Upon returning to the opening she stared down the long corridor. She raised her voice within earshot, "Oh, he's not here. Let's try the open stalls."

Professor Golden had recovered, with a slight limp she cheerfully followed, "Okee-Dokey," she responded.

Near the entrance of the outdoor stalls they abruptly ran into Jube and the Vet. He had his hand up the tail end of a mare with Jube holding her halter to calm her. Jeanay and Professor, surprised, pulled up short and stopped, both let out a shocked "Oh."

Jube offered, "We're doing a pregnancy check."

Jeanay nodded her head up and down in multiple little nervous nods.

Professor looked to see what was making Jeanay nervous. The direction of Jeanay's gaze was not where Professor assumed it would be, but on the handsome face of the Vet.

Suddenly Jeanay started giggling. Professor Golden looked at her in disbelief. *What is wrong with you girl?!*

Jube reached out and grabbed Wags awkwardly while holding onto the mare's harness. She shoved Wags toward Jeanay. He nuzzled Jeanay's leg, whereupon Jeanay being distracted absent-mindedly started to pet him rhythmically. Her giggling slowed and softened. Dr. Masters smiled with his back to Jeanay and Professor Golden having sensed what was going on. Pulling his arm out of the mare he announced, "Tell the happy owner she's four months along."

Jube smiled, "She sure WILL be a happy owner this is a prize mare! That stud fee wasn't cheap! This should be exciting, a new foal. Wow!"

Once Dr. Masters' arm was free of the mare he pulled off the long plastic glove that went up to his armpit. It slapped off free of his arm.

"Let me introduce you to Professor Golden, Jeanay's aunt, this is Dr. Masters." Jube then turned away to tie up the mare.

Dr. Masters turned to Professor Golden and held out the same hand the plastic glove had been on to shake hers, "Nice to meet you, Professor."

The Professor paused, "Oh," she breathed sharply. She eyed his hand carefully then convinced it was clean she shook it vigorously. "Yes, so nice to meet you too."

Jeanay nervously cleared her throat and looked away.

"So you've already met my niece."

Dr. Masters smiled broadly at her and then Jeanay. "I most delightfully have had that pleasure."

Jeanay gave a little breathy, "Oh," and glanced at him then away again. She started gently tipping back and forth on her toes and heels rocking like a child.

"I see." Professor Golden studied the situation.

Jube interrupted, "Perhaps, Professor, you and the Dr. could talk over there," she indicated a bench. "Jeanay would you get me a glass of water from the house. Just inside the back door you'll find a cooler and cups."

"Yes, I remember," Jeanay nodded and walked away.

Dr. Masters walked over to the bench. Jube leaned over to whisper to Professor Golden, "The dog helps." Professor nodded she understood, but she didn't want to say anything to bring more attention to the matter. Jube went to the mare to untie her and lead her back into her stall while Professor Golden went to sit with Dr. Masters.

Out in the driveway a white SUV rolled in on the gravel crunching the small rocks beneath it as Jeanay passed by. She noticed the sound and a child's face in the car, the child waved to her. Jeanay smiled and waved back as she headed toward the house on her contrived commission to get a glass of water. The SUV parked across from the pipe stalls, by a corral, in a lone designated parking spot. The driver and child got out of the car. The woman was dressed in a riding habit. The little girl was in a school uniform holding a guinea pig. It sent out its charming whistles, beeps, and clicks. It had an incessant chatter. Possibly it was excited about its surroundings, or chatting to itself, or to the little girl. The mother, hearing the creature's small noises and loud whistles, turned to her daughter. "Now Dot, I let you bring him with us, but you need to put him back in his ball and keep him in the car."

"Oh mom," Dot whined, "Please let me go sit over on the bleacher with him. I get so bored!"

"You know some of the horses get spooked with his noises," she chided her.

"No one is around. I'll just sit over there all by myself. If someone comes I'll go sit in the car. P-l-e-a-s-e," she begged.

Her mother cupped her child's irresistible, little face in her hand, "Promise?" She stared into her child's eyes like a laser to let her know she was indeed serious and to ferret out her child's honesty. The innocent child nodded completely committed to keeping her word. Convinced her mother replied, "Okay," and dropped her hand. She turned to go then spoke as she walked away. "I'll be watching you while I put Sugar through her exercises in this corral." Her arm shot out pointing to the corral her car was parked in front of and to the adjacent bleachers her daughter was to sit on, "Go sit."

"Yes, momma," Dot obediently went over and sat down cuddling her little creature.

Jeanay came out of the back of the house with a cup of water in her hand. She stopped a few feet out and looked around to see if she could see Jube? She did not, so she proceeded to walk in the direction of the path between the stalls and corral. Intent on finding Jube she crunched on the gravel past the bleachers not noticing its occupants. A low-pitched, long, loud beep warning issued from the bleachers causing Jeanay to jump. She stopped, turned her direction toward the sound, and to her delight saw its source.

"Oh, I'm so sorry, did he scare you? Dot asked worriedly. Jeanay nodded her head.

"He does that when people come near me, to warn me, but then he's okay after that," Dot reassured, nodding her head as she spoke making her curls bounce around her face.

Jeanay quickly stepped over to them. The fuzzball started up his chatter and whistles. "Oh, he's so cute!"

Dot's eyes got big and happy. "You like him?" She looked quickly around to see if there were any horses close by.

"Oh yes, he's adorable, reminds me of my aunt. Oh, I guess I shouldn't say that," Jeanay giggled.

"Why? Really he does?"

"Yea, my aunt chatters when she's nervous, or upset, thinking hard, or explaining things."

"Oh," Dot nodded as if she understood perfectly. "Yes, Squeeker does talk even more if he's upset or worried."

"Squeeker?" Jeanay asked.

Dot nodded her head.

"That's a cute name. Sure fits. What's yours?"

"My name is Dot."

Jeanay held out her hand to shake hands, "My name is Jeanay, pleased to meet you Dot, and Squeeker."

Dot clasped her hand. They shook hands vigorously and giggled together.

Jeanay set the water down. "Dot, hum, that's a cute, unusual name. How'd you get it?"

"Oh, it's short for Dorothy. My momma said I started out smaller than a dot. And she wanted a "dot" real bad, so she picked the name Dorothy just so she could call me her Dot."

"That's so sweet," Jeanay smiled. Jeanay sighed not wanting to leave them, but she chose to pick up her water duty. "Well Mr. Adorable," she put her head down looking into Squeeker's eyes, "I gotta finish my errand." She got up and waved via a little hand twist, "See ya later."

Dot nodded "yes" emphatically and smiled big. Her eyes turned away to follow her mother posting to her horse's trot in the arena. The diminutive, white horse lived up to her name Sugar.

Professor Golden and Dr. Masters were deep in conversation about the history of the horses that had symptoms. When that subject was exhausted Professor switched questioning to the length of time he had been the attending vet.

Dr. Masters went on to explain, "I purchased the prior vet's practice upon his retirement about the time Jube became the owner here."

"Did the vet or previous owner mention any history here at the stable?"

"I don't recall that either of them did. The owner was not well and was eager to sell and leave quickly."

"Do you know the nature of the illness?"

"No, I don't think that was any of my business…Why?"

"If the problems here are related you might have wanted to make it your business."

Dr. Masters' eyebrows lifted, "Oh!" He sat there thinking for a minute with his elbows resting on his legs, hands clasped, fingers intertwined. "So you're running tests… When do you think you will get the results back?"

"Hopefully tomorrow, if not, in a couple of days."

Jeanay came around the corner of the stable with the cup of water.

She spied her aunt. "Have…" She stopped short upon noticing the vet and started to flush pink and stutter, "Ha-hav y-you seeeen Jube?"

I sure wish I had! Professor Golden shook her head, "No." She then mumbled in a whisper, to herself nervously, "No,no,no,no,no," because of Jeanay's erratic behavior as if that would stop her through osmosis. Jeanay held the water in her hand and turned her head away from them staring off. The silence was awkward. Professor Golden rubbed her forehead. *Where has my stable, solid girl gone?*

Dr. Masters stood up, "Maybe I can find her."

Jeanay mumbled, "Um-hum." She glanced at him with a shy smile and turned her head away again. She pursed her lips together in frustration and one heel started thumping up and down.

Dr. Masters, taking notice, slapped his hands together with a bang, "Well, I'll be right back."

Jeanay jumped at the sound.

Professor Golden looked around furtively for something to do or say. *Where's that dog!* From the entrance walked in a lone clucking hen. *Ah, a distraction, thank God!* She quickly went over to the little chicken and picked it up. The startled hen clucked more loudly. The Professor moved quickly to Jeanay's side. The bantam got Jeanay's attention. Professor grabbed Jeanay's free arm and tucked the hen under her arm. She then took the water cup out of Jeanay's other hand.

Jeanay started petting the little hen, "Oh, you're so pretty." The bantam nestled into Jeanay's arm both soothing each other. Looking up at the Professor she pondered out loud, "I wonder how it got out here?"

"I don't know," Professor Golden smiled, *but I sure am glad. Good, she's thoroughly distracted and coming out of that stupor.*

Jeanay stepped close to the Professor and whispered, "I am so embarrassed… I don't know what is wrong with me. I can't seem to help myself." She stroked the chicken. Looking around she started chewing on a fingernail, "He's going to be back soon. I'll go put the hen in her coup." The Professor nodded her approval.

Professor Golden stood there with the water cup in her hand looking around trying to figure out what to do with it when Jube walked in the entrance. The Professor handed her the drink. Jube looked at it quizzically and then it dawned on her what it was about. She asked the Professor, "Did it help?"

The Professor nodded with a sigh.

"Good, but we have another problem." The Professor looked at her immediately worried. Jube continued, "I asked Derek, I mean Dr. Masters, to take a look at Goldy, my horse. She's just developed a sudden, large growth on the underside of an eyelid," she sighed in distress.

"Oh no! That beautiful Palomino, we met you riding on, in the forest?"

"Yes." Jube looked miserable and took a drink.

"How suddenly?" Professor Golden looked mystified.

Jube shrugged, "I don't know maybe it was there and I didn't notice it till now?"

"Lead the way I'd like to see it."

"Sure." They walked away together.

In one of the outdoor stalls Dr. Masters had the Palomino tethered under its shaded awning. The horse, shy of having its eye examined, did not want to stand still for him. "Oh good, you're here, would you please steady her. Take this lip lasso and twist it around the upper lip." He handed the tool to Jube.

"Okay, Goldy be a good girl. Now doc has to take care of that eye," Jube spoke soft and soothing into her horse's ear, on the opposite side of the bulging eyelid, as she applied the loop twisting it.

Professor Golden cringed, "What does that loop do? It looks painful." Professor Golden's heel started tapping the dirt. *Oh dear, did Jeanay get that from me?* She was accustomed to having owned horses, but not having the need for this type of large animal medicine.

Dr. Masters was too busy studying the eye to answer. Jube filled in the hanging silence, "It doesn't hurt, for some reason, it calms them." She patted the mare's neck.

"Oh," Professor was surprised her heel tapping slowed to a stop. The reassurance about the horses comfort kept Professor from descending into her nervous rambling-mumbling. She moved closer to inspect the lump which was half the size of a golf ball.

Dr. Masters was pulling the lid back to study it. "This appears to be a soft tissue problem. Perhaps she got some grains of sand or dirt in there. Jube, do I have your permission to remove it? It's soft so it won't be difficult."

Jube nodded her permission, reluctantly, for the procedure.

Professor Golden squirmed watching the procedure start and then decided to turn away. "When you have it all removed would you biopsy it, please. We can compare it to the report I'm waiting for."

"No, problem," Dr. Masters answered as he kept his attention on his patient.

Professor continued her questioning, "Did you find the animals to have elevated white blood cell count in their tests?"

"Yes," he replied.

Jeanay had been looking around for her aunt. Once she got to the arena where the little girl sat she could see further ahead. Not far away she spied her aunt with the vet and Jube collected around a Palomino. She looked at Dot and asked, "Would you and Squeeker come and walk with me?" *Maybe with them my nerves will be a little better.*

"Oh, I can't do that! My mom would get mad."

"She would? Why?"

"Squeeker's squeaking upsets some of the horses."

Jeanay reassured Dot, "But his whistles and toots are so cute. We'll stay on the path and avoid the horses. See that one over there with my aunt? When we get near you just stay back a little, okay? And you'll still be within eyeshot of your mother."

Dot looked a little torn and then made her decision, "Okay."

They walked over to the metal pipe stall. "Hi," Jeanay called out.

Dr. Masters looked back over his shoulder and shot her a smile. *Oh no, I hope that doesn't start this all over again!*

Jeanay gulped, "Ha, ha, how, what ah, are you doing?" Jeanay's fists shot down by her side in frustration her head turned skyward as she rolled her eyes. *Boy, am I glad his back is to me!*

Professor Golden sprang into action to help her niece when she spied the little girl, behind Jeanay, her eyes landing on the little creature in her arms. She advanced quickly toward her. Dot took an alarmed step backward. Squeeker started his alert signals. Thankfully the horse was too busy with its nose tweaked to notice. Professor Golden stopped short of her because of the furry creatures objections. She held out her hands hoping to take hold of it, "Please, Please let me hold him."

"What? No!"

Professor Golden gently laid her hands on the little girl's hands and a tug-of-war ensued. "Please."

"No, my mommy will get mad. You're making him too noisy," Dot retorted in a protective, frustrated voice.

"Please, he will help calm my niece."

Dot stopped pulling and looked at Jeanay and then up into the face of Jeanay's aunt. "Oh." Then quietly she complied and let go of her pet realizing the greater good.

"Thank you, thank you, thank you," Professor Golden softly puffed. The Professor quickly stuffed Squeeker into Jeanay's hands. The little fellow made his disapproving presence known. This totally distracted and charmed Jeanay as she stroked his ultra-soft fur which in turn quieted the little fella.

Dr. Masters was finishing up with antiseptic eye wash cleansing the horses repaired eyelid. He noticed Jeanay's transformation. "You have a way with animals, or they have a way with you," he observed approvingly with a chuckle.

Jeanay smiled and looked up at him as she continued stroking her little friend. "Yes," she answered. Determined to act natural she looked the vet directly in the eye, but only for a quick second. His gaze lasted a little longer.

Oh, this is an improvement and a good note to end on. Let's not press this any further. Professor Golden linked Jeanay arm in arm and shot out to Dr. Masters, "We've got to be going. You have my number. We'll be in touch." She turned Jeanay briskly around almost knocking Dot over. They all strode together back toward the bleachers.

Jeanay leaned over to her aunt and whispered, "Thank you."

Professor nodded her head in acknowledgment, "Affirmative."

Jeanay handed Dot her pet, "Thank you so much!"

Dot took him back happily, "You're welcome. Will I see you tomorrow?" Her curls bounced as she looked back and forth between the faces of her new friends.

Jeanay looked at her aunt and then back to Dot, "Probably." She pet Squeeker on the head, "Bye-bye."

Waiting Game

Jeanay kicked off her shoes. She swirled her body onto the bed collapsing on her back with her feet shooting up in the air kicking. "Ah, that feels so good! It's good to be back in our motel on a full stomach. What was the name of that restaurant? Shabob, kabob, thingy."

Professor Golden added, "You wouldn't expect Indian food up here, but they seem to have all kinds. Dinner was devine."

Jeanay paused and then started to giggle, "Isn't he dreamy?"

"Have you been watching the 40's movies? That term is before even my time. Who do you mean? Oh, of course. He's a 'looker' alright!" Professor Golden rolled her eyes. She looked at her cell phone on the nightstand, "No email yet!"

Jeanay turned around to look at her aunt and laughed at the descriptive word 'looker.'

"What are you going to do about your problem?" Professor Golden spoke as she started changing into her robe and slippers.

"I don't know!" Jeanay sounded disappointed. "I don't get that way with guys my age. I am really surprised at myself. I've got to figure something out to get over this. I can't have stuff like this popping up in my career." She groaned, "It could be a disaster a real career breaker."

"You could imagine he's married." The Professor sat down on the edge of her bed.

Jeanay gasped, "Oh dear, do you think he is? I didn't even look for that."

"No, he's not. I checked, especially after the way you acted," Professor gave a hearty laugh.

"I'm sorry Auntie. I feel so stupid."

Professor Golden spoke in a firm tone, "Don't you ever say that again!"

A startled Jeanay looked at her.

"Don't speak words over yourself that bring a curse. Only speak GOOD words over yourself and others."

Jeanay took the information to heart, "Oh, if you say so!"

Professor Golden mulled over her thoughts, "Ah, another thing that might help is for you to get behind your camera or notepad. That will help you stay in a professional mindset, keep your thoughts off yourself."

"Oh yes, that might work. And I still have time to video the animals and that mare with the eye problem."

"Yes, you do. We can all redeem ourselves until lifes over. That is a certainty! I don't want to tell you how many times I've flubbed up," Professor Golden looked down humbly as she spoke.

"Really? You? You mean other than your phobias."

"Oh Jeanay, it's the human condition. And yes, other than that," she looked pained.

"Hum, okay," Jeanay let out a sigh of relief and resignation.

Professor started busying herself tidying up the night table by her bed. The rearranging of objects was a little OCD as she nervously confessed, "I gave up trying to be perfect a long time ago. It takes too much effort. Besides I've gotten accustomed to my...quirkiness. I know I can be a little irritating sometimes, but oh well. And I just like talking, especially to myself, when I'm alone 'cause then I feel like someone's there listening."

"I'm sorry that I was insensitive," Jeanay reflected. She decided to venture a question with apprehension. "I was wondering, I mean if you don't mind me asking? You don't have to answer if you do."

There was silence. Both of them were waiting for each other.

Jeanay took that as an indication to venture her question. She hesitantly spoke, "Sometimes you don't get directly to the point of a subject you take a rabbit trail that honestly seems not related to the subject at all. And I was wondering…what that's about?" She looked at Professor hoping she hadn't hit a nerve. She had.

Professor Golden remained quiet, except for fidgeting fingers that were now in her lap, and then she decided to answer the question. She stopped fidgeting and spoke slowly and carefully. "My mind works in a loop. As memory comes up around something it takes me through a maze of sorts. Through memories of people, or events that happened in that same particular timeline. That helps me remember what I am trying to explain. If I try to jump the track, so to speak, I get lost. It doesn't feel good to get lost even though people wish I could get to the point faster. I just have to do it that way. Other times, when I get upset, I do jump the track and I'm all over the place. I can't seem to help it."

Jeanay went over and sat down next to her aunt and hugged her. "I love you!"

Professor placed her hand on top of one of Jeanay's hands as she smiled gratefully into Jeanay's eyes. "I love you too."

Jeanay kept respectfully silent.

Untimely

A new day dawned. Professor Golden looked at her cell phone, "Still no email?!" She looked pensively at Jeanay then turned away her mind twirling. Having pounced upon the next course of action she announced, "I think we should take a little trip to the County Records Department. I saw it along the highway."

"What are you looking for?"

"I'd like to find out background information on the stables property and the previous owners."

"How do you get access to that kind of information isn't it private?"

"No, it's not, should be, but it's not. All records are open to the public even, astonishingly, the outstanding mortgages. I think it leaves people open to predators making cheap offers on their homes when they are in trouble."

"Doesn't that help some folks?"

"Perhaps, but if people give things time and reach out for help they might find better ways to deal with their situation. I did say cheap not fair. When people are tired and worn out, and an offer comes easy even though it's a bad offer, they succumb. I've seen it too many times with older people. Oh, don't get me started." Her mind started buzzing and it was too late to stop. "Those reverse mortgages, gag me, so you get to take money out of your house, right?"

Jeanay looked mystified and shook her head indicating she didn't know about reverse mortgages.

"It's taking money out of your house's equity without paying it back while you're alive and in your senior years. Maybe if you're sick and you think you have no other way to turn its plausible, but that is very unusual with today's Medicare that covers exorbitant medical costs and drugs." Professor's head tipped back and forth as she considered and reconsidered the ideas that popped into her head. "And there's welfare, oh that's right, if you're on welfare you might not own a home, or you might, it still might help in dire circumstances, and it should ONLY be used in dire circumstances. Or you're too young for Medicare, I suppose that happens too, but then you wouldn't be a senior, hum. I don't know how that would work. You might need a reverse mortgage, to offset what Medicare doesn't cover with assisted living, but only at the end of your life. Now, that's a nice way to go--assisted living. So if you don't need assisted living, or if you only need it for a short while, which is at life's end any way you still have something to leave for an inheritance. Otherwise, you use up the equity in your house to do what, play? What about an inheritance?" Professor Golden's voice rose in a feverish pitch with dogmatic overtones, "The Bible says to leave an inheritance to your children, and your children's children." She waved her hand in the air agitated, "Oh don't get me started!"

"Too late!" Jeanay whispered under her breath. Jeanay touched her arm hoping it would derail her aunt. "And you were telling me about checking stable records?"

"I'm getting there."

Jeanay turned away to roll her eyes, undetected, a conscious reaction to help dissipate her impatience.

"It's just perfect nonsense unless you don't have children to inherit from you, or bad children. It's just downright selfish to take away an inheritance for your own pleasure."

"But you don't have children!"

Professor Golden gave Jeanay a penetrating stare, "Oh yes I do."

"Oh!" Jeanay realized at the inference to herself. *I feel guilty n-o-w.*

As soon as the Professor had sufficiently wound down she abruptly stopped and changed course, "So we need to go to records and get some help. Which hat do you want to wear?"

The jump in subject took Jeanay by surprise. When Jeanay caught up cognitively, a few seconds later, her spirits brightened. She walked to the closet and pointed up on the overhead shelf to the desired hat. "I saw this lovely cloche in your collection which means I could dress up a bit. They look so lovely on the actress that plays in the English murder mystery series Miss Fisher Murder Mysteries. She's got that classy 20's look down great! And…I can do that today since it doesn't look like we'll be going out to the stables."

Professor Golden stood up and retrieved the desired cloche handing it to Jeanay. "Yes, that would look perfect on you! For me I think…" Professor Golden rested her chin on her fist in a thoughtful pose, "I think I'll go for my Tilley hat." The hat had a classic look with a medium brim. She placed the Tilley hat on her head and pulled the hat down over her thick hair. She then tipped the brim to one side slightly over her eyebrow.

They got in the car with Professor Golden driving. Jeanay inquired, "You haven't told me what you're looking for at the record's office?"

"I'm suspecting something isn't quite right about the land. The vet says that the horses involved have in common elevated white blood cell counts, but no fever."

"I don't know that much about biology, but I think you said that means the immune system is struggling?" Jeanay recalled.

"Yes. I can't figure anything out other than the environment affecting them. Oh my, I forgot about the feed possibly being contaminated! I think you mentioned feed samples one time. We'll need to get samples of the hay, and find out if they commonly use the same grain? How will we isolate whether the feed has gotten contaminated on the property or, unlikely, from the manufacturer? And if there is any foul play involved? Oh my, this is getting very complicated." Professor actually seemed energized by this stream of thought.

"We're not dressed for the ranch," worried Jeanay looked down at her lovely dress and high heels.

"I'll pop out and gather the samples. You can wait in the car I'm wearing flats. I better do it right away." Professor Golden made a quick tire squealing 'U' turn. "Hang onto your hat," she grinned.

Jeanay looked over at her aunt startled to see her in such rare form. "Alright Professor, you go!"

They pulled in the long drive to the back of the ranch passing the nosy llamas, inquisitive donkeys, and grazing horses. The llamas walked over to the fence, with hay sticking out of each side of their mouths, eyeing the occupants in the car. It was so whimsical that both ladies burst out laughing. Professor Golden remarked, "Aren't they a hoot!"

"Uh-huh," Jeanay agreed.

They pulled up behind the vet's van. Jeanay stared at it. Then she noticed a fish decal on the bumper. *Oh!*

Professor reassured her, "I'll be quick." She jumped out and went to the feed store. She purchased a bag of grain remarking how heavy it was. The clerk offered to carry it for her. Jeanay noticed them coming to the car and popped the trunk button from inside where she sat waiting. The helpful clerk hoisted the bag into the trunk.

The clerk offered, "I can carry it to where your horse is."

Professor Golden replied, "Thank you. I don't have a horse."

The clerk gave her a peculiar look. Professor Golden gave her a smile and a tip of her hat. The clerk walked away mystified.

Professor Golden stuck her head in the window, "Please hand me my gloves. I'll be back in a minute." She walked over to the bales of stacked hay and selected pieces of straw. She stuck them in one of the small brown bags she garnered from the tack and feed store. She proceeded to pick hay up from the ground that had fallen just outside of a stall, from a messy horse, during feeding. She then found leftover hay inside a feeding crib. She put each in separate bags. "I'll label these when I get back to the car," she mumbled to herself, "Good job Natalie, good thinking!"

As the Professor rounded the corner she saw Dr. Masters opening the back double doors of his van. He spied Jeanay and waved, she nervously waved back. Professor Golden increased her gait to reach him quickly. "Checking on the eye surgery?"

Startled the vet turned around, "Yes."

"How is it?"

"Good, she looks much better now."

"Good, good, can I call you later for the biopsy results?"

"Sure. See you." Dr. Masters gave her a wave. Professor Golden nodded at him as she got in the car. She looked at Jeanay who couldn't keep her eyes off the vet now that she felt protected behind a hood and car windshield. Professor offered, "Alright?"

Jeanay answered with a quick nod, "Alright!"

"Okay, off to the recorder's office girl."

The car crunched up onto the gravel driveway of the Department of Record's office. "I guess they like gravel in this town," Professor Golden noted.

"I like the sound of it, crunchy."

"Eh," Professor Golden shrugged her shoulders, "Don't like walk'n on it."

The office was empty of customers. The Professor looked around, she mumbled, "Good. Don't like crowds." She walked up to the only clerk.

The clerk looked bored. She lifted her head saying, "Yes, how may I help you?"

Professor Golden passed a piece of paper to her. "I'd like to know about this property. What was on it, who has owned it?"

"Okay, give me a couple minutes." The clerk turned to her computer and typed in the address. After the file loaded she turned to the pair, "Okay, the property was purchased from San Bernardino County in the 1800's."

The Professor stopped her to ask, "Wasn't that the time period of the gold rush here?"

The clerk nodded "yes," but pointed in the opposite direction of the stable. "It was over in those hills. They built a few cabins they called a town. There is a plaque at one of the foundations, a historical site. They all burned down in a fire after the area was abandoned. Tourists visit it." She laughed, "One of those cabins was a brothel, prostitutes!" She shook her head amused with the idea.

Professor Golden frowned, "Prostitutes always get a bad rap. What about the guys, the what-cha-ma-call-its, Johns." The clerk realized she had hit a nerve. The look on her face expressed whoops can I duck out of here? Professor was winding up, "If it weren't for those dick-heads"—Jeanay gasped, and looked horrified at her aunt. Her aunt paid no attention and continued, "There wouldn't be any of those women doing that. Most of them because of that male-dominated society couldn't get good jobs. They had to resort to that to survive, makes me so mad!"

The clerk jumped in, "Yes, yes, you're right," hoping that this would end the conversation.

Professor Golden pounded her finger on the counter. "Yes, and they're just now getting around to treating prostituted women as victims and not as lawbreakers, took 'um long enough! Sticking innocent women in jail!! Hump! …Men!"

The clerk looked helpless at Jeanay and to her relief the Professor was finished. She stared at Professor Golden and then feeling that it was safe to proceed read the information in front of her. "A shed was built on it by, it says, a miner who panned some gold at the lake. Then he eventually sold it to a mineral company who then sold it, when they finished mining, to an individual. Oh, a former Mayor of our town, I recognize the name."

"Is he still alive?" Professor Golden was intrigued.

"Oh no, he died a long time ago. And then it goes on to a few other owners."

"Who is the present owner on record now of the ranch house and stable?" The Professor was intrigued.

"Let's see." She looked at the record carefully and then went back over it frowning. "Did you say ranch house and stable?"

"Yes, is there a problem?"

"Well yes," she hesitated, "I see a shed, but not a ranch house or stable. I guess it's zoned properly for a stable, but I doubt a ranch house. Wait a minute let me go check in the other office with our land tax inspector."

Professor Golden nodded her head in compliance. The clerk left the room. Jeanay was trying to make sense of what they had just heard, "What do you think is going on?"

"I thought there might be something unusual about the properties location. It is a beautiful spot. Beachfront location not far away, such a huge patch of land that is undeveloped? Strange the land is bald compared to all the pine tree growth around here. Houses on the lakefront would pay the county higher taxes than a stable, so let's see what she has to tell us. I have a hunch."

The clerk came back into the room looking perplexed. "The tax records show a minor's shed for storage not a ranch house, or a stable. It is zoned appropriately for horses and for storage, not for a home, not for living in. But the taxes are being assessed and paid on time since the new owner took it over this year."

"Do you mean the taxes were late in the past?" Professor queried.

"Yes, there was a default in taxes. The current owner caught all that up when the property was purchased. Our tax assessor will be going out to the property to reassess its value so the taxes might be going up. And it looks like the zoning needs to be addressed too as it is commercial, not residential."

"The owner has a surprise in store it sounds like," Jeanay looked unhappy, "Thanks to us."

"I would say so!" the clerk answered.

"Okay, thank you, you have been most helpful," Professor Golden concluded.

"You're welcome." The clerk went back out of sight. They walked out the building toward the car silently until the building's door closed behind them.

Jeanay groaned, "Oh no, we've made a problem for Jube!"

"Maybe not," Professor Golden frowned and answered in determination.

Jeanay cried out, "What do you mean?"

"The county would eventually find out and then Jube would have to come up with back taxes, better that she find out now. Also, there is property in this county that is zoned commercial slash residential, permitted for an assisted living facility. They could do the same with this situation, allowing for living on-site, to care for and protect animals. They could also 'Grandfather' it in which I know they have done with a lot of these old cabins that don't pass current codes."

"Wow, how do you know so much about this?" Jeanay was awed.

They got in the car and Professor answered her question as she looked both ways down the highway waiting for a chance to pull out. "Your uncle and I looked for investment opportunities in different counties. We even had some rentals for a time. We learned about different variances in different counties and this county is one we studied. But without him it was too much for me to keep up, and not all tenants are delightful people to deal with. I sold them. But it took a great deal of investigation before we decided where to plant our money."

"Ah, maybe you can help me invest someday?" Jeanay had a new respect for her aunt's wise financial moves.

"Not someday. Now! You need to be putting money into an IRA of some sort and in silver or gold. Silver and gold give you a measure of protection if other things fail. Live by the 70-30 Rule, that's how people become millionaires on average incomes."

"Really! What is the 70-30 Rule?"

"Live off of only 70 percent of your income. Save 10 percent for emergencies, give 10 percent to God--who gave you everything any way, and 10 percent in 'don't you touch' investments. That's how to be a millionaire by the time you retire."

"Okay, I'll start doing that with my next big story check."

"You do that! Living with me you can put more than that away."

"I guess so." *I'm not so sure about that. I'd like a little freedom to spend after being so frugal in college.*

"Where are we headed?" Jeanay wondered out loud.

"First, I need to get these samples in an overnight postal box to the lab." Professor Golden looked at her car's clock. "It's getting late and the lab still hasn't gotten back to me," she frowned. "I guess that's okay since I'm adding to their technical analysis, but I sure would like to know what they've found so far." She shook her head, but then added, "It's good, it's all good, it's going to be okay!"

Jeanay brought to recall, "And second?"

"Second what? Ah, oh, let's go to that restaurant we went to the first night. It had an interesting menu."

"Blue Skies Restaurant?"

"Yes, that's it, not hard to remember with so many places here being called Blue Skies this and Blue Skies that."

"Yep!"

They both laughed as the winding scenic road bent before them.

Revelation

The lake situated at the top of the mountain, approximately 5,000 miles above sea level, reflected and magnified the sunset as they drove along the main highway passing it. Blue Skies Restaurant the sign loomed up above them. Its royal blue neon color illuminated brightly against the pink, lavender, and fading blue sunset sinking behind the lake's mountain range.

"I'm hungry!" Suddenly Jeanay thought of the bartender. "What if that bartender works tonight? I don't want him to recognize us. Let's take off these hats. We won't be as noticeable that way!"

"Sure," Professor Golden responded.

They put their hats in the back seat just before they locked up the car and proceeded to the entrance. Just inside the door was a line of people waiting to be seated.

Jeanay sighed, "Oh good, there's a lot of people here, he won't notice us."

"Maybe so, but that means we won't be served as fast," Professor complained.

The hostess gave them the customary smile and took their names. A few minutes later she walked toward the waiting customers with a platter of fresh warm bread. "I'm sorry we are so busy tonight, here is our fresh-baked garlic bread to help the wait, enjoy!" She smiled at all the standing crowded customers.

"Oh wow, this is great! Have you ever seen this before?" Jeanay took the warm bread eagerly.

"Hospitality!" Professor Golden nodded approvingly while trying to manage her discomfort from being crowded so close to strangers.

After a while and a few pieces of bread later their turn to be seated came. "Good, we can't be seen by the bar," Jeanay breathed a sigh of relief noticing their auspicious location as she slid into the booth.

Professor Golden, unconcerned about their seating location, announced, "Good, we're going to eat!"

They looked over the menu and ordered their selection.

"Okay Auntie, p-l-e-a-s-e fill me in on the information we got at the record's office today. I could sense something about it had relevance for you."

"Nothing is for certain, yet. I need the lab results to confirm my suspicions, but I will tell you gold mining has its bad side. Cyanide compounds are widely used by the mining industry to assist in the extraction of both precious and non-precious metals from rock. In gold mining, a dilute cyanide solution is sprayed on crushed ore that is placed in piles, commonly called heaps, or mixed with ore in enclosed vats."

"Yikes, that's poison!" Jeanay's eyes widened while receiving this information. "Does it evaporate over time? I mean that was a long time ago? Right? Ew, we could be breathing it, or getting it on our skin!"

"Exactly, I'll have answers to that when the lab results return, or at least I'll have a better idea. I can't rule out anything at this point."

"Oh no!" Jeanay gasped, "This could ruin her."

"Could ruin who?" A loud male voice broke into their space.

Looking up a pudgy man stood before them, in a rumpled suit, chewing on a corner of his cold limp cigar. Their startled reaction prompted him to remove his rumpled Fedora. "Let me introduce myself, my name is Doger Reech. I work for the local paper here."

The pair peered up at him their faces expressly annoyed.

Upon no reciprocal name exchange Doger cleared his throat, "Yes, well, and let me tell you something." Doger leaned down as if to whisper and then decidedly plopped himself down square onto the same seat as Professor Golden who immediately let out a startled noise. The look on her face showed incredulous disbelieve, she scooted away from him wedging herself into the corner as far from the dodgy occupant as she possibly could. *How dare he. Downright rude!* He leaned forward on the table with both elbows his belly touching the edge of the table. He looked directly into Jeanay's eyes. "Your story was fantastic!"

Jeanay sat back pushing away from the table and leaning as far away from him as her seat would allow. *Odorous person go away!* Firmly and tense she asked, "How do you know what my story is, or for that matter who I am?"

Pointing, with his brown cigar stained finger, to the doorway that connected the restaurant to the bar he then nodded toward a figure. Their attention turned to the doorway where the figure of the dreaded bartender stood. Cocky, with his arms crossed he leaned against the door frame. Smiling, he saluted lazily then sauntered back to the bar.

"Ooooh!" Jeanay sounded like a disgruntled tiger as she glared in the direction of the empty doorway. She sat rigid and crossed her arms in defiance.

When Professor Golden saw the familiar figures impudent salute to Jeanay her eyebrows knit into suppressed anger.

"Oh don't be that way," Doger chided. His tone and words made the hair on the back of the ladies' necks rise. "You don't need to be worried about ole me, I'm harmless." He talked with his hands as his animated cigar bobbed between his fingers. Though it had not been lit in a long time, an old, musty, nauseating stench clung to it. "I thought, well you know, this is a clever young lady doing this investigative article. And then I heard you hadn't left town."

Both of them looked at him hard.

"Nah, Nah, ladies don't be upset! Look, you're still here right? So I figured you found something else to interest you. And now I hear somebody might be in trouble? This is what I figure. You scratch my back I'll scratch yours. You're young and need a break so let's share. What could it hurt?"

Jeanay could see the ire swelling in her aunt's face and she was in no mood to be blown over either. She decided to take an unusual tack to this offer much to her aunt's shock and consternation.

Jeanay demurely replied. "So, let me see, you want to know something new you could publish?"

Doger nodded grinning, "That's right, but of course I would only publish it here. I don't have any great plans for a career outside of this town. Just wanna keep my job. You publish it out there." He waved his cigar in a roundabout fashion to indicate the world.

Professor Golden followed his, dirty cigar, motion dizzily with her eyes.

Jeanay continued, demurely, as Professor Golden's eyelashes batted rapidly and her head started bobbing, "So I do all the work, investigating, putting the evidence together, filming, and writing it." Doger nodded. Then Jeanay suddenly crescendoed, "And you get all the credit and first printing. Are you nuts!" His Cheshire cat grin started to fade.

Now, Professor Golden looked on in amazement as Jeanay continued, "You have a lot of nerve intruding on us. You think I'm some stupid, naive, little college graduate." Then she became very angrily animated. "My aunt and I uncover a serious situation that even the police were stalled on. I am not some witless--twerp--" She sat forward and thumped him on the chest thrice with her finger as she spoke, "Like...you...think!"

Doger slid out of the bench to get away from her fury. He held up his chubby hands, "Okay, Okay, but if you change your—" He was interrupted by a sharp pain in one ankle.

"She won't!" Professor Golden had just delivered a severe blow with her foot.

"Ow,ow,ow," he hopped up and down grabbing his ankle, "You didn't need to do that!"

"Oh yes I did!" Professor quipped back in rare form seldom delivered except in the confines of a human angry mother bear protecting her young.

The ladies looked at him and started to belly laugh. He looked at them as if they were crazy and exited quickly.

Jeanay slapped her aunt's arm. "You were great!"

Professor Golden returned the fun slap. "No girl, you go girl, you were great! They laughed out of relief, and disbelief, and above all victory. The commotion had not gone unnoticed by customers sitting close to them. They got smiles, thumbs up, and a few hand claps. Jeanay and Professor nodded back with a smile.

Jeanay cocked a thumb toward their approving audience, "They must know him!"

Professor nodded in agreement. "Under different circumstances I would pity him, but this time I do think he got his just desserts." As they watched him limp out of the restaurant professor remarked, "He does reek of miasma. I feel a foreboding!"

The waitress came and placed their platters down in front of them. She nodded toward the door. "I see you got rid of our town buffoon. I hate the way he tries to hit on all the pretty girls. He thinks he's such a celebrity journalist," she shook her head and rolled her eyes.

Jeanay asked in surprise, "Oh, he does?" Professor Golden and Jeanay laughed. They looked into each other's eyes.

The waitress looked confused. "Wasn't that what he was bothering you about?"

Jeanay nodded her head up and down. "Oh yes, of course, you got it."

Professor Golden added, "Yep, you got it! Thank you, the food looks great!"

The waitress nodded approvingly and left them to stuff their mirth down with food. The ladies stifled snickers here and there that kept resurfacing until they finally were able to settle down and concentrate on their food.

"Say, Auntie, what would you say to getting back, somehow, with that ridiculous loser bartender?" Jeanay's expression looked crafty.

"Hum," Professor thought a second, "I'd say…games on!"

They smiled wickedly at each other.

The next day dawned with the beautiful scents of spring air. The, seemingly, long-awaited email message bearing tidings had arrived. Professor Golden breathed the air deeply as she stood, stretched, and yawned outside the motel room in her robe. She was hoping the air and sunshine on her face would help take the dread out of her before looking at the message. This trail of clues did not look good. She knew there was a probability that something was not on the level with the property and the recorder's office. Her suspicions about the land had been melding in her thoughts creating a foreboding that entangled her heart and mind. Jeanay was not the only one who was forming an attachment to the people and animals at the Rim of the World.

Professor Golden stepped back into their room where Jeanay sat on her bed, with feet propped up, enjoying her Facebook account on her cell phone. Begrudgingly she picked up her own cell phone from the bedside stand and opened the text. Jeanay looked up at her questioning its content with her eyes.

"Yes, it's from the lab," she answered Jeanay's questioning gaze.

Jeanay got up and stood in front of her aunt watching her face for an indication of the content that would hopefully give them the answers they needed. Professor Golden remained expressionless as her eyes read the messages. She then turned the phone around and held it for Jeanay who briefly read it and sighed heavily, "Oh, noooo."

Professor Golden sighed, "Not that we didn't expect some of this, there's a lot here. Let me use your computer to read this further. I need to open up the pdf files they sent me with the individual lab results."

"Okay." Jeanay opened up the laptop for her aunt. They both sat down on the bed to read. After they worked their way through the material Jeanay asked, "What do we do now?"

"I'm going to call Dr. Masters with this information. We can compare it with the tests he's been running. He may want to meet us at the stable to lend support to Jube. I think you need to get out there and get your videos of the animals quickly. Make your report. Then we'll sit down and talk to Jube."

"Alright," Jeanay agreed. She rubbed her chest where her heart thudded.

The lovely, familiar crunch met their ears as they pulled off the dirt road onto the ranch's entrance. This time they hardly noticed the snoopy animals coming over to gawk at them as they drove past. Professor Golden pulled her car into a parking space and helped Jeanay unpack her video equipment. "Now you remember how well you stuck up for us with that man last night. You are a reporter. Remember that!" Jeanay nodded, "Yes," solemnly. Silence felt most comfortable at this juncture.

Professor Golden helped Jeanay set up and move to each horse. She recorded Jeanay speaking to the camera about the horses' conditions. Professor made sure the subjects remained square in the frame of the lens. When Jeanay put the mic down, after the last one, she said, "I need to get some front footage and the ranch's sign." They quietly went together to the entrance of the driveway. As they were finishing up Dr. Masters van entered the property. The solemnity of the situation toned down Jeanay's reaction to encountering the vet.

Professor Golden turned to Jeanay, as they waved at Dr. Masters who reciprocated the gesture, "Remember you are a reporter!" She repeated herself to encourage Jeanay that she could be just fine around the good doctor. Jeanay nodded she understood and agreed with the intention of the reminder.

They walked behind the van to the bleachers. There was the usual activity going on at the ranch with horses and owners, employees and work. Jube walked out the back door smiling, "You're here." They gave weak smiles in return. She looked at their solemn faces, "You know something!"

Dr. Masters got out of his van and came over to them. Jube asked, "Did an owner call you out?"

"No, I'm here for you," he answered calmly.

"Oh!" Jube sounded like she had the stuffing knocked out of her, "I better sit down."

Jeanay put on her professional demeanor, "I need to set up my video equipment to record the conversation." She gave Dr. Masters a small nod, with a shy smile, as she went about her business.

Professor waited quietly sitting beside Jube. She gave her a reassuring pat on the hand, at the same time, she wished someone else was delivering the news to her. Derek took a seat on the other side of Jube. Jeanay signaled that she was ready.

Professor Golden started directing her comments to Jube. "Jube you contacted me and Jeanay Golden about your lovely ranch stables to look into various ailments with some of the horses here. We were called after the vet you consulted could not figure out why some of the horses had strange, unrelated symptoms. As you know we have taken samples of different areas on your property, and we have their analysis to share with you."

"Yes, thank you, Professor Golden," Jube nodded looking very distressed.

Jeanay interrupted speaking boldly from behind the camera, "Dr. Masters, as the vet of this stable, do you have anything to say at this point?

Dr. Masters reacted in surprise not realizing Jeanay had turned the camera on him. "No," he shook his head, "Not at the moment."

Jeanay turned the camera back to Professor Golden and Jube. Professor took a deep breath and proceeded, "The reports from the lab were sent to my email address this morning. And they will also be sent to your ranch address in the mail. The reports indicate, in all the soil samples and some of the feed samples, that in varying degrees there is cyanide evidence."

Jube caught her breath.

Professor Golden continued on, "The samples taken show the concentration of the cyanide starting at the lake to decrease in incidence as you get nearer to the stable. What I am saying is the strongest concentration is on the beach of the lake. There are other abnormalities in the soil as well which fits with the information we got about how this property was used in the 1800's on into the early 1900's."

Jube was breathing quicker and lighter than usual and looking peaked, but she responded, "Yes, go on."

The counties records show that gold was found in this part of the lake and it was panned here. The only structure on the property was a shed, the shed located next to your ranch house which was used to store equipment in, or for spending a night.

Jube nodded, "Yes, the shed looks original, very old." Jube looked confused she shook her head in disbelief, "What is the connection?"

Professor Golden decided to skip over the property zoning issue for now and continue with the most pressing problem. "Gold mining has a 'dirty' side to it. Cyanide compounds are widely used by the mining industry to assist in the extraction of both precious and non-precious metals from rock.

Jube gasped in shock, "No!"

Professor Golden continued, "In gold mining, a dilute cyanide solution is sprayed on crushed ore that is placed in piles, commonly called heaps, or mixed with ore in enclosed vats. Probably the former was done here in heaps. The heaps were spread out over this whole area, but more concentrated near the lake. That is why this area was not zoned residential, but commercial."

"They contaminated this ranch so we're being poisoned here?" Jube was incredulous. She did not catch the significance of the zoning in the face of dire life threatening implications.

"Yes slowly." Professor Golden turned toward Dr. Masters, "The lab report shows the feed has been contaminated probably when it fell to the ground and the horses ate from where it fell."

Dr. Masters nodded as he thoughtfully contemplated the ramifications of the symptoms. "That would account for the throat problems."

"And the rashes from laying in the dirt," Jeanay spoke from behind the camera.

"Oh my God," Jube covered her eyes and started sobbing. Dr. Masters moved closer and put his arm around her shoulder. "What am I going to do, I'm ruined! …The horses are sick because of me!" And what does this mean for me?

Professor Golden looked away, disturbed, moved by the distress Jube was experiencing.

"The horses are sick because of me!!" Jube repeated in abject agony.

The Professor turned back to her quickly, "No, they're not!" Professor reacted strong and firm, "The problem came before you! It came with the county! It resulted in the failure of many land owners and is now thrust, innocently, in your lap."

"What am I going to do?" Jube wiped the tears from her eyes. She looked into the Professor's eyes with her tear streaked face pleading for help.

"Oh," Professor Golden, taken back started to stammer, "Well…I don't know—oh—'um, right, well, th-there have to be answers…" Speaking more to herself than anyone, "There have to be answers—I'll—I'll." Then nodding "yes" with her head, and then switching to shake her head "no." Her eyebrows went up into 'think' mode her head started to bob. She stammered, "I'll have to study into this!"

Jube looked hopeful, "You will?"

Professor Golden looked around baffled, hard pressed, and then—earnestly to Jeanay for help.

Jeanay called out, "Dr. Masters you've checked the animals do you have anything to add?"

Dr. Masters caught up in all the emotion looked unhinged. He dropped his arm from Jube's shoulder and returned his arm to his lap. Both of his hands moved to each knee rubbing the top of his leg nervously unaccustomed to being in such drama. "Ah, Ah," is all he could get out.

Professor Golden got her breath back from Jeanay's redirection. The time lapse gave her the presence of mind to ask the vet, "Dr. Masters you took biopsies on the horses, and you have been studying the situation. Did you find cyanide in any of your samples?"

"No, I did not," He shook his head.

"Oh, then maybe this isn't connected," Jube threw in hopefully.

Dr. Masters continued, "I really wouldn't expect to find the actual cyanide in the tissue samples. I wouldn't have been testing for it anyway. And since I don't have information on cyanide symptoms that is if cyanide can have the affects that we found, I really can't say more than that right now."

Jube turned away disappointed.

Professor Golden answered, "We will continue to work on this."

"Okay cut." Jeanay found this a good point in which to shut the camera off. She waved for her aunt to come to her. "You haven't addressed her being on commercial property, her home it's not zoned for her home."

"Yes, no, I haven't, but since she didn't catch that part. She's in such shock. I don't think this is the time to bring that up. I don't want her fainting or throwing up, or something." Professor waved her hands, palms down, signaling her discomfort over the idea. "Do you have enough? Can I just talk to her with-without…about this without…you know…the camera," nodding toward it.

"Sure, it's off now." They walked over together to sit with Jube.

Jube turned to Dr. Masters, "Derek what did you find?"

He answered her question gently, "I found elevated white blood cells. You already know that. Their immune systems are fighting a pathogen, or alien substance that came through the skin, or the air. I'm sorry Jube that at this point I can't be of any more help to you."

Professor Golden thought out loud, "Let me go over some of the possibilities that we've touched on. I would suspect that the animals that have skin issues lie down more than the others. And the coughing and tumors came from breathing stirred up dirt or eating contaminated feed."

"Jube countered still not wanting to believe the inferences, "If this is true then why aren't all the animals sick?"

Dr. Masters surmised, "The horses not affected may have better immune systems, and each creature has individual genetics just like humans."

"The llamas, donkeys, and horses in the front corrals may be sufficiently distanced from the toxic areas to not affect them," Professor conjectured. "In hind sight I should have gotten samples from their area as well.

"We haven't noticed a problem with them," Derek added.

Jeanay turned on a light, "And the chickens are elevated up off the ground on chicken wire, wood, and straw. So they wouldn't be touching the dirt, hum, but they would be breathing it."

Jube offered, "I give them antibiotics occasionally like pet shops do, maybe—"

"That protected them!" Dr. Masters finished her sentence.

"Well maybe. We don't know much about this kind of thing. It will need more study." Professor Golden didn't care for speculation without facts and hard evidence.

Jube held out her gloved hands. "What about the rash on my hands?"

"That could be from all the dust even in your store. Your employees all wear gloves and you didn't always?" Professor asked considering the evidence.

"Right, we touched on that a few days ago."

"Oh right, right, you did." Professor acknowledged bringing the conversation to her memory.

Jube continued, "I sometimes help with the hay feeding twice a day. My helpers wear gloves because the bales are strapped together with wire. When they clip the wire it recoils. The end is sharp and could pierce flesh so I insist they wear gloves."

Jeanay turned to her aunt, "I noticed Jube also keeps the dust down better than any stable I've been in with her tractor-trailer, water barrel sprayer. That must help keep the exposure down."

Jube turned to Dr. Masters in her shocked stupor and asked, "What about Goldy's eye? That didn't have anything to do with this right?"

Dr. Masters replied, "Under microscope I found a grain of dirt that was surrounded by inflammation. It could, of course, been contaminated with cyanide, but not necessarily so."

"Oh." Jube turned to each of them and implored, "What am I to do?"

In response Jeanay reached out and put her hand on Jubes hand, "Don't worry my aunt will figure out something."

Professor Golden started to get up when she heard Jeanay offering Jube her unequivocal assistance in astonishment she just about fell over. She steadied herself as one leg almost gave out from the shock. She stamped that leg down hard. She looked up at Jeanay with a most pained expression and an ever so barely-noticeable head shake "no."

Jeanay looked straight into the Professor's eyes and in answer nodded her own head emphatically up and down, "yes." Both their eyes locked, and then both of their eyes got even bigger and then narrowed in intensity. A barely, visible, mental battle with each other ensued. Jeanay, repeatedly, nodding ever so tiny "yes," and Professor simultaneously doing the same, but indicating "no."

"Jeanay may I speak to you?" Professor Golden pulled Jeanay aside, "What are you doing to me?

"Nothing, I have implicit trust in you."

"Your innocent trust in me is astounding. There is too much involved here to be certain of any outcome!" The Professor shook her head in disbelief.

Dr. Masters patted Jube's hand and gave her a final shoulder squeeze. "I'll leave you to figure this out. I'm going to go put on a mask, we must be sure to wash surfaces and our hands. And I need to isolate my clothes when I leave here." He smiled and walked a few steps. Then he turned back, "I suggest you all do the same!"

Jube sat down hard, "Oh! What will people think?"

Jeanay offered, "Tell your workers to wear masks. They're already covered everywhere else. If none of your owners have medical problems, and the workers who are coughing stop coughing, wait just a little while for Professor to work on this before you make any announcements. Right, Auntie?"

"Right," Professor Golden sounded exhausted. "If they don't stop coughing it wouldn't hurt to have your employees go on antibiotics while I figure this out. A medical doctor wouldn't give them any, but maybe your vet can help out with this. There should be some cross-over antibiotics that would work."

Jube spoke sadly, "Okay, I'll ask him. If all else fails I can give them my chicken antibiotics. I've used them to get over infections, it works. I'll go back on it."

"Ew, really?" Jeanay shivered.

Professor Golden rubbed her forehead and judiciously added, "If they have to go on antibiotics tell them to take probiotics to counter the loss of gut bacteria." Jube looked mystified over this information, but nodded. "And Jube will you please excuse us. My brain is mentally on overdrive, shifting back-and-forth, analyzing this and that. I'm in this mode, gotta be alone, no distractions. I hope you understand, understand," Professor repeated herself and the rambling started, "Pressure, so much pressure… It's okay, it's gonna be okay, it's all good, it's all good."

Seeing the signs, Jeanay quickly stepped in. She went to Professor's elbow and announced, "Yes, we've got to go. Professor thinks better alone."

Professor Golden continued muttering to herself in concentration as Jeanay guided her. "Help her, the soil, change the soil, how do you change soil? Find ways to neutralize toxins." Jeanay guided her all the way to the car and was seating her. The Professor became more and more oblivious to her surroundings. Her mind was in high gear revving like a hot rod. The Professor suddenly popped up from her seat, the car door had not been closed yet, and rose her hand up in the air to Jube, "Detox, you need to detox. Herbs, poultices, intravenous food grade hydrogen peroxide. I'll get back to you, your-your workers, detox--"

"Okay Auntie, okay. I'm shutting the door," Jeanay interrupted her. "Work it out in the car. Please!" Jeanay strained to keep patient. When she had her aunt contained, with the door shut, Jeanay then turned to Jube and yelled, "She's already figuring things out." She ran over and grabbed her equipment and tossed it into her trunk adding loudly, "Don't worry just don't worry, okay?" She banged the trunk closed.

Jube, so involved in her ranch's problem, didn't notice anything about the Professor as she waved goodbye.

The absentminded Professor didn't notice to return the wave. She was caught up in spinning thoughts and emotions her mind traveling through it's lobed mazes. Her brain isolating points on an invisible white board, like a detective, she plotted out a crime scene and its suspects.

Jeanay relieved to get her aunt out of there spun the car's wheels splaying the gravel.

Professor Golden sat in her seat oblivious. She mumbled out ideas and possibilities as her mind spun. Her brain urgently arced through brain crevices synapsing, pulling, from the gray matter filled deep from years of scientific study. Introspective, gears switching, she sat with her eyes riveted to the floor, her fingers interlaced, her hands folded in prayer.

Time Is Short

"I'm going to get us pizza Auntie," Jeanay announced loudly. It was as if talking to a blind and deaf person. Professor Golden remained huddled in her seat in deep concentration even to the point of obsession. She felt immense internal pressure and nothing could relieve it until her brain was satisfied. Jeanay pulled the car into the driveway parking lot of a Sharkys Pizza.

Professor continued her incessant mumbling as her brain worked through its maze of ideas and possibilities. "Sand, possibly, or that new composite has possibilities. Detox, fluids, I wonder, hum, would sealant alone work? Definitely detox people, animals, she'll lose business, oh-my-my, minimize losses, educate. The county needs to cooperate. Get contacts, meet the right people. Figure out zone changes. Difficult, very--very difficult," she spoke shaking her head, "Not impossible, proof of intention, legalese, County-get County to offset losses, yes, yes, hard, but possible…maybe? Submit documents, work out details—

"Auntie," Jeanay called out frustrated.

Professor Golden mumbled on deaf to Jeanay.

Jeanay had parked and was listening intently to Professor Golden hoping she could follow her line of thinking and pick up some clues to where this might be leading. Her aunts recycling made no sense to her. "Auntie," she tried again to get her attention. She put her hand around Professor's upper arm, this time, and shook it lightly, "Auntie!"

Startled, Professor Golden looked at her and responded, "Yes?"

"We're here, pizza parlor, Sharkys. I want to get pizza and I'm dying for a cold, stiff Coke. I need a swift shot of caffeine. I don't think you need Coke, nope, no upper for you, nope, no need there."

"Okay." Professor Golden dazed opened the car door and stepped out. She came up short, hard, with her step out. She looked down, "Oh, finally some cement, nice!"

"Ahh," Jeanay let out a sigh. *She's returning to earth.*

There was no line inside. They placed their order. Jeanay gave her name. They sat down to wait. An employee brought Jeanay her Coke in an ice cold glass. As Jeanay took it from her hand she looked up surprised. "Oh?" She looked at the self-serve beverage bar and then at the employee.

"Special for you, the owner told us who you are. I really enjoyed the article. We all sorta know the scientists at the observatory. They come in here like everyone else in town—

"Everyone else in town? Professor Golden noted and interrupted.

The helper nodded and continued, "We're happy Oleg is okay." Then she added, "You're a celebrity here!" The young employee spoke in an animated voice, "We don't usually get much excitement here, the towns so small, except for that shooting a few years ago. A couple of old-timers got into a fight outside of the bar. Shot his friend dead," she stated deadpan.

"Oh, no," both Jeanay and Professor flinched and echoed.

Ignoring their sentiment the employee continued looking inquisitively at Professor Golden. Staring at her she asked, "Would you like anything since you're with Jeanay Golden?"

Professor Golden chuckled.

Jeanay quickly spoke, "This is Professor Golden we did the investigation together. She worked behind the camera."

"Oh Golden, you're related," the girl looked impressed.

Professor Golden grinned, "Yes. And, I'll just have water thank you," she smiled and nodded.

"Okay, be back in a jiffy with that and your pizza should be out soon."

Professor Golden held the girl's attention to ask, "So when do we pay?"

"The owner said it's on the house."

"Oh, really? How nice. Can we thank him?" Professor looked at Jeanay who did not look especially surprised. Professor thought, *that's odd.*

The employee turned around to look inside the pizzeria behind the bar and then back to them, "Looks like he isn't here yet. He has five other Sharkys. He's not here every day, but we do expect him in before long to check on a couple things."

"Thank you," Professor Golden responded. *Everyone in town comes in here. Hum…I might not have to sit here all week trying to run in to the right person. Maybe I can get some contacts from the owner since WE'RE celebrities. That comes in handy!*

"Wait, did you say he has five other pizzerias…in this little town?" Professor looked skeptical.

"Oh, no, the others are down the hill," the girl laughed.

Professor Golden nodded, "That makes more sense."

The employee walked away smiling. Jeanay chuckled, "Well how do you like that? Feels good, huh, we sure can use the levity and celebrity."

Professor Golden looked amused, "Ah, huh!"

"I wanted to surprise you. Cathy the owner of the gymnastics' business well her husband is the owner of Sharkys. She called to congratulate me on my video documentary about Oleg. She said to be sure to come here and they would treat us with their compliments. Since her husband isn't here all the time she said, 'Just give me a name and we'll let the employees and manager know to look out for you.'"

Professor Golden sighed with pleasure, "Nice. It feels good to relax. I've been in such a state."

Jeanay smiled demurely. *Isn't that for sure!* She took a quick drink to cover up her opinion, and then she drained the almost empty glass.

The employee, with the scent of pizza sauce on her clothes, came back and placed water for two on the table. She turned to Jeanay, "I thought you would like some water too. Can I get you a refill on that Coke?"

"Oh, I ca—," Jeanay stopped, looked at the coke dispenser, and then back up to the employee. "Yes, that would be nice."

Another employee came out with their pizza held up high, over their heads, and silverware with napkins in the other hand. "Here you are!" She placed the pizza before them with a big flourish and smile. The first employee returned with Jeanay's freshened drink. Then both employees stood back and grinned at them, gapping. They gave no indication of leaving. Jeanay and Professor Golden sat blinking at them.

"Ah, okay, thank you," Jeanay tried to break the spell as she and the Professor waited patiently for them to leave before starting their meal.

The manager came to the rescue as Jeanay and Professor Golden stared up into the employee's faces not sure what else to do. He leaned over the cash register counter and called them, "We need your help back in here!" That did it--they smiled again at the sitting celebrities and returned to work. One had looked like she was going to curtsy, but then sheepishly thought better of it.

Jeanay and Professor Golden looked at each other and sniggered with delight when they were out of earshot. They picked apart the pizza eating until their appetite was satiated. In between chewing Jeanay started questioning the Professor, "What have you been able to figure out?"

"Only hypothetical possibilities, so we need to use your laptop for me to do research."

"Sure, I'll go out and get it when I'm finished."

"It's in the car?" Professor looked incredulous.

"It almost never leaves my sight for very long. In fact, now that you mention it, it makes me nervous to leave it in the car. I'll be right back." Jeanay quickly removed herself and returned with the laptop. She placed it down in front of Professor Golden. "All's safe and sound," she said as she sat down.

"Would you get it going? I don't have your password."

"Oh, sure," Jeanay said between bites. As she was logging in a tall, fair haired man, with a smile, advanced toward them from behind the counter.

"Hello, you are our town's visiting celebrities aren't you? I'm Cathy's husband Bruce."

Both ladies looked up and smiled. Professor Golden spoke first, "Thank you for this delicious meal."

Jeanay nodded, "Umm-good, thank you so much!"

"You're welcome. Well, I'll leave you to finish." Bruce started to step away.

Before he went far Professor called out, "Oh wait!"

"Yes?" he answered politely turning back.

"Bruce, I hear you get everyone in here that is in town, all the locals?"

"Yes, I do."

Jeanay wondered what her aunt was up to.

"Do you know the Mayor?"

Bruce looked surprised, "Yes, as a matter of fact, I do. He comes to the civic business' men and women monthly meeting."

"What's he like?" Professor Golden asked.

"What's he like? Huh," he repeated her while thinking about the man. "He's nice. He's very meticulous and concerned about the reputation of this city. He does a good job."

"Would you be able to introduce me to him?"

Jeanay was thinking. *What? This is embarrassing asking for a favor.*

The owner was taken aback at such a presumptuous, brazen request. He wasn't usually flustered, but this was a new one for him. Bruce paused to think then he looked at Professor Golden calmly, "May I ask why?"

Professor Golden decided to let him in on why. She signaled to a chair, "Please sit down. This is going to take a little explaining." Bruce took a seat. She and Jeanay explained what had happened out at the ranch. They discussed the information discovered at the record's office. He sat back listening intently.

Bruce shared his concern for Jube's situation and then he asked, "How can the Mayor help?"

Professor Golden shared, "First, I have to put together what can be done to fix this situation for the ranch. Then I need to look into some possible zoning changes that would have to go through the cities board. Their vote would be needed. If this is presented right, knowing what you told me how appearances and reputation are so important to the mayor, I think we could get his help to save her business."

"I see," Bruce stroked his chin in thought. "It's tough being a business owner, so many challenges. Yes, I think I would like to help."

Jeanay almost jumped out of her seat in excitement. Professor Golden beamed with satisfaction.

"I am a large contributor to many of the Mayor's pet projects. I think I could arrange a meeting in his office for our 'celebrity reporters.' You would need to make a tidy presentation." Bruce turned to Jeanay, "And you have an advantage since he likes to impress the press!"

"Oh, how nice!" Jeanay felt flattered somehow.

Professor explained, "I'm doing my research now. I will present it in a report along with a trajectory of what can be done to make her land safe and the means by which we need to accomplish that."

Bruce responded uncertain, "Means, ah-yes well… He can be a tightwad if it's not his special project."

Jeanay piped up, "Then we'll make it his pet project!"

"Okay, then I'll leave you two investigators to do your work. You've really got it cut out for you. Glad I'm not in your shoes." Bruce stretched his long legs, got up, nodded, smiled and walked away.

Professor and Jeanay smiled at him and then turned to each other. Professor adamantly stated, "That was a courageous declaration!"

Jeanay answered with a timid, "Yes," as she nervously cleared her throat.

Professor Golden turned to the laptop, "Let's get going. We've got some help now on our team. Pray I can figure this out."

"Will you tell me what you have in mind?" Jeanay pulled her chair closer to Professor Golden, so she could watch what was on the different links Professor was pulling up on the laptop.

"Alright, we need to neutralize the cyanide."

"Right, is there some kind of spray chemical that can do that?" Jeanay was hoping this would be simple.

"No. Boy that would be nice! It probably could be done, but I don't think there's enough call for that. You know not enough money in that kind of research." Professor typed while she spoke, "What needs to be done is to seal it. The immediate crisis is the stable, not the trails. It would be too costly to do the trails. Besides most of them are in the government park forestry jurisdiction. The price of a sealant is going to be tough, or even out of the question for Jube."

"Yes, her ranch is very large. Then there's the zoning too don't forget," Jeanay added.

"First things first, look here at this quarry site for rocks, sand, pebbles. They even have a quarry for lime, up here, to sell to the cement companies. San Bernardino has a plethora of outlets from many quarries. Now, what I'm thinking is the aggregate composite used under my porch paver's might be perfect."

Jeanay queried, "How is that? Paver's would be too expensive to cover that whole area."

"Yes, and they would break under the hoofs striking them also. No, that's not what I'm thinking. Emanuel was helping me and he knows I like to save money and repurpose materials. He had a load of cement composite material that was used in a stall and the horse owner wanted to replace it. He said it was good for horses in loose form, but it could also be wet and compressed with a large, heavy industrial roller. It would, virtually, turn the loose material into cement. When he dumped it at the house it was loose. It looked a little like pea gravel, but jagged. So he wet it and then pressed down the paver's on top of it sealing it all together. It worked beautifully holding everything in place. It would be easy to bring it in, in truckloads."

"Oh, that sounds really good!"

"Yes, it is promising. Look at the price it's cheaper than gravel, but still we need a lot. I'm trying to figure an angle that would get Jube help from the city to pay for it."

"What about from the county instead?" Jeanay suggested.

"What do you mean?"

"Didn't you say the county forestry service helps keep the brush and trees under control by matching half the amount residential owner's pay to clear the required debris away from their homes for fire safety? Now, why wouldn't they want to keep the community safe on this level too?"

"Yes, very good thinking!" Professor Golden pondered this information for a minute. "You said residential. Our twist is that we have commercial property."

"And you're thinking to get the Mayor to change that I bet."

"Right, but I don't think the stable will fit the zoning for residential even though it has a ranch house on it. But since the same county, down the hill, has unusual and different zoning under commercial I am going to try for that. Jeanay would you call several of the companies selling the composite and get estimates for me?"

"Also, you'll need to call Jube and get her square footage so we can figure the cost." Professor Golden added, "Let's not bother Jube with the details until we find out if we can get her some kind of financial help. I'm feeling a little hope here."

Eagerly Jeanay agreed, "All righty, will do!"

Mayor's Report

The printer made, "Katoosh, katoosh, katoosh," clicking noises as the pieces of paper sailed through the machine.

"Would you collate and bind the pages in a presentation folder for me, please. That black one would be just fine." Professor Golden smiled and pointed at the black binder.

"Yes, ma'am," the attendant replied.

Professor waited patiently for the clerk to complete her work.

"We're almost ready, aren't we?" Jeanay tapped her fingers on the counter impatient to go. She confided, "I'm nervous we might get kicked out of the Mayor's office."

"You are? Really, I'm surprised Jeanay. Why?"

"I know Mr. Sharky said he likes publicity, but still he might not like me videoing a sensitive subject."

"Oh yes he will after I'm done with him. I've never seen a politician who doesn't love his ego stroked even the shyest ones. And if he goes for my proposal we're going to make sure he knows he'll be a hero!"

Jeanay laughed, "Ya think!"

"I think! ...Okay, it looks like we're done."

The clerk handed Professor Golden her presentation folder in a bag. They paid and left.

"Next stop, the Mayor's office," Jeanay announced loudly. She shook her hands trying to shake off nervous energy. Looking at her aunt she entrusted, "Building up confidence."

Bruce Sharky was already in the parking lot when Professor Golden and Jeanay pulled up to the city building. They greeted each other.

"I'm looking forward to hearing your presentation to the Mayor," Bruce said genuinely intrigued. Then he turned to Jeanay noticing her video equipment, "Do you think he'll let you video the meeting?"

Jeanay weakly responded, "Oh, you don't th--" Then getting a hold of herself she switched to, "I don't see why not!" Jeanay spoke to embolden herself as she and the Professor gave each other the eye. Jeanay had the tripod and camera in the black bag over her shoulder. She stood erect and puffed out her chest to force herself into a confident posture with hopes it would transition into an inner truth.

They walked onto the portico entry with its neat columned pillars. The two-story building structure was modern for the area. They entered through the double glass entry doors. There were long, faux, marble counters, and neatly situated behind them were several secretaries. One looked up and greeted Bruce with a nod, "Yes, go on up he's expecting you."

They took the elevator up to the second floor. It hummed efficiently which Professor Golden was silently praying for with bowed head. Being in a tight space with the potential of falling didn't appeal to her any more than being on the wide expanse of water. Upon a gentle landing she opened the door quickly and gratefully exited first. Bruce held the door for Jeanay to clear her equipment from the elevator. Immediately in their vision sat a large, dark, walnut tree desk in the middle of the room. An attractive, tidy-looking lady in dressy casual clothes sat behind it.

"We have an appointment with the Mayor," Bruce spoke to her.

"Yes, Mr. Sharky," she stood up and nodded at each person, in turn, then walked around her desk to them. "He is awaiting you, Professor Golden, Reporter Golden, please go in." They returned her nod with a smile and followed her through the paneled, pine, double doors. The panels were stained dark walnut and held carvings of elk, moose, coyote, mountain lion, bear, squirrels, birds, and local flowering plants. Pine trees and mountains rose above the animals in the background. Professor Golden and Jeanay found them to be distractingly beautiful as they walked through the doorway.

In the middle of the next room sat a large, carved, walnut desk matching the one in the outer vestibule. A carved, high-back, walnut chair accompanied the desk. An immaculate, tie and suited, middle-aged gentleman rose from the chair with a cheery smile and offered his hand to Bruce who preceded the visitors.

Bruce turned to Jeanay, "Let me introduce our journalist. You read her article with the impressive investigation of our observatories missing scientist. This is Jeanay Golden." Then Bruce gave a wink to Jeanay and introduced the Professor. "And this is the esteemed Professor Golden also involved in the investigation." Jeanay smiled in recognition that her suggestion was used.

Professor's eyes twinkled, and batted in delight. She stood a little taller with her perceived status of recognition.

The Mayor came around his desk and shook their hands heartily. "This is such a pleasure you wanted to meet me, I'm honored. Please take a seat. Oh, and I see you brought recording equipment." He brushed at the side of his graying temples, with both hands, making sure his hair was in place. With a whimsically, pompous air he added, "You wish to record me?"

Jeanay breathed a sigh of imperceptible relief, "Yes, we are doing additional journaling of Big Bear. I might use this visit with your permission." Jeanay pulled the camera out of its bag to distract from her last sentence aimed as a statement rather than a question.

"Of course, of course," the Mayor swept out an inviting arm and effused, "Why yes, by all means, feel free to record."

Craftily concocted my little niece! Professor Golden cheered. She discreetly gestured to Jeanay her approval.

Jeanay finished setting up the tripod and viewfinder, while her aunt made small talk about how lovely the town and mountains were. Jeanay gave Professor a wry smile happy with her own ingenuity, and then the nod, when she was ready.

"Mayor," Professor Golden began, "We have made friends with the owner of the beautiful stable at the far edge of town by the lake's end."

The Mayor looked at Bruce questioningly. Bruce filled in, "Lake's End Stables."

"Ah," the Mayor smiled and nodded to continue.

The Professor continued, "The stable has had some unusual, unexplained illnesses that the owner asked us to look into. Her veterinarian could not find the reason for them."

The Mayor looked at Professor Golden quizzically pondering why this was his concern? Then he waited in silence fumbling for words to respond with the correct political response. Buying some time he repeated her statement, "The stable has unexplained illnesses…" He cleared his throat and grabbed a pen to twist around in his hands. "I don't see how that is my area of expertise?"

"There are also symptoms among some of the employees," the Professor added to create concern.

The Mayor sprang to alarm, "Are we talking community epidemic?

Professor Golden jumped in startled surprise that he could leap to such a conclusion, "Oh no, no!"

The Mayor, sat back, shook his head in relief, "Good, good!" He paused searching with a frown, "So is it treatable?"

Professor was relieved he was coming back to where she needed him to, agreeably, be thinking. "Yes," she responded in anticipation.

"Is it contagious?" He asked, becoming worried again.

"No, not contagious, per say, but there is a type of pathogen, you might call it. We can treat the symptoms, but not cure it with standard treatment, because…there is no standard treatment."

"I don't understand," the Mayor questioned as he turned to look at each person.

Professor led on, "We didn't either until we did some tests. We took samples from the property and we had them analyzed. We found that the soil is contaminated with cyanide and that that is the probable cause--"

The Mayor cut in, "Cyanide? Cyanide! How is that possible?"

"Jeanay and I wondered that too and so we went to check out the history of the property at the county records office." Professor took a deep breath. Bruce and the Mayor listened intently. "We discovered that the property had been panned for gold in the 1800's then sold to a mining company in the 1900's."

The Mayor gestured his hands spread out palms up in question, "How is that a problem? Panning the water is harmless and safe. I've done it."

Professor Golden answered, "That is true if you're using a simple pan and that is the only method you are using. However, mining companies use means to make their investments work faster than time-consuming panning. They heap the sandy soil taken from the water along the banks. Then they apply cyanide and other toxic chemicals to separate the gold out chemically."

"Wouldn't the chemicals dissipate?" Bruce asked.

"Only slowly over hundreds of years," Professor answered cryptically.

The Mayor, tense, shifted in his seat, leaned forward, and asked nervously, "Has this contaminated our lovely lake?" Then he turned to Bruce, "It couldn't have. We have a wonderful fishing season. Why my family and I have enjoyed numerous meals from the lake over the years." His mouth dropped open aghast. He stopped, and a petrified look overtook his features, "Is our food being poisoned?" He felt around his body neurotically for a symptom.

Jeanay had to contain herself, behind the camera, from bursting out laughing. Bruce looked away amused turning red from his attempts to keep from laughing. Jeanay noticed Bruce's reaction to the mayor, and then she had to stifle a roar of laughter. She looked in amazement at Professor Golden. *Auntie, how can you sit there so straight-faced?*

Professor Golden could feel victory start to raise its head. *Oh, this is better than best. He just gave me more ammunition.* That realization squelched any humorous reaction she may have had to the Mayor's squirrelly behavior. Delight coursed through her small frame. Without skipping a beat Professor Golden continued, "The contamination might be contained to that part of the lake. Your fishing is at the other end of the lake so hopefully it's not infected. However, we need to make certain." The professor could barely contain herself with a straight face over his changing facial expressions transitioning from concern, to relief, then uncertainty, throughout her discourse. He was in the palm of her hand just where she wanted him.

The Mayor sat back staring at the top of his desk not sure what to think. He looked up hopefully, "So what can be done about it? You wouldn't be here if you didn't have answers."

"Oh, okay. He's not a dummy," Jeanay noted.

"Right," Professor Golden got up from her chair. She picked up her report from her lap and carried it over to his desk. "I have the sample report and my analysis here for you to go over. This does take some extraordinary effort and help from you and the county to make this right." Professor transitioned from informative to a lecture in abrading, attorney, tactical form. "The property should never have been sold without this information. A residence should never have been permitted by the county to be on it, and animals should never have been allowed to live on it. A former mayor who owned it should never have sold it without addressing these hazards and zoning improprieties. The present owner could sue the city and the county."

The Mayor looked rebuffed, chagrined, he wrung his hands. Then he challenged, "What do you mean by this?"

Jeanay was getting great footage. *You go, Auntie! You got 'im right where we want him!*

Bruce was taken aback, at the same time, he was amused to see this demure little woman become, both, demonstrative and demanding wielding such power over his mayor.

Professor Golden turned into an actress. She leaned over the Mayor's desk and got up close to the Mayor, whereupon, she planted both palms face down on the top of his desk. Peering into his eyes she proclaimed with grandiose dignity, "This, your honor, is where you become the h-e-r-o… Your city needs you! Your city needs a Hero." She let that sink in for a few seconds and she held her breath. Their eyes were locked.

"How?" Was all he could manage to exhale, completely mesmerized.

Professor Golden walked back over to her seat, for effect, and sat down. The Mayor's eyes were riveted on her. She crossed her legs and then placed one hand on top of the other on her knee. In a husky voice she spoke assertively, "This is how you become the Hero…" She paused, again, for effect and then, slowly, continued in her professorial voice, "Jube will not take any action if you get the county to seal the cyanide, zone her property commercial to include her home as an on-site premises caretaker. The county already has this zoning for commercial, assisted-living facilities."

Jeanay looked on in wonder thinking, *is this, my aunt? She's acting more like a MI5 agent than the aunt I know. Huh, wow, I don't believe this.*

Thinking out loud, shaking his head, and rambling worriedly, "I might be able to get the zoning changed, but I'm not sure I can get the county to do anything."

Jeanay spoke from behind the camera, "I could start an investigation into the impropriety of city-county zoning, and who may have paid off whom over a dangerous land environment, and also illegal property development and sale."

The Mayor waved his hands excitedly, "Oh-no-no-no! I'll have to figure something out. You said you have solutions to this?" He picked the report up off his desk.

Professor Golden explained, "Yes. The county forestry seems well-heeled by the looks of its incentive program offers to home owners to keep Big Bear and the adjacent mountain areas clean and safe. They may not mind helping if you present the case I have laid out before you."

"Don't forget you can be a "hero." And I can do an article on YOU saving the day," Jeanay added.

The Mayor, reticent, gave Jeanay a one-sided smile not convinced yet, but she had hit his happy button. He looked at Bruce in a manner to suggest "how could you do this to me."

Bruce's hands flew up in his defense, "Don't blame me I didn't know everything about this!"

The Mayor rubbed his forehead. "Okay, just give me some time to think and work on this. Leave your number with my secretary so I can reach you." Turning away from Bruce and the Professor he looked straight at Jeanay pointing his finger and announced in no uncertain terms, "And no articles on this till you give me a chance, right?"

"Right, Absolutely! We're counting on you." Jeanay flashed her pearly whites and gave him her most endearing, charming smile. That had the desired effect. The Mayor finally produced a real smile, small, but genuine. She shut off the camera and lifted it off the tripod. She put it in its small black bag and then placed it in the larger over the shoulder bag along with the tripod. Professor Golden took the cue and stood up as did Bruce. Jeanay and the Professor shook the Mayor's hand and then they all made a hasty exit.

On the way out the front door Bruce commented, "You didn't tell me you might be getting me on the wrong side of the Mayor!"

Professor Golden, weary, smiled wryly, "It's all good, all for the better good!"

Bruce pursed his lips thoughtfully, "Umm, yes. I never saw him jump through so many hoops in my life." That got a giggle out of the Professor. Then a few beats later Bruce added, "Take care I'm sure I'll see or hear from you ladies again!"

Jeanay smiled confidently, "You will, we'll be able to increase our celebrity status, with this one."

"In that case, you'll be up for another treat," Bruce said as he waved good-bye.

Waiting

Professor Golden sat on the dry, spray-washed bleachers overlooking the largest corral. She pulled her wide-brimmed, floppy hat down firmly to shade her eyes from the sun. Her shirt had a high collar that she pulled up to cover her neck with her gloved hands. She tipped her head up just enough to watch a rider circling in the damp soil around the arena.

The horse and rider pulled up short in front of her. The rider spoke forth, "Isn't she just lovely? Her name is Honey just like her color and her disposition." Jeanay patted the horse affectionately.

"Yes, she's perfect. What is it with these names, Goldy, Honey? My horse's name had nobility, Imperial Ambassador."

"Ha, you called him Amby, for short, from what I remember. I could have ridden Salt or Pepper, but if their namesake describes their personality, well, I choose this one."

"Hemp, Little Miss Know-it-all," Professor gaffed in jest.

Jeanay retorted speaking in mock high and mighty tones, "I wonder who I got it from?"

The charade continued, "Your mother!"

"Ha! …But really, are you sure you don't want to ride? It's just wonderful! Such a lovely day."

"I'll think about it. Now put her through her exercises. Let's see what you can do."

"Oh my goodness, look!" Jeanay pointed, giggling, at a funny spectacle headed their way.

Professor Golden started laughing as she saw Wags doing a high-step. Each paw had a boot on it, a doggy boot. He lifted each paw up with a jerk, and did a prance arching each leg in the air like a gaited horse. Every now and then we would hold a paw in the air looking at the boot and try to shake it off.

"Oh, my word he's got booties on!" Professor Golden jettisoned into a belly full of laughs.

Jube stuck her head out from around the corner of the barn wondering what all the commotion was about. She came over to the bleachers, laughing, getting there about the same time as Wags. "I was afraid for my dogs to walk out here. I found these at the pet shop. Aren't they cute?"

"Funny is more like it!" Professor Golden tried to contain her mirth.

Wags stood there with his tongue hanging out of his mouth breathing a little heavier from the extra exertion. His tail wagged happily to see them. Their attention afforded a little distraction, for him, from his cumbersome attire.

Professor Golden reached out to pat Wags, a reward, for the laughing spell he gave her. Squeezing Honey's sides lightly Jeanay encouraged her horse to start walking. Jube slapped her gloves together to shake off some of the dust. She lifted one corner of her cowboy hat and wiped the sweat from her forehead with her arm. "I think I'll take a load off for a minute." Jube sat down by the professor.

Jube sighed, "I wish the boots were enough for Sadie, but she is older and insists on lying around in the dirt. The irritation hasn't cleared up since she won't use her bed.

Professor Golden turned to Jube having listened to her while watching Jeanay. "I don't remember another dog here even though you mentioned her."

"Sadie, yes she's the one I mentioned that had a rash on one side of her belly, so happens it's the side she lays on the most. She likes to sleep alongside the chickens and watch them. She is so funny! They are like her pets, or children." Professor looked at her quizzically as if she were nuts. Jube continued, "If one comes close to the wire she'll go over and lick the chicken. It just lets her!"

"What?" Professor was astonished.

Jube nodded, "Yes, uh-hum."

"Are you sure she doesn't think they're food and likes the taste?"

Jube laughed, "That's what you'd think, but no. If one gets out she cuddles it under her chin until we put it back in the cage."

Professor's tune changed, "That's hilarious!" She shook her head and laughed.

Jube nodded again, "I know, I know." She paused for a few minutes to watch Jeanay cantering on Honey and then commented, "She seats that horse well."

"Jeanay's a good rider. We all miss not having horses anymore. Kids grow up, life gets in the way."

"You're welcome to ride here, any time, if we still have a place for people to ride," Jube sighed.

"All's not lost you know! We have a good plan, have a little faith. Prayer always helps me." Professor Golden pulled a piece of paper from her pocket. "Here's something to encourage you. The Old Testament quote is from me. The New Testament one is from my niece."

Jube read silently, "Isaiah 41:11. 'Fear not, for I am with you; be not dismayed, for I am your God. I will strengthen you, yes, I will help you, I will uphold you with My righteous right hand. 1 Peter 5:7. Cast all your care upon Him, for He cares for you.'"

Jube clasped the paper to her chest and sighed, "Thank you so much." Professor reached out and gave Jube's knee a knowing, comforting pat.

Crunching gravel turned their attention to the driveway. Dr. Masters had an impressive six-horse travel trailer in tow.

In surprise Professor Golden asked, "What's he doing here in that?"

Jube spoke reluctantly, "He's taking the sick horses to his place to board. I can't in all conscience keep them here. And I can't tell the owners why this happened to them, or it will create a stampede exit out of here if you know what I mean. I feel so helpless waiting for answers. They agreed to let him care for them at his place."

The Professor looked impressed, "That's marvelous of him, he's quite the exception don't you think?"

"Yes, a vet that really cares and doesn't cost an arm and a leg. You know some vets charge so much that retirees and others can't get their pets treated properly for lack of money." Jube sighed.

Professor was all over this, "I know. It's terrible! I heard of a woman who had to pay so much for her pet's painful mouth problem that she couldn't even pay for her own two broken teeth to get fixed. That's unconscionable! Greed, so much greed! Makes me so mad! They have no right—

Dr. Masters came over to them interrupting Professor Golden's ensuing tirade with a package in his hand. He handed the package to Jube, "Here's salve for Sadie."

"Thank you. I'll go get your patients and help you load them."

"Okay, great, thank you."

"It's the least I can do. Oh, and I'll forward the rental income to you from their owners.

Derek looked at Jube and shook his head, "That won't be necessary."

Jube looked incredulous, "What? Why not? You're boarding them now."

"Yes Jube, but it's just temporary, and besides they are paying me for their medical expenses. I'm good!"

Jube looked speechless her eyes misty. Before she could choke up she replied, "Thank you so much, you have no idea," then she hurriedly walked away.

Dr. Masters turned to Professor Golden, "Are you going to be able to help her?"

Professor Golden looked him in the eye and replied, "Possibly, we're giving it a good try. You're quite the champion taking the horses."

"I like to help where I can."

Professor Golden stared at Dr. Masters thinking. Are *you for real?*

Jeanay had noted Dr. Master's presence out of the corner of her eye. She decided it was time to say hello. She guided Honey to the gate, sidled her up to the latch, and unhooked it. Unlatching it she guided Honey out and trotted over to the bleachers.

"Hello, Dr. Masters," Jeanay bravely looked him in the eyes.

"Please call me Derek."

Professor Golden gave him the 'eye' and a 'once-over' look. *Hum, well, he is coming across very well still she's my niece.*

"Okay, Derek." Jeanay managed a pleased, shy smile.

"You handle that horse well," Derek complimented her.

In a small voice she answered, "Thank you," and looked away shyly. Derek did the same not sure what to do next. There was silence, and then she hesitantly broke it, "Did Auntie tell you what we came up with?" Derek instantly turned back to look at her equally interested in her and the subject.

Professor Golden looked up at her with a frown.

"Oh come on, you can tell him," Jeanay cajoled.

Professor shook her head, rolled her eyes, and looked away.

"No, she hasn't," Dr. Masters commented with interest. Professor Golden kept her head turned away from him in refusal. "Ah, come on!? He rubbed his hands together in anticipation looking at the Professor.

Jeanay looked at her aunt for permission.

Professor gave a huff, "Well go ahead if you must!"

Jeanay's horse started fidgeting impatient at standing still which helped to distract her from nervousness in the doctor's presence. "Auntie figured a way we could seal this place and get the mayor and county to pay for it!" She ended with a distracted flourish whilst addressing the horse's defiance with hand and leg corrections.

Dr. Masters leaned back with a grin, "Impressive!" in reference to Jeanay's equestrian skills and the Professor's clever work.

Both ladies grinned over the complement thinking it was intended for oneself. They simultaneously said, "Thank you," and then looked at each other. They both turned in question to Dr. Masters who, amused, just smiled.

Satisfied that he meant the compliment for her Professor Golden still felt it necessary to chide. "Jeanay we don't know if what you explained will work, yet. We can't get Jube's hopes up too high. I couldn't stand to disappoint her. I'd rather it work out to be a surprise."

A little embarrassed being chastised in front of Derek Jeanay muttered, "Oh."

Dr. Masters gave Professor Golden a playful shoulder nudge, "Don't you worry my lips are sealed. That's better than I had hoped to hear."

Professor Golden gave Jeanay a, direct, roll of her eyes.

Jeanay looked up and away not sure what to make of her aunt.

Dr. Masters got up slowly and said, "I've got to get the horses loaded. Jube probably has them lined up by now." He started to leave and then turned to Jeanay, "Would you like to help us load?"

Jeanay's eyes lit up, "I'd lo—," she cleared her throat and then thought better of finishing that word. "I'll just put Honey away and be right there. I'll brush her down later she's not that sweaty."

"Great!" Derek smiled, slapped his hands together, and left.

"That was a bit flirty!" Professor criticized with a ruffled tone not yet over the pressure to disclose her information.

Jeanay had started to turn her horse to leave. She stopped Honey and turned in the saddle toward Professor Golden. "Seriously," Jeanay gaped at her annoyed, "Seriously? Oh Auntie, don't be ridiculous, I was not."

"Oh. Are you sure?"

Deciding not to become haughty in defense and in light of her aunt's mistaken reaction, Jeanay laughed. "Auntie you need to lighten up!" Jeanay laughed again shaking her head in amused disbelief.

Professor Golden not quite sure how to take it frowned in speculation toying with the idea she might not be right. After thinking about it she threw her hand in the air in a back-handed wave, "Oh, all right!" Not wanting to give it any more brain strain. "Your uncle used to keep me straight. You go on." The clip of hoofs sounded as Jeanay did so.

By the time Jeanay got to the trailer, Jube and Derek had half the horses loaded. The fourth one was balking as she pranced around the ramp, but not on to it.

Jube offered, "Let me go get a carrot."

Jeanay stood alone with Derek as he held the lead to the, now, quiet horse. *How can I put lovely Jeanay at ease?* Not being able to think of anything he offered, "Would you like to take the lead?"

"Oh, no, that's quite alright. I'm good, thank you," she shyly answered as she stood tensely with her hands clenched together behind her back.

He awkwardly toyed with the lead. "No Wags…chicken…guinea pig?" He lightly teased.

Jeanay blushed, "No." She lightly shook her head as she looked down at the ground. *Okay, cut this out. Think of something to say. Don't be an idiot. Oops, Auntie wouldn't approve of that self-talk.* She took a deep breath and looked up with her lips pursed in determination. "I admire what you're doing for Jube. That says a lot about a person to go out of the way like this."

"Oh!" Derek was caught off guard he had felt like he stuck his foot in his mouth and did not expect a thoughtful, genuine compliment. Now, it was reversed, he was the shy one. He said slowly, "Ah, I don't know what to say. Thank you."

They both smiled at each other. Derek finally broke the silence and asked, "Would you have time to go to coffee? I know you're all busy investigative reporting after that article."

Jeanay's eyes got big, "You read my article?"

"Yes, I enjoyed it AND I enjoyed your documentary, but that's NOT what I asked."

At that very, inopportune, moment Jube returned with a handful of carrots. She spoke without noticing their conversation, "Just in case we need some for the others." She plopped the carrots down, and with one in her hand she waved it under the nose of the obstinate horse. Then she got in front of it and walked backwards up the plank, enticing the horse, oblivious to what she had interrupted. Jeanay and Derek stared at each other. Jeanay cleared her throat and looked away. *Darn.*

They safely boarded the rest of the horses into the trailer with a little help from the leftover carrots. Derek slammed the gate closed behind the horses and lowered the guard arm into its rocker to secure the gate of the trailer. He turned around and dusted off his gloves rubbing them together.

Jube waved, "Thank you, Derek," and turned to go.

"You bet!" he answered and then turned away to get in his van.

Jeanay unexpectedly, and to her own surprise, grabbed his arm. He, in turn surprised, looked down at her hand on his forearm. Jeanay whispered, "Coffee would be great."

Derek nodded, speechless, as he locked eyes with her and smiled. They both felt a jolt. Jeanay shivered with goosebumps and shyly smiled and then she noticed her hand on his arm. "Oh," embarrassed she pulled her hand away. She abruptly turned and as she walked away she blindly waved and giddily announced, "A horse awaits a rub down!"

Derek, thoughtful, watched her walk away. When Jeanay was gone from his sight Derek grinned as he got in his van and started the engine. Putting it in gear he hauled the horse trailer around the looped driveway circling the ranch house as he eased the horses out onto the main highway.

Horse Fever

Jeanay sat atop Honey watching Jube train a beautiful, black horse in the small arena. The arena was made for using a 12-foot lunge-line attached to the horse's halter. Jube stood in the middle of the arena holding a 12-foot long handle whip. The tight quarters gave the trainer maximum ability to keep the horse's attention. Jube gave a voice command to the horse and when needed, to reinforce her voice commands, she touched its flank with the tip of the whip. If the horse turned in toward her she would use the whip to tap it on the shoulder which convinced the horse to turn away from her and return, back in step, to the outer edge of the circular ring.

Two little girls, age 7, came running up to the fence to watch. They stood on the bottom rail each girl gripped the top rail barely peering over it. Jube noticed the horse was slightly kicking up dust that was going their way even though she had the arena sprayed down with water. She called out, "Girls would you please move around to the other side where the dust won't get your clothes dirty?" The little darlings complied, nodded, and ran to the other side.

"What's the horse's name?" The little, blonde pony-tailed one asked.

"His name is Spirit," Jube answered then clicked her tongue for the horse to go faster.

The pig-tailed brunette asked, "Did you pick that name 'cause he lifts his legs so high?"

Jube smiled, but kept her concentration on Spirit. "I didn't name him, he's not mine. I'm just training him."

Then Jeanay became curious, "What are you training him for?"

"He needs to be green broke." Jube pulled the horse up short to take a rest. He was wearing a saddle, and over the halter that the rope line was attached to he wore a bit and bridle. The reins were loosely attached to the pommel better known as the horn on the saddle.

"He looks a little old for that."

"Yes, he is a little older, six years. His owner bought him from a racing farm. He just finished his career as a trotter pulling a buggy on the racetrack."

Jeanay was very surprised, "Really? I didn't know they did that anymore. I thought that was a thing of the past, way back in the past!"

"They still buggy race back East."

The little blonde, in her high, little girl voice asked, "Does that mean he can only trot, and can't run?"

Jube laughed, "Oh, he can run alright! But he's specially bred to trot high and fast. Do you like how he makes his legs look like a square when he picks up his hoofs?"

"Oh, yea!" The girl's squealed, "It's beautiful."

"You can say that again!" Jeanay admired.

Jube patted the black, glistening neck below his long, flowing mane. "He's got a great attitude, he's gentle, a real winner! The owner is hoping he'll bring in winnings at our amateur shows."

"What? You have shows here?" Jeanay excitedly asked.

The blonde, little girl answered back, "Yea, my momma competes in the Gymkhana competitions. She even won a prize once!"

Jube spoke of her hopes, "I'd like to bring in some professional shows, but at least I've been able to get us advertised on the amateur circuit. We raise money for different groups that are non-profit. And we have cash prize winnings for the riders too."

"We gotta go," the brunette announced. The girls hopped down from the fence since there was nothing to watch now. They in unison yelled, "Bye, bye."

Jeanay and Jube both smiled at them, and they yelled back, "Bye-bye."

Jube spoke when the girls were out of earshot, "I feel so guilty having them walk around here. I feel like I should be warning everyone."

Jeanay chided her, "No. You don't go and do that. Wait just one more day. It doesn't hurt for this to go on a few days more."

"I just feel so guilty!" Jube mourned as she stroked Spirit's muzzle.

Jeanay got riled up, "Guilty-guilty! The people who are guilty are dead. The county is responsible, not you! You just hang on, this will be over soon!"

"That's true they're dead. I hope your right. And I hope whatever needs to be done I can afford." Jube was a veritable gloomy-gus.

"I know it's hard to keep positive, but try. It only makes you feel worse dwelling on the negative."

"Right!" Jube shook her shoulders hoping to shake off the attitude. She switched her attention back to training. "I think Spirit is ready for a rider. Would you like to give him a try?"

"Me? Get on a horse that's never been ridden? Are you kidding?"

"No I'm not. I don't think he'll be a problem. I'm going to ease into the stirrup and give him my body weight. Then if he doesn't move around I'll throw a leg over and then if he's still okay I'll sit on him. If he's good with that you shouldn't have a problem. I will work with him from the ground while you're up there. It makes learning for him easier because he's learned all his cues with me first. Then you add the weight, hand, and foot cues to that, and he'll catch on fast."

"Well okay, if you're sure." Jeanay was still hesitant.

"Oh you'll be fine, it'll be exciting! Just wait till you feel the fantastic power and speed of his different gaited trots."

"That does sound exciting!" Jeanay was warming up to the idea.

They both turned to look as they heard a van drive up to the corral. Dr. Masters got out and waved. Jube turned to Jeanay, "I wonder what he's doing here? I didn't call him. Maybe one of the owners called him?" He stood in the door of his van watching them. Jube shrugged, "It must not be important since he's just standing there. Let's do this."

Now Jeanay was doubly nervous with Derek watching her. She got off Honey and tied her to a wood hitch by the corral. She came into the corral and introduced herself to Spirit by looking him in the eye. Jeanay gently blew into one of his nostrils as horses do with each other when first meeting and getting acquainted. Then she pet his head and muzzle with gentle strokes. "Easy boy, you better be good to me," she spoke gently to him. Spirit's eyes watched her.

Jeanay stood there holding his halter while Jube put one boot into a stirrup then she added a little of her weight into the stirrup. Spirit turned his head to look at Jube. Jube waited for any other reaction, but none came. She gripped the saddle horn pulling herself up with her full weight in the stirrup as she brought her other foot up next to the foot in the stirrup. Her entire weight was, now, in the one stirrup leaving the other leg free in case she needed to jump down quickly. She bent over the saddle waiting with one hand on the horn and the other on the saddle rim. Spirit snorted lightly still looking at Jube then he brought his head straight forward. He moved his legs out slightly to compensate for her added weight and stood quietly. Jube nodded at Jeanay, "Good sign." Jeanay nodded back, and then Jube swung her leg over Spirit's back and gently eased herself down onto his saddle.

Spirit inquisitively turned his head, again, to look at her and sniff her boot. He stepped forward. Jube called out, "Whoa," and he stopped. Jeanay kept a tight hold on his bridle keeping his head tucked toward his chest in an attempt to help correct any sudden move. He could easily start tossing his head and rearing up. They all froze each in place.

"Okay, I think we're good Jeanay." Jube got down slowly while Spirit watched her from the corner of his eye, his curiosity peaked. "You're up girl! Try to stay calm they sense it you know." Jube switched places with Jeanay.

Jeanay nodded she understood and then nervously, gently she eased herself onto the giants back and sat quietly.

"Okay Jeanay, I'm holding the lead line, and I'm going back to the center of the ring. If he starts to move forward tell him, "Whoa." If he won't obey your voice command alone lightly pull on the reins till he stops and then drop them. I don't want to teach him with reins at this session."

"Okay," Jeanay nodded as she watched Jube slowly back up to the center of the ring. Spirit stayed still and quiet. He took his eye off Jeanay and watched Jube.

"Told you he'd be good, he's had a lot of lunge-line training in his day. I just needed to remind him and set him in the trainee mode. You probably know all this, but I want to make sure we are on the same page. Now, when I ask him to stop lean back slightly and give no leg pressure. When I ask him to walk squeeze your inner thigh slightly and shift your weight forward slightly then relax when he obeys. When I ask for him to trot lean forward and squeeze your thighs again and maintain a light firm pressure. If he goes faster than you want him to ease off the pressure until he keeps the pace you want. To move him into his slow, gaited trot give him an upper and lower leg squeeze, then release most of the pressure once he's in it. We'll save his faster, gaited trot and canter for the bigger arena since he couldn't manage it in this small space. When we turn him lay the rein lightly on the side of his neck that you want him to turn away from along with pressure from that same side with your leg."

Jeanay nodded okay. She glided through the rest of the exercises from walk, to trot, to slow-gaited trot, to stop and then they turned around to go in the other direction. The experience was exhilarating. *Darn, the fastest gait and gallop will have to wait for that larger arena.* Spirit was excited and glistening from the easy workout which was not one to make him breathe, or sweat too hard. "Whew, that was absolutely marvelous, thank you Jube." Jeanay patted Spirit on the neck and then slid off onto the ground landing on both feet.

"Thank you Jeanay, that really helped me."

"He's amazing!" Jeanay let herself out the gate to return to Honey. She gave a shy smile to Dr. Masters and offered a, "Hi."

Derek returned the greeting. With purpose he walked to her side and smiled. Before he could say anything Jeanay asked, "You here for a patient?"

"No," he answered, "I'm here for you!"

Jeanay looked startled and then she jested, "Are you stalking me?"

Derek laughed, "Maybe you'd like that."

Jeanay didn't know what to say. She turned pink and looked amusingly befuddled.

Derek came close, "Coffee, remember coffee?"

"Oh," Jeanay exhaled softly with a laugh, "Yes."

"I had a little break between clients and thought I'd stop by here to see if you could join me. There's a little, mom and pop, coffee shop down the road not far. They have great homemade, triple-layer, double chocolate cake."

"Oh, my word," Jeanay was overcome by the prospect of all that wonderful chocolate. "I'm in!" She nodded her head decisively then she laughed nervously.

"Great you're a chocolate lover," he laughed, "Me too!" Derek looked around, "Where's the Professor?"

Jeanay offered, "She gave me the car for the day. She wanted to relax, for a change, at the hotel. They have pretty good coffee and a nice view of the mountains. A few squirrels to keep her company."

Derek walked around to open the door for her, "Then shall we?"

Jeanay cleared her throat and laughed, "I do have a horse to put away unless you plan on fitting the three of us in there." She lightly laughed, again, as she looked amused into his eyes and then diverted her gaze away uneasy.

Derek was embarrassed, "Oh, a little ahead of myself, would be a tight fit." He laughed amused at his mistake.

Ah nice, I'm not the only one with a case of the nerves. He does like me! ...I guess, I think, maybe? Jeanay giggled nervously a little giddy. "I'll meet you in a flash just let me get her to her stall. We didn't get a chance for a ride so I don't need to brush her down."

"Guess I came too soon."

"No, it's fine. You saw what a great time I had. You've got…" Jeanay paused a little searching for the right words, "Perfect timing!"

Derek grinned fully redeemed by Jeanay. He got in his van and backed up to the stalls, while Jeanay mounted Honey and headed for her stall in the same direction.

City Meeting

Professor Golden's cell phone chimed, she looked at it and then called out, "It's time!" She opened up the text as Jeanay walked over.

"It's time? That's funny!"

"Why?" Professor didn't look up to ask.

Jeanay laughed, "That's what women say to their husbands when they're pregnant, and it's time to go to the hospital to deliver."

"Ah," Professor looked up and cracked a smile. "Same way I feel right now, I guess, come to think of it, it fits. The Mayor has called a meeting and asks us to be there in one hour."

"Not a problem. I hope I can video this."

"Just set up and assume you can. It was a little different, but when I first taught I wasn't much older than the students. So I decided to pretend to take charge. I shrugged off my insecurities, but only time and experience really got rid of them. It will be the same for you. It's that way for any young person starting out in the world. Or, for that matter, anytime we are thrown into new situations we don't, really, feel prepared for."

"Like today?" Jeanay queried with a lifted eyebrow.

"Huh!" Professor Golden responded, "Yes! Like today!"

They stood at the front door of the Civic building. Professor Golden reached to open the glass doors to let Jeanay through with her equipment. Her hand froze and started to shake. "I-I-I'm not feeling so good. I need to sit down, the stable, so much pressure, so much work. How did I get myself into this? I need help—

"Auntie, Auntie—" Jeanay was fumbling with her armload as she tried to quickly, but safely set it down. The equipment thudded to the ground. Jeanay grabbed Professor's hand, "Come here Auntie it's okay, sit." They sat on a bench by the door. "Let me pray for you." Professor nodded her head "okay" and then she looked up to the sky, in Jew fashion, while Jeanay bowed her head, in Christian fashion. "Dear Father, please help good things to happen today for everyone. And help Auntie to feel okay. In Jesus name amen." Professor Golden looked at Jeanay when she finished the prayer having used Jesus' name, she sighed. When Jeanay opened her eyes Professor nodded a "thank you." Jeanay smiled and nodded back.

Along came a man dressed in a suit. He looked at the equipment on the ground blocking the door and the ladies that were sitting on the bench. He turned to them and asked, "Oh, did you need some help here?"

"Sure, I wouldn't mind your help." Jeanay got up, grabbed her backpack and her aunt, and allowed the gentleman to carry the camera tripod bag and open the door for them. Professor Golden gave the man a "thank you" smile as he opened the glass door. He smiled back.

The man inquired, "Could I venture to say you are here for the same meeting I'm going to? I can't imagine equipment of this nature for any other purpose. You look new? Not a local reporter."

"Right, I'm not. I'm Jeanay Golden, and this is my aunt Professor Golden."

He brightened, "Oh I know who you are. Great article! We seldom have anything that attracts national news." He shook his head in wonder. "But this sure did! I still want to look at the documentary, just been so busy."

"Why thank you," Jeanay smiled tickled with the compliment.

Pleasantly distracted from her own feelings Professor Golden puffed up in pride for her niece.

A secretary greeted them, "Please join the rest of the people in our conference room." She pointed to the door across from her.

"All right, thank you," Professor Golden said and took the lead through the doors.

A long, oblong, mahogany table spread out before them. Jeanay immediately set up the tripod and camera by the door since she noticed the Mayor at the other end of the table. She kept busy with her head low checking angles with her camera. Two legs covered with crumpled suit pants stopped beside her. Her eyes followed up one leg to the head attached to it. Startled, she pulled herself erect quickly and shifted her feet in a little stomp. "You're here!" Grinning, the reporter kept his unlit cigar clenched between his teeth and saluted her with his pencil to his forehead. He proceeded to a chair near the door not far from her. He caught Professor Golden's attention, out of the corner of her eye, as the Mayor greeted her.

The Mayor indicated for Professor Golden to take a seat near him. He put several gentlemen on either side of him one of which was the ladies door opener.

Jube walked in the door, looked around, and took a seat by Professor Golden who was signaling her. She smiled at the Professor nervously and then she smiled at Jeanay. Bruce came in the door and smiled at them taking his seat with other council members.

The Mayor started the meeting when he saw that all were seated waiting for the proceedings to begin. "Thank you, all of you, for being here today," he spoke. "Yesterday we had an emergency board meeting that included the fire authority and our zoning commissioner." He indicated the men on either side of him. "We studied the gold mining operation issue that is responsible for toxic grounds at the lake adjacent to Lake's End Stables."

The Mayor turned to Jube compassionately, "I know this has been a very trying time for you. We are here on your account. We have put a great deal of endeavor into helping one of our citizens and valued business owners." Jube, looking up, gave him a weak smile. The board members nodded in solemn agreement.

The rumple suited reporter was writing furiously on his notepad. He turned on an antiquated, palm-size, audio recorder. Jeanay was happily videoing relieved that she had not been stopped or questioned. People were oblivious to her being caught up in the serious nature of the unfolding drama.

The Mayor paused, for full effect, and then continued, "I want to acknowledge Professor Golden and thank her for putting a concise report together that has helped us to formulate a plan."

Professor nodded seriously gratuitous. *I hope this acknowledgment brings a good solution. I can't smile until then.* Her leg bounced under the table.

The Mayor riveted his eyes on Jube. "I am happy to assure you that we will be changing your zoning. It will be changed to a special commercial code. The commercial zone change will include a caretaker resident dwelling on site." Jube sighed in relief. He added, "Now that does increase the taxes above the present zoning which is for a shed only." He looked at her waiting for a response.

Jube's relieved sigh ended in "Eh?" *Uh-oh, oh no,no,no!*

Jube looked at Professor Golden with big eyes wondering how good could that be? Professor nodded back to her several times with intent to encourage that it was a good thing. Jube watched Professor Golden, and then Jube nodded her head, "okay," at the Mayor. He smiled.

The Mayor became a little more serious. "Now, on to the toxic soil that is NOT the fault of anyone presently alive. The forestry service has agreed--" pausing dramatically, "Like they do for owners clearing out trees and vegetation, to include, in this unusual circumstance--" He took a big breath before he finished delivering the news. "To agree to pay half the cost it takes to clean up this problem."

Jube let out a distressed sound looking up at the Mayor pleadingly. Professor Golden patted Jube's leg to get her attention and shook her head ever so slightly "no," with a smile, indicating that it wasn't the appropriate response, or time to talk.

The Mayor continued, looking at Jube and holding up the report. "We know that it will amount to a great deal of money to make your grounds safe. So, I have talked with a local bank that is represented here. I have encouraged the bank to give you a loan on your property. Since you recently purchased it there may not be enough equity in it to secure the loan. But, I strongly encourage the bank to work with you as it will be good for the community. Please talk with her before you leave." The Mayor took a deep breath and sat down adding, "Questions anyone?"

The room was silent. You could hear Doger's wrinkled suit rustling as he rose. He had decided it was his time. Doger put down his cigar, and drew the attention of the room, "You know what I'm getting here is there is some hanky-panky, under the table stuff, going on from our illustrious town council. What kind of zoning issues are you covering up?" He waved his pencil as he spoke.

The Mayor looked flushed at the question, and he started stuttering, "Well I-I—"

The zoning commissioner, who had helped them at the front door, stood up placing his hands flat on the conference table looking directly at the newsman. He stated firmly, "Mr. Reech, I can assure you nothing irregular has occurred with our rezoning at the zoning department. Changes are an acceptable order of business when it's for the greater good along with the board voting for it." He remained in his imposing stance with his hands on the table ready for battle.

"Humph," Doger placed the pencil behind his ear. He picked up his cigar waving it taking the challenge. He spoke in a loud obnoxious voice. "Then our illustrious predecessors have a black mark against them! Under the table dealings, I would guess? Ha, ha," he laughed amused. And, for effect he put the cigar between his yellow teeth clenching it in a wide, toothy grin. The blustering, self-aggrandized reporter stood there enjoying the full rooms, unequivocal attention. He then pulled his cigar from his mouth and asked, "Mayor, sir, how can you ensure that this toxic situation will be made safe? ...That it can be properly taken care of."

The zoning director gritted his teeth at the odious reporter.

The reporter did not react. It was as if he was used to getting on peoples bad side, and enjoyed it.

Professor Golden stood up, "If I may?"

In a combative gesture, eye to eye with Doger, the commissioner changed his hands into fists and lifted them from the desk. He turned his glare from Doger and gave the Professor a nod of approval.

The Professor turned to the Mayor, "May I?

The Mayor's immediate response was, "Yes please." Relieved he gestured for her to take the floor. The zoning commissioner, with crossed arms, decided to take his seat.

Mr. Reech remained standing as Professor Golden delivered in professorial manner her findings. "I have studied into the elements of this situation. The immediate area can be sealed and, thereafter, if necessary tested for any offending agents. But I am certain, after the seal is made, there will not be any more leakage from the ground. The air will clear with the next heavy wind. No one can be certain when that will be and no one can be responsible for that! The whole lakeside cannot be sealed, but human and equine do not consistently inhabit it. Nor is it the property of Jube, it is the property of the government since it is a reserve."

"The highest level of contamination is predominantly at the edge of the lake were piles were made and treated. The further one travels from the lakeside the less the contamination, thus indicating that animal and foot traffic carried cyanide particles away from the main site. The lakeside and trails are the jurisdiction of the federal government. Again, that would not be Jube's, or the city's responsibility, but the forestry's jurisdiction. Am I right?" The Professor turned to the forestry agent.

The forestry agent squirmed in his seat and nodded. The Mayor looked relieved and gave a nervous chuckle. Professor Golden sat down as did Doger.

The Mayor got up and spoke, "Let me remind everyone that we have no case of death reported from the area and it's been in this condition, possibly, for over 100 years. Now my term as Mayor has brought this to light. I will be bringing, as we all will be bringing, a safer Big Bear City to our residents and vacationers." The Mayor addressed this to the video for his posterity. Jeanay giggled behind the camera.

The reporter flicked his cigar, as if it was lit and he needed to get rid of the ashes, his one last arid gesture of theatrics.

The Mayor sat down and looked at Jube compassionately, "I hope you are pleased with what we have, wholeheartedly, worked out for you. This took a lot of deliberation and planning."

Professor Golden leaned over and whispered in Jube's ear. Jube then turned to the Mayor and those around the table. "Thank you for everything you have done. I am most grateful!" She did her best to smile though still worried about what the financial implications meant for her.

The Mayor smiled and answered, "You are most welcome! And now if there are no other concerns, we can adjourn?" He held the gavel up in one hand waiting. There was silence. "Then we are adjourned, good day!" He brought the gavel down hard on the pad sitting on the table.

Everyone got up to speak to each other. The zoning commissioner came over to Jube, put his hand on her shoulder for a second and then shook her hand congratulating her. The banker came over to shake hands with Jube. She handed her card to Jube letting her know to call at any time. The forestry agent came over to shake her hand and give her information on how to get reimbursed for half the sealing costs. Doger and cigar, gruffly, left without so much as a nod in the direction of anyone. The Mayor came over to shake Jube's hand and wish her well. He then turned to Professor Golden to shake her hand.

Professor Golden asked as she shook his hand, "Jeanay was the only person videoing this meeting, any particular reason?"

"Oh, yes, definitely, she's the only one I could trust to do a quality documentary." He ended his sentence with a wink and a smile.

Professor Golden gave him a bright hearty smile. "Thank you, you have been most helpful!"

"That's what I'm here for." The Mayor then turned to schmooze with the members and others who remained.

Professor Golden joined Jeanay. Bruce walked over to them smiling, "Well, you two make a great pair. You've done a lot for our little town."

Jeanay added, "Thank you, your contribution made it all possible."

Bruce answered in surprise, "Me?" He laughed and shook his head. "You did bring some excitement into my life," he admitted. "Well, I'm headed home now. Cathy will find this all very interesting.

Professor Golden stopped him, "No, no wait a minute. Would you be interested in donating some pizza for a good cause?"

"Well that depends, just what do you have in mind?"

"I have ideas for Jube. She's going to be in need of raising funds, probably desperate need. Would you help to sponsor a horse show? How about it? Are you in?"

Bruce laughed, "I'm in! Just have someone give me a call. A tax deduction is always welcome."

Professor Golden beamed, "Wonderful, thanks!" Bruce gave the Professor a pat on the arm and left for home.

Jeanay rubbed her hands together gleefully. "Auntie, I got the most amazing footage for my video package. What a news story this will make!"

Professor Golden gave her a huge smile of happy acknowledgment.

Jeanay was all packed up, and ready to leave as Jube walked over to them. She looked relieved and confused. She walked out with them quietly. Once out of hearing distance of any board member she confided, "I don't know how I'm going to make this work financially?"

Professor Golden patted her on the back. "I know. Jeanay and I have some ideas for you to raise money for your half. All is not lost! Look at what just happened! It's a miracle, be happy! You're more than halfway there. It's going to be okay. Let's go get a bite to eat while we tell you what's on our mind. I think you will be very pleased."

Old Town

"Please let us treat you to Thai food Jube," Professor Golden encouraged.

"Oh yes, we saw a lovely little place, in old-town, across from the art gallery and postal store. We'd like to try it." Jeanay was effervescent in her euphoria over the town meeting results.

Jube nodded, "Yes, I know where it is. I've been too busy to try it. I'll meet you there.

Professor headed to the driver's side of the car, "You're so worked up. I've decided to drive till you aren't so...

"Amped?" Jeanay finished and took the passenger seat. She bounced in the seat as she spoke, "Oh, Auntie I got the greatest footage. And to think, I'm the only one who has it. Wasn't that a hoot! That--that buffoon reporter, he made this a great piece. Why I may need to thank him," she added in surprise.

Professor looked over at her in abject shock not sure what to think about her niece doing that.

Then Jeanay shivered, "No, forget that!"

They both burst out laughing.

The three ladies met in front of the restaurant. The friendly waiter seated them at the window. Not that there was much of a choice with only a few tables inside. It seemed more like a place built for quick sandwiches to go, or an ice cream soda shop which was down the street and around the corner. The crew was pleasant, the place sparsely decorated in attractive Asian influence. The menu looked delicious. They made their selections quickly and the waiter took their order.

Jeanay rubbed her hands together, "Boy, am I looking forward to this!"

Jube was subdued, "I know I should be thankful for all you've done and the town councils done, and I am, but I'm also just stuck. I don't know how to move forward. I sunk all my money into my stable and its upgrades."

Professor Golden smiled, "We have a plan for you."

"So you said. I'd like to feel like my glass is half full instead of half empty," Jube confessed and tried to speak hopefully, but she wasn't succeeding.

"In fact, we already have one sponsor on board." Jeanay smiled her eyes lit with anticipation.

"What do you mean?" Jube gave her a speculative glance.

Professor Golden, animated, sat forward to lay out their plan. "You presently have competition shows at the ranch. We propose you increase the number of them. Have local businesses donate prizes. You keep the fees for entering the competitions instead of giving that money away until you're solvent. You use that money to help make your place safe. Put ads in the town newspaper about the show. Charge a small audience fee to get in. Explain it's to raise funds to save the stable. Have a big banner at the ranch asking for donations. Have vendors come in with their goods and share the sales with you."

Jeanay took her turn. "You can donate lessons for riding and horse training as prizes, and auction them off. Bruce Sharky, the owner of Sharkys, will donate pizza as a prize. I bet the pet shop would donate dog food, or something else. Ask other store owners to do the same. And I will write a story that I can guarantee will get in the news. It will get people to your event. And I bet some great supporters will come out of it too," Jeanay explained bubbling with excitement.

Jube still wasn't convinced. She spoke as if she hadn't heard anything. "I'm going to lose business. People will be scared and take away their horses. They'll be afraid to have their children there!" She was overcome, "I can't see the corn for the peas," she covered her eyes.

Jeanay looked quizzical, "Huh?"

Jube uncovered her eyes, and answered offhanded, "An old saying…on my family farm." She rested her elbows on the table with her chin in her hands, and sighed, "Ugh. Oh, I don't know."

Professor Golden intervened cajoling her, "Now you just wait a minute you're not listening. The bank will help. You can use that loan to cover expenses. When some people don't stick by you don't worry they WILL come back as they see that the news is correct that the stable grounds are not toxic anymore. Some people will wait to see if there are any more incidences of toxic symptoms and many will stay. Jube you know you have the best facility up here. You've done a great job. I mean it's every bit as professional as stables I've seen down below where it's more lucrative. You can be proud of what you've done."

Jube started to perk up as she was lectured to by the Professor. She started nodding her head in agreement with the Professor's encouragement.

Professor Golden patted Jube's hand, "It's all okay, it's good, it's good!"

Jeanay added, "Yea, it's all good!" Then Jeanay remembered a piece of information. "Oh, oh, and I know of several fundraising Internet sites."

"What's that?" Jube wondered out loud. "I really don't have much time for the Internet except when I send out announcements to official show registries. They place ads in horse magazines announcing different ranch arena competitions."

Jeanay explained, "Okay, so these fundraising sites have a website where you set up an account that explains what your mission is. There is GoFundMe and Fundly. People can donate right online to your project. It works really well. I've seen thousands and thousands of dollars raised. Then we advertise the sites on your Facebook business page as well as advertising your upcoming shows on Facebook's AdWords or some other venue. I'll add that information to my Facebook page, and you ask your friends, and patrons to do the same."

"What patrons?"

"The patrons who come and support your fundraising site, and the borders who rent stable space from you."

"Oh, ohhh!" Jube was finally catching on. Her eyes got big, "I see. Oh my goodness, you two are amazing!" Like an empty balloon filling up with air Jube became invigorated. Other ideas started coming to her. "And I can, also, bug the horse associations to get me on their professional, not just amateur circuits, calendar. The fees to compete in the professional category are really high, and the stables keep a nice sum of the money." Jube's normal, confident, personality was returning.

The waiter interrupted them with their food. The aroma was titillating. "Wow, smells delicious!" Jeanay sniffed the steam rising from her plate.

"Looks really great too!" Professor commented.

"Uh, hum!" Jube added. The waiter smiled broadly enjoying their comments. Jube picked up her chopsticks, and the waiter left.

Professor Golden interrupted, "Please indulge me." Jube paused, and looked at the Professor. She continued, "I'd like to offer a blessing before we eat."

"Oh," Jube set her chopsticks down, "Okay."

Professor Golden looked up. Jube looked up wondering what the professor was looking at? Jeanay closed her eyes after she noticed Jube following Professor's upward gaze. Professor began, "Bless this food, the hands that prepared it, the people at this table and throughout the restaurant. Thank you God, amen."

Jeanay opened her eyes, and she whispered to Jube, who was still looking up, "The Jew always looks up watching for a sign from God."

Jube looked at Jeanay, "Oh, I was wondering... I like that." Jube shrugged with an expression of that's cool.

Jeanay asked Jube while they were eating, "Do you think Spirit could compete professionally?"

Jube decided to switch her chopsticks for a fork, "Ah, I'm not so good as you with these Professor." She stopped fiddling with the utensils and turned to Jeanay, "I'm not sure his owner has that in mind. He sure can stop on a dime and move fast. He'd make a formidable barrel racer maneuvering around those barrels in tight formation."

"Sure would and then, man, what a fast race down the final strip he'd make! I can't wait to see him in action," Jeanay added.

"What are you talking about Jeanay?" Professor Golden queried.

"Oh, this incredible black beauty, he has beautiful conformation, a long flowing mane and tail, gaited, gentle, and fast! Used to be a buggy racer."

They continued enjoying their food fare and talking 'horse talk.'

Getting Even

Jeanay was pulling on and off hats as she tried to figure out which one to wear. "How's this cloche? Or this Hunter cap?"

"I'm going to wear my turban scarf," Professor Golden determined. It tied to the side at the nape of her neck, thus she wore the end draped down her front.

"I should go for the gypsy-fortune-teller turban. That fits my idea nicely. He is about to squirm like crazy!"

"I think your idea is a perfect payback, or should I say lesson, ha, ha," Professor laughed gleefully.

"Yep," Jeanay laughed giddily, "And let's wear long skirts, the ones we got in town. Old fashion western wear can stand-in as gypsy clothes, don't you think?"

"I think we can make it work. I always wondered what wearing a petticoat must have been like?" Professor Golden pondered, "Though...we didn't see any of those to buy."

"Nope, that might have been interesting. We need to wear our boots."

Professor Golden studied herself in the mirror, and then looked over at Jeanay, "Ready to go?"

"Yep!" Then bowing, "I mean yes ma'am," Jeanay tried to keep a straight face.

They grabbed their boots, pulled them on at the door, and headed out to the car in the cool, pleasant night air. "This is so perfect for a late spring evening," Professor Golden remarked as she pulled a shawl around her shoulders.

"So perfect I might not need this short jacket," Jeanay had a denim jacket slung over her arm. "I'll drive."

It was a short distance to their destination the 'infamous' restaurant-bar they first came across as newcomers to the town. Once inside they went straight to the bar. They were the only persons to sit there.

"Now you follow my lead, Auntie."

Professor Golden nodded. They went to sit on the high bar stools. The bartender turned around to place a napkin before each of the ladies. Jeanay let out a disappointed, "Oh!" Professor remained silent. "Where is the other guy?"Jeanay whined.

The barkeep answered, "He'll be here to spell me soon. What can I get you, ladies?"

Jeanay and Professor Golden exchanged looks and shrugged. They had nothing else to do, but wait.

"I'll have a glass of rosé wine, please," Professor decided.

"Sure, and you," he turned to Jeanay.

"Could I have something with fruit, a virgin drink?"

"I can mix you up a cranberry spritzer, no wine, with soda water?"

"Yes, that sounds good."

The barkeeper noticed the other bartender come in. "I'll give him your order, I'm off now." The ladies nodded. He gave the other bartender their order, who, then proceeded to make their drinks without further ado.

The bartender they were waiting for brought their drinks over and placed them on the napkins. He looked up, "Ah, uh, oh!" He stepped back a little from them as if to protect himself from getting hit. He looked around trying to figure out what to do, and looked at their odd clothing as he bit his lip.

Professor Golden and Jeanay were thoroughly enjoying his reaction to their presence. Jeanay spoke first, "Yes, it's us! S-u-r-prised?" He cleared his throat not knowing what to say and definitely not wanting to admit anything. He grabbed a white towel, used for wiping the bar, and rubbed his hands nervously on it. He picked up a glass and started wiping it even though it was dry.

Jeanay began, "What are you up to tonight? Of course, you're such a busy fellow calling the press reporting on two little women. She spoke in mock tones of helplessness. "Such a big guy like you picking on little ole us, my, my. Whatever shall we do?" Jeanay turned to Professor Golden for a second then she turned back to him. "Oh, I know," she pulled a globe out of her skirt pocket, "We'll tell him his fortune."

Professor Golden nodded bobbing her head jerkily, "Yes, I agree, he needs to hear his future. I know the last person you read met their Maker earlier than they thought." Professor Golden was stepping to the tune of the pied piper in her head.

"Ah...Maker?" He shook his head, "No, I don't think so," he turned to go.

"Oh, bartender, you can't go, you need to tend to your customers. You don't want to get your boss upset now do you?" Jeanay chided and teased. He turned back to face them unhappily.

Jeanay stroked the globe she set on the bar passing her hands over it looking into it as if she were seeing things in it. Every now and then she pronounced, "Oh," as if she were viewing something important.

Professor Golden leaned over peering at the globe. "Oh, yes, he doesn't realize what a short lifeline he has."

Jeanay whispered quickly to her aunt, "That's palm reading, not globe reading!"

Professor Golden sputtered realizing her mistake, but then covered it over haphazardly, "Yes, Jeanay found, in her globe, that even though the palm reading had been given she also read his misdeeds and his certain doom."

The young man shook his head, "I never had my palm-DOOM?" The young man switched his tone stricken.

Jeanay picked up on it, in a spooky voice she hissed, "Yes, doom! You walk in the ways of darkness. You weren't good to your fellow ma-women. Now, what do I see for you?" She ran her hands over the globe peering at it with great intensity. "Aw, I see, um, uh-hum. I see red flames!"

The bartender stepped forward to swish the rag across the bar doing his best to peer into the globe. "That's ridiculous!"

Professor Golden tapped her forefinger on the bar. "And do you presume to know the future young man?" She spoke in a pretentious voice, "Only God knows your future. It is written, no man knows the day he's born, or the day he'll die, destiny, des-tin-y."

Jeanay leaned over to whisper to her aunt, "I think that's a western song?" Professor Golden shrugged. Jeanay decided to continue the songs theme. "Yea, you never know the day you're gone, done in, kaput!" At the word, "kaput," her hand flew up into the air, for emphasis, startling him. "Ah, but you can change your destiny."

"This is just one big charade." He paused, and then asked skeptically, "So how do you change your destiny?"

"No, YOUR destiny," Jeanay bounced back.

"Yea, that's what I said," he shot back.

"No, that's not what you said. I just hate it when people can't claim things for themselves, but use the 'Your' instead of the 'My or I'. How can I change my destiny?" She hotly protested.

He threw his hands up in frustration, "I-I-I, then!"

Jeanay, quietly, settled back on the bar stool. "Okay, then!" She paused. He shifted, impatiently, back and forth on his feet with his arms crossed. She studied him and then waited until he looked most upset before she continued, "The Good Book says, 'Do unto others as you would have them do unto you.'"

"What? It does not! What Good Book? That's the Golden Rule." He looked scornfully at Jeanay.

Jeanay's expression showed she had messed up. Professor Golden leaned over and whispered, "He's right."

Jeanay whispered back, "Thanks a lot. Help me here!"

A man yelled across the room from his table, "Come on we've been waiting here for some service!"

The bartender looked up angrily taking his frustration out on the customer. He yelled back, "I'll be there in a minute!"

The interruption gave Jeanay a second to recover. "The Golden Rule was first introduced by Christ, in the Sermon on the Mount, and then later coined The Golden Rule. Yes, that's it!" She nervously countered.

"What?" The bartender looked confused.

Professor Golden flew in to help cover for Jeanay not knowing what she was talking about. She blustered, "Yes, most definitely, I'm a scientist and I should know everything…I know!" She flung the words out not putting any real thought into them scrambling for some kind of mental order, but none came.

A man stepped into the doorway behind the bar, he hissed at the bartender, "What's wrong with you? Get that customer," pointing to the man at the table.

"Oh, right, right!" The bartender went quickly over to the man.

Jeanay whispered to her aunt, "What are you doing?"

Professor Golden whispered back, "What am I doing? What are YOU doing?"

They both sat there silently trying to decipher the last round of words. Jeanay confused over the Golden Rule not positive where it came from, and Professor Golden wondering about Christ. That twist of information was new to the Professor. She asked, "Did it say that in your New Testament Bible?"

Jeanay's memory kicked in, "Yes, but not in those exact words, and He said even better stuff about forgiveness and being humble, how we get blessed. You should read it Auntie, Book of Matthew, Chapter 5."

The bartender came back and filled the man's order of beer. He grabbed and pulled the handle of the beer dispensers tap. After he came back from delivering it he tried to hide in the corner away from the ladies. He pretended the other end of the bar needed wiping down with his towel.

Jeanay lifted her hand in the air, "Yi-who, bartender, Yi-who," she called. His groan was palatable as he twisted his upper body toward them, but not his torso. "Come here please," Jeanay called. He slowly came over and stood before them with his lips firmly pursed his face ashen.

"It is time for you to know your fate," the barkeep paled, his arm steadied himself against the back wall of mirrors and liquor storage. "You will die soon," Jeanay paused a second for dramatic effect, "If you do not repent of your ways!"

The bartender, completely duped, and engaged, put his hand over his heart. Seeing this Jeanay gave the bartender a sly smile and salute like the one he'd given them the night he stood at the door leaning against the molding when the reporter sat next to them. Professor followed suit and gave him a salute as well. The bartender's appearance graduated from scared to the realization that he had been had.

Jeanay and the Professor got up quickly. They grinned at him then smiled at each other and exited the bar. When they reached the hallway exit you could hear their roaring laughter.

"We got 'im good didn't we!" Jeanay proclaimed.

Professor Golden nodded, "Yep, we got him good!"

Jeanay did a little jig snapping her fingers up over her head, "Celebrate, celebrate!" She sang out, "Dance to the music."

A Month Later

Jeanay held the video camera on the car window ledge for balance as she shot the scene before her. She set the camera down on her seat when the car stopped. She stepped out and threw her western hat up into the air. "Yahoo! Just look at that crowd. And the banner, look at that banner!" The large banner hung at one end of the crowded arena. She read it out loud, "Help! Don't let us lose our stable!"

Professor Golden stepped out of the car. "Sure is hard to park with all these cars here."

"I think that's what we want isn't it?" Jeanay smirked, "Silly."

"Oh yes, right!" Professor Golden corrected herself.

They both were dressed in full complete western wear from the top of their cowgirl hats down to their boots. They drove up the less congested back road from Professor Golden's home to the top of Big Bear. This was a shorter route to the ranch since it was on the opposite end of Old Town Big Bear and the ski slopes.

Professor Golden stretched and complained, "Oh, my aching legs. Why didn't I let you drive? I need to let you drive up here next time, or take turns driving."

Horses were everywhere. They were washed and combed with braided and non-braided manes and tails. Their coats were brilliantly shiny from being brushed over and over. The very best tack and saddles were brought out and proudly displayed on the horses. The arena was surrounded by private and commercial vendor's selling brownies, cookies, tacos, tostadas, hamburgers and beverages.

"Look!" Jeanay pointed to the people behind the booths serving and helping. "People donating time Auntie," Jeanay clapped her hands gleefully causing Professor Golden to smile.

"Listen," Professor Golden cupped her ear, "I think Jube's the announcer."

"Oh, your right! That is her!" Jeanay looked around for her. She picked up her camera, shut the car door, and started her camera rolling. As she walked a little ahead she filmed the people and horses moving around going this way and that. There were riders, in the medium and small arena, warming up their mounts. Jeanay spotted the booth pointing it out. "She's over there!"

Professor Golden shaded her eyes, "Ah, yes, I see. Shall we go say hello?"

Jeanay shook her head, "No, not yet. I'd like to get food first." She turned back to the car, "Let me get the tripod from the trunk." When Jeanay returned from the car they walked over to where the food booths started. Standing in line were Cathy and Bruce. Jeanay walked quickly over to them. In turn to Cathy and then Bruce she said, "Hi, hi. You're here! I mean I knew you'd be here since you've donated. I mean, here, in this line."

"Sure, wouldn't miss this," Cathy smiled and pointed, "We're over there." She pointed to a booth with a Sharkys sign over it. "We're only keeping what it costs us for supplies the rest goes to the stable. Our employees are donating their time. Aren't they great?"

"They sure are," Professor Golden nodded.

"Wow, they're absolutely great! Jeanay's eyebrows arched in curiosity, "How come you're in this line and not your own?"

Bruce laughed, "Mexican food, a nice break for us."

Jeanay replied, "Ahh." They all nodded in understanding and laughed.

Bruce asked, "Do you notice anything different?"

Professor Golden looked around intently. "We see a lot different. You must mean something significantly different."

"Take a deep breath," he clued them. They took a deep breath. "Do you smell it?"

"Yes, I do." Professor Golden nodded taking another deep breath, "Yes, uh-hum."

"No, I don't get it?" Jeanay looked around clueless.

"Exactly! You don't smell it," Bruce laughed.

"Clean air, no dust, f-r-e-s-h!" Professor Golden stamped her foot hard, triumphant, on the solid surface they were standing on.

Jeanay sniffed the air. "Ah, oh yes!"

Professor Golden announced proudly, "It's working!"

Bruce added, "Yes. She didn't lose many of her borders either and she also has new ones. And some who left are coming back to rent space again."

"Wonderful!" Professor Golden felt giddy even though she handled the news in stately fashion.

Jeanay took the tripod out of its bag and attached her camera to it. She slung the bag over her shoulder deciding to carry the tripod under one arm for quicker access. The line became smaller as people's orders were filled. Soon they were at the cash register ordering food. They got their food and headed toward the bleachers.

The competitions were well on their way. Situated at the bottom step of the bleachers was a lead rope tied between two portable hitches blocking access. Standing there was a friendly guard who asked, "Have you paid your $2.00? May I see your tickets?"

Professor Golden and Jeanay looked at each other grinning, and said at the same time, "She did it!" The guard smiled, she looked at them peculiarly not expecting this response.

A familiar voice came to their ears. "Let them pass. They are the ones who made all this possible!"

They turned to see Jube behind them smiling. The guard immediately responded, "Of course." She presented them with two tickets, "In case you need them to get in and out of the bleachers later." She couldn't figure out how to hand the tickets, or program of events to Jeanay whose hands and arms were full of equipment and food. After failing a silly attempt to squeeze them into Jeanay's full hands, or under her arm she gave up and handed everything to Professor Golden.

"Thank you," The two ladies replied looking amused at her consternation. Balancing their plates they both reached out to give Jube a big hug with Jeanay having a special problem hanging on to her tripod.

"You've done so great! Professor congratulated.

Jeanay nodded, "You've done really great, look at you!"

Jube let out a breath, "Yes, it has been a lot of work, I can't begin to tell you how much, but it has paid off!" In excitement she jumped and clapped her hands, "And we're three-quarters of the way paid off! Can you believe that?" Bubbling over she added, "And the professional circuit is considering us."

"Oh, that IS exciting. Good for you!" Professor Golden beamed.

"Wow, great! We're going to come more often for all this, this is so fun!" Jeanay bubbled.

Jube squeezed both of them again. "Okay, I've got to get back to the announcer's booth. Watch for Spirit, he's in rare form today. He just might take first place in barrel racing. And he's a good contender in intermediate jumping. We found out he had hidden talent there."

Jube held up her hands, "No gloves. I have beautiful hands again, so wonderful! She sighed and walked away waving. Professor and Jeanay grinned broadly and nodded.

Professor Golden and Jeanay scooted into a bleacher to watch. They heard Jube's voice over the loudspeaker. "We have a special guest today. Please welcome our city's esteemed Mayor. Give him a round of applause." The Mayor stood up waving and smiling.

Professor Golden and Jeanay snickered.

"Of course, making his rounds," Professor offered as she clapped.

Jeanay looked at his suit crowned with a cowboy hat. "Dress to impress, good ole politics." She clapped as well.

Professor Golden leaned in toward Jeanay, with all the applause going on, so she could hear. "Yes, but he did do a good job on this one!" Jeanay, happy as an equestrian could be, nodded "yes".

The competition resumed as the afternoon events began. They had missed half of the competition that morning driving up the mountain.

Jeanay read from the program to Professor Golden. "The next event is barrel racing. Oh look, Spirit is the first contestant." She pointed to the program schedule and then looked down at her folded tripod sitting next to her. "I think I can get Spirit on video without the tripod, we should be up high enough." Spirit came prancing into the arena, alert, snorting in excitement. Jeanay bounced on her seat. "Wow, he's awesome!"

"Impressive," Professor Golden admitted under her breath.

Jube announced Spirit by name and the number on his rider's back along with the owner's name and rider's name. "On your mark, get set, go!" The timer clicked his stopwatch. Spirit shot down the course-way and made a tight close turn around the first barrel. As he turned around the second barrel the crowd started clapping with excitement. He was flying around the course in such perfection that when he reached the third and final barrel the crowd stood, and whistled, and screamed for him, "Go, go, go!" The rider leaned forward and slapped her cowgirl hat on Spirit yelling, "Ya, ya," to urge him to run with the wind, full-out, as he headed down toward the finish line. The crowd burst into cheering. He had given it his all, and it was astounding. Spirit was a true performer, excelling, driven on by the roars of the crowd.

Jeanay stood to her feet trying to film around the moving heads in front of her. She put the camera down, after Spirit crossed the finish line, and jumped up and down clapping with all her might yelling, "Wow, wow, wow!" She threw a fist into the air in triumphant exhilaration, "And to think I helped in his training."

Jube yelled into the Mic, "And that folks is going to be a hard score to beat. A flawless ride! What a performer!"

Breathless Professor Golden sat down after having being swept up in the cheering. "He didn't touch one barrel. You're right he turns tight and fast, really sweet!"

"I told you so. Man I wonder how well he'll jump?" Jeanay and the crowd took their seats.

A little while later, after the last entry to the barrel racing, the loudspeaker announced, "And now our esteemed Mayor has agreed to give out the ribbons. Can we have a round of applause for our Mayor?" The audience obliged.

"Again?" Professor Golden and Jeanay burst out laughing as they, in good form, clapped.

"I'm going to get closer. I want to record the winners." Jeanay picked up her tripod along with her camera. "I'm leaving my tripod bag with you," she informed the Professor. Then she jumped down the bleachers, in between people, to set-up her tripod at the arena's fence. She centered herself in the middle where the participants were lining up standing quietly for the announcement of the winners and presentation of the ribbons.

Jube, in her most eloquent entertainment voice, spoke. "I want to thank our town businesses for donating prizes for our winners as well as for our auction. Sharkys, Pets Galore, Blue Skies Restaurant, Blue Skies Realty, Gazer Gallery, Fetch & Stay, Betty's Gift Shop, Alex's Auto Shop, and the donations of our partners, and our friends at the food booths, and our patrons. This wouldn't have been made possible without all of you. I am so deeply grateful and touched."

"And now, here it is, our first place winner is…Spirit!" Jube yelled into the microphone. The crowd went crazy! Spirit pranced up to the Mayor who then placed a large blue ribbon on his bridle. He shook hands with the rider then he handed the rider an award envelope. Spirit loved it. He threw his head up and down showing off the ribbon. That was met with the audience's laughter and applause. One by one the participants were awarded first through third place while Jeanay captured them on video. Then she rushed with her camera in hand, leaving her tripod behind, over to the gate to record their exit.

The Mayor, also, exited behind all the horses. He came over to Jeanay. "Hello, nice to see you here. When do we get to see your docudrama of our fair city?"

"Soon, I'm just finishing up the happy ending by adding this event to it," Jeanay assured him.

"Great! Great! Looking forward to it," the Mayor smiled broadly and shook her hand. "I don't suppose you filmed me giving out the ribbons?"

Jeanay chuckled to herself. She smiled at him. "You bet I did!"

The Mayor smoothed his hair, gave her a happy nod, and walked away quite self-satisfied.

Jeanay couldn't keep herself from giggling all the way back to her tripod. Retrieving it she went back up to the bleachers to sit with Professor Golden. When she got there the Professor asked her, "I saw you, what was so funny?"

Jeanay started giggling again. She placed a hand on her aunt's arm, "The Mayor, he's so, so, what's the word?"

"Predictable?" Professor Golden filled in.

Jeanay laughed out loudly, "Yes! Yes. That's it! He wanted to know if I included him in the video of the awards being given out."

Professor smiled, jesting, "Who would 'a thought!" They both laughed in great fun.

"Oh, we're so bad, laughing at another's expense," Jeanay added.

"Yes." Professor tried unsuccessfully to make a straight, contrite face. "No," she shook her head as she bent over continuing to laugh, but at the same time trying to hide her mirth.

They sat for several hours watching the different events. The pair took a break to go get humongous pretzels. Jube caught up with them on her break. "Honestly, the mayor, don't get me wrong I'm grateful to him, but the real heroes are you two."

Jeanay and Professor Golden looked at her surprised and smiled. Professor spoke first, "Why, thank you, that's very nice!"

"Thank you," Jeanay seconded. "By the way, it's so cool you got business owners to donate to the winners as well as the auction." Professor Golden nodded in agreement.

Jube grinned, "Thank you, since I wasn't going to give them cash winnings I just had to come up with something for them. They do work so hard."

Jube continued, "I'm so glad I hired you. I just don't know when I can pay you, or for that matter how much you're going to charge me."

"You mean you haven't gotten our bill?" Professor asked, and elbowed Jeanay at the same time.

Jube with wide-eyed innocence blinked and shook her head looking pensive.

"Well that's because we haven't sent you one." Professor gave her a mischievous smile. She cleared her throat and spoke, mock, seriously, "I don't know if you can afford us." Jeanay looked at her aunt in surprise and frowned at her. She continued, "Because it will cost you," she paused to elevate anticipation, "Lessons for Jeanay every time we visit."

Both Jeanay and Jube gasped in surprise, they let out a sigh of relief. Jube planted a kiss on Professor Golden's cheek. The professor couldn't have been more startled or pleased. Touched, she placed her hand on her cheek where Jube had planted the kiss.

Jeanay laughed watching her aunt's reaction. She turned to Jube, "Besides I plan on making a pretty penny with this video package I'm putting together. Some very interesting stuff here." She patted her video bag.

"That's terrific Jeanay I hope you make a bundle. Well, I've got to get back. Our last event is up, jumping," Jube announced. "Want to place any bets?" Professor Golden and Jeanay shook their heads. "Oh, have you seen Derek?"

Jeanay perked up. "Is he here?"

"I thought he would be, especially since he knew you were coming," Jube kidded.

Jeanay blushed in silence.

"Don't worry he probably got called out to tend a patient. He's going to be really upset that he missed this!" Jube conjectured.

They returned to their seats intently watching the arena as the props were replaced with hurdles. A figure quietly came to sit by Jeanay's side. She turned to look at who the stranger might be and then burst out, "Derek!" Jeanay turned away in embarrassment. Her spontaneous, unabashed enthusiasm caught Jeanay off guard. Professor Golden had seen him sneak up, so she was already smiling. He gave Jeanay a quick hug. "Oh!" she gushed and smiled at him.

Derek saluted the Professor, she chuckled. Derek explained, "I got called out, had to pull out a bunch of piglets stuck in a sow, they let the pig get too fat so she couldn't get them out." He shook his head, "Could've killed her and the piglets! They know now."

"Eww," Jeanay shivered at the prospect of the pregnant sow had she not been assisted.

"Cute little things already snorting and oinking, that's the fun part of my job."

Jeanay nodded her head noticing he seemed a little nervous around her. That, strangely, calmed her.

Jube called out over the microphone, "Okay folks, the events that we saved for last are finally here. Thank you all for your wonderful support! Please look forward to more events like this one and come join us. Tell your friends and family how much fun we all had today. Again, thank you for the donations that made this so special for our winners and above all for helping to save our ranch!" Then switching to her announcer's voice, "Now, for our last event, jumping!" She went on to explain the three categories.

The beginners jump event was filled with grade school children. The jumps were a pole between one and two foot high hurdle bars. A few of the horses stopped and balked at jumps although their patient riders urged them to obey. The intermediate event was set up with the hurdle bars graduated to three feet high. The contestants consisted of grade school children and adults. Some of the horses were old pros at jumping and others were new to jumping. At times the horses knocked the top bar down while at other times they cleared the bars. The enthusiastic "oohs" and "aahs" of the audience could be heard at the appropriate times. The awards were handed out to the top three winners in these two categories.

Jube spoke into the Mic, "Wasn't that exciting folks? You're looking at our future big competition riders. Now we will up the railings for our advanced jumpers." These jumps graduated from three to four and a half feet high. "And now here comes our first competitor, S-p-i-r-i-t!"

Remembering Spirit the crowd clapped loudly. Then they got very quiet so that the horse and rider could concentrate. Spirit was prancing with high steps, but then at the signal of the rider he set his head in concentration.

Jeanay exclaimed, as she rubbed her stomach, "This makes me so nervous."

Spirit cleared each hurdle perfectly with massive muscles rippling in melodious movement. His steps were synced, his tail flipping in the air as he made a perfect arc over each obstacle. Arching his neck proudly he knew he had done well. He was a real crowd pleasing performer. The crowd was beside themselves cheering.

All the jumps were completed. He now faced the flat, open home stretch. Spirit's rider gave him the signal for a full speed gallop, but something got confused in the signals, or maybe it reminded him of his racing days, but nonetheless, Spirit went into his high speed, fast-gaited racing trot. The audience reacted as they gasped in dismay. They knew the finish was supposed to be a high-speed gallop. As they watched and heard the massive pounding of his hoofs furiously beating the dirt their "oh no's," crested like a wave to "aah's" in surprised thrill. He fairly flew in racetrack time and speed. He made loud breathy snorts in excitement and strained effort. The finish was powerful! The crowd jumped to their feet yelling. They had never seen anything like this before. It was magnificent! And then as Spirit touched the finish line a loud buzzer blew signaling a foul. Spirit had won the hearts of his audience, and they "booed" loudly at the sound.

Jeanay was bouncing like a rubber ball, up and down, with excitement till she heard that buzzer. She turned to Derek in consternation. "What was that?"

"That's too bad, it will take time off for him, a foul of some kind," Derek surmised.

"Yes, but if no other horse has as clean of jumps and isn't faster he could still win couldn't he?" Jeanay spoke hopefully.

"True," Professor Golden added reflecting her hopes.

"That was a spectacular performance folks, but we're sorry..." The crowd was "booing" so loudly that Jube paused. She finally spoke, "Please, please quiet down." The crowd moved about restlessly. "I know, I know folks, but the rule is the horse must finish in a cantor or gallop, not a trot. You have seen our talented former buggy racehorse in action, a truly great sight, but we have to stick to the rules. Please wish him and his rider the best for their spectacular ride." Applause broke out little by little and then gained in tremendous thundering and stomping of feet. In spontaneity rider and Spirit took an excited, high-stepping, slow-gaited trot around the ring. Spirit swayed to his steps in a dance. The rider waved thanks as she and Spirit ate up the attention.

"I sure didn't expect that rule," Jeanay grouched.

"Me either," Derek admitted.

Professor Golden nodded her head in absolute agreement.

Spirit finished his lap and exited the arena. The audience settled down.

Another beautiful equine specimen walked out proudly. "Isn't that a beautiful dapple gray," Jeanay sighed.

"Uh huh, that is also a hurdle winner from past shows, tough competition," Derek informed them.

"Oh, this jumping event makes me so nervous!" Jeanay started chewing her nails.

Professor Golden looked on amused. The dapple gray gelding perfectly cleared all the jumps and galloped to the finish line. He had cleared the hurdles, his score was perfect, but Spirit had been faster.

The score came up and the crowd applauded. "Unless someone can beat that time and not touch a hurdle that's the winner," Derek announced.

"Aw," Jeanay was disappointed. "I sure wish they'd given Spirit a second chance. Oh well!"

The ring was cleared out, the show was over. The competitors were being brushed down and escorted back to their stalls, or exiting in their horse trailers back to their homes. A tired, elated Jube wound herself through the crowd to find Professor Golden, Jeanay, and Derek. "You made it," she commented to Derek. "Spirit was impressive huh. He picked up a first with barrels, and he got a first in confirmation. Not bad for his first training season. I think the prizes might make up for the cost of his training sessions."

They all smiled nodding in agreement. All four walked over to the parking lot together. Professor Golden opened her car door and got in, "You're driving Jeanay." Jeanay got in on the driver's side and rolled down the window. Derek placed his hands on her open window to say good-bye.

Jube indicated she wanted to speak to Professor Golden. Professor rolled her window down. Jube spoke in a hushed voice, "I want to mention what a few of my borders have, quietly, mentioned to me."

Professor looked at her concerned, "Yes?"

Jube paused, a little embarrassed and whispered, "They say they have felt like they're being watched out in the hills where they have been riding."

Jeanay and Derek overheard the soft whisper and stopped talking to listen.

"What do you mean? Was it a trail group ride?" Professor Golden asked hesitantly.

"No, individuals who were riding out alone, but it has been a few riders.

"Horses do get spooked by people and animals," Professor mused.

Jube continued, "One rider thought she saw something moving, her horse reacted as if it were a predator, but there was no bear or mountain lion spotted.The way they talked it kind 'a spooked me. It didn't sound normal. Jeanay said you have a science background and some knowledge of the paranormal. I thought you might want to check it out."

"I see," Professor Golden was intrigued. She looked over at Jeanay's worried face. "Okay, thank you. It's probably nothing. People can imagine weird things, and if it wasn't several people seeing this at the same time. Well, it's not creditworthy, but let me know if anything else develops."

Okay, bye-bye now, till next time," Jube gave a warm double tap on Professor Golden's door where she had been leaning.

"Goodbye Jube." Professor Golden smiled big back at her with a wave of her hand. "Great day," she commented to herself.

Jeanay added in cowgirl slang, "We'll be back fer sure!"

Jube nodded, and she turned walking away. Professor rolled up her window. Derek looked at Jeanay and Professor Golden. Jube's comments were in their thoughts.

Jeanay spoke up, "For God has not given us a spirit of fear, but of power, and of love, and of a sound mind."

Derek added in a decisive voice, "2 Timothy 1:7, Sounds good to me!"

Thank you for reading

Professor Golden Mysteries Volume 1

**If you liked the book please consider leaving a positive review on Amazon. It is of great help to any independent author, and I'd love to hear from you.
jeanettedesigns1@gmail.com**

ABOUT THE AUTHOR

Jeanette Jensen B.A. is an accomplished artist of many years and has been writing novels and screenplays for the last five years. This is Jeanette's first published novel. She is also the artist for the novel's cover. Her background includes acting, directing, and writing in a traveling stage play group that she created. Her credits include being a winner in the 2014, 2016, 2017 and 2018 National Novel Writing Month competition. She has a stage play called Psych Me Out about a detective at a concert hall who is trying to find out what happened to the first seat violinist. He and his girlfriend along with his friends who are attending the concert delve into the mystery. This funny free for all play has moral revelations and is a great who-done-it. Jeanette is also working on several screenplays, faith-based novels, and Professor Golden Volume 2.

Jeanette has a yearly Solo gallery show in Tustin, California. Several newspaper articles have featured her artwork. She has had numerous art shows, art walks, artwork in high end boutique stores, and greeting cards in shops and Postal Annex stores in 13 states. Some of her genre is faith based other subjects are nature, figures, portraitures, landscapes, and florals. She paints in oil on canvas, watercolor on paper, oil on antique windows, and vivid acrylic flowers and fruit on tote bags. Her original artwork, prints and a signed copy of her novel can be purchased at Jeanettedesigns.com. At the website you can also follow her blog and join her newsletter announcing new gallery shows and book signing events.

Another venue for Jeanette's art is Instagram, Facebook, LinkedIn and Pinterest at Jeanette Designs. Check out Jeanette Jensen artist on Google for one of her 'featured artist' newspaper articles.

www.ingramcontent.com/pod-product-compliance
Lightning Source LLC
Chambersburg PA
CBHW081356090726
47908CB00011B/2693